SILENT GAVEL

SILENT GAVEL

MERISSA RACINE

Silent Gavel

Silent Gavel is a work of fiction. Any reference to real places are used fictitiously. Names, characters and events, other than those in the public domain, are from the author's imagination, and any likeness to places or persons, alive or dead, is completely coincidental.

ISBN (paperback) 978-0-9993033-0-6
e-ISBN 978-0-9993033-1-3

For information contact author Merissa Racine
www.merissaracine.com

Book Design: Maureen Cutajar

In Memory of Harvey
Who finally found his forever home and was by my side
on the couch while I wrote the first draft of this novel.

Chapter One

The Volvo bounced hard at the end of the driveway. Lauren backed out into the street, ignored the posted speed limits, and drove the short distance across town. With little traffic to contend with in the early morning, she turned onto Bridger Avenue and pulled up in front of Judge Murphy's house in under fifteen minutes. A quick glance at the clock on the dash told her she was late. Six-fifteen. *Damn it.* The garage door getting stuck in the closed position, and her trying to figure out how to open it, ate up more time than she realized. In the seven months Lauren had lived in her very first home she was learning that being a homeowner wasn't all about picking out paint samples or curling up in front of a cozy fire. Another chink in the joys of home ownership.

Lauren sat in the warmth of her car and waited for her boss to join her. A minute passed. Light shone behind the closed curtains but no sign of Judge Murphy. She took her phone out of her bag and texted, "I'm here." *At least it won't be all my fault if we don't show up on time for the nine-thirty hearing.* She checked the weather forecast from her phone one more time. It hadn't changed since she checked it at five o'clock that morning.

Another two minutes went by. No judge. No reply. Lauren looked at the house again and huffed, "That's nice. You warn me about being on time and now I'm waiting for you." She placed her phone in the side pocket of her purse, got out of the car, and hurried up the porch steps.

The front door stood slightly open. Judge Murphy's dog appeared on the porch and yipped.

"Hey, Percy. Did your mom let you out to do your business?" Lauren lifted the Papillon. His fur was wet, and she placed him gently back on the ground.

Percy yipped louder.

"I'm sorry, little guy. I can't show up for court in a dirty suit."

A sliver of light seeped through a crack in the curtains, illuminating the small section of porch where they stood. Lauren rapped on the partially open door, stuck her head in the foyer, and called out, "Hello?"

No answer.

"Your Honor, it's me, Lauren. Hello?"

No response.

This time, her voice louder, "Your Honor, Judge Murphy, it's me." She hesitated, not wanting to enter uninvited. She rubbed her arms, wishing she had thrown her coat over her suit. A few homes across the street had interior lights on.

The chill in the air made up Lauren's mind for her and she stepped into the foyer. A crunch under her feet made her take a quick sidestep. She glanced down and saw pieces of broken glass scattered like pebbles on the oak floor. She hugged herself and took another step into the house. "Your Honor—" Lauren stopped mid-sentence when the toe of her teal pump hit something. She looked down and sucked in a sharp breath. The silhouette of a body lay on the floor. "Oh, my God. Your Honor?"

No reply.

Lauren backed up, groped along the wall, found a light switch, and flipped it on. Judge Murphy lay in a fetal position, her side soaked in the maroon liquid that had pooled beneath her. The bile in Lauren's stomach rose and burned the back of her throat. It threatened to escape. She forced herself to swallow.

Percy whimpered. She stared at him trying to think. *What should I do? What the hell should I do? Get out of here, now? Yes, yes, yes. No, I should stay. Check for a pulse? Yes. No, I can't check for a pulse. I can't get that close to her. Call nine-one-one? Yes.* All these thoughts in her head jockeyed for first place.

She turned away from the lifeless body and suppressed the overwhelming urge to bolt out the door. A small lamp next to the sofa illuminated the living room. Lauren focused on the surrounding area, looking for a landline or cell phone. She saw neither, and slowly backed out of the house, spun around, and fled to her car. She pulled her phone from the side pocket of her bag. It slid from her fingers and fell onto the seat. She reached for it, her fingers trembling. It took three attempts to unlock the screen, and two tries before she managed to punch in three simple numbers.

"Nine-one-one. What is the address of your emergency?" asked a calm voice.

Chapter Two

The dispatcher's voice sounded far away, almost dreamlike, as she asked for her name, the nature of the emergency, and instructed her to stay on the line. Lauren shivered in the October predawn air. She grabbed her winter coat from the back seat, threw it on, and sat in the passenger seat waiting for help. She thrust her hand into the glovebox and patted around until she touched the familiar rectangle stashed inside. She reached in again and felt for the lighter, kept there for winter emergencies, she had always told herself. With a quick pull of the tiny red tab, Lauren unwrapped the cellophane covering and with it, unwrapped the nicotine addiction she had been fighting for close to a year.

The lighter's blue flame brought giddy anticipation but before she could light the cigarette the nine-one-one operator's voice came back to life. She flung the lighter and cigarettes back in the glovebox and slammed it shut, feeling like she had been caught stealing a candy bar. "Lauren, is Miss Murphy still breathing?"

"No. I… I don't think so."

"Can you check? Can you do that for me?"

She stared at the phone, thinking surely this woman is crazy. Go back inside?

"Miss? Are you still there?"

"Yes, I'm here. I'm pretty sure she isn't breathing, but I'll check." Lauren inhaled a deep breath of courage and went into the house. Percy followed. She steered clear of the blood and knelt beside Judge Murphy. A piece of glass dug into her knee. Lauren ignored the pain. She noticed for the first time that the bottom pane of glass on the front door had been broken out, only jagged edges remained. A glance around the living room revealed nothing else out of the ordinary.

Pieces of broken glass lay on her boss's body. Lauren instinctively wanted to tidy her up, pick out the tiny shards from her tangled mass of blonde hair, but she could not bring herself to touch her, not even her hair. "Tamper with a crime scene? Am I freakin' insane?"

The dispatcher broke into Lauren's monologue. "Miss, I didn't hear you. Did you say she's breathing? Miss?"

"Uh, no." Lauren studied Judge Murphy. No rise and fall of her chest. Blood had ceased pumping through her veins and settled in a dark, irregular-shaped puddle. Lauren stood quickly. It made her dizzy. She stumbled backwards into the wall, pressed her hand to her mouth, and breathed through her nose, afraid she was going to lose her breakfast.

"Miss? Is the victim breathing? Lauren, are you still there?"

"Uh, yes... I mean no. She... she's... there's blood *everywhere*," Lauren sobbed into the phone. "I can't... I can't touch her." She turned her back on the lifeless body but not before the image of Judge Murphy's vacant stare had been seared into her mind like a bad tattoo.

Percy pawed Lauren's leg. She gathered him in her arms, ignoring his wet fur, and pressed his trembling body to her chest.

Sirens sounded in the distance and broke the morning's silence. The quiet street came alive as first one, then a second, and finally a third police cruiser screeched to a stop at the curb. An ambulance was on the heels of the police cruisers, and a fire truck came up the street from the opposite direction. The kaleidoscope of lights blinded Lauren.

"The police are here." Before the dispatcher could speak, Lauren ended the call.

Three officers, weapons drawn, approached. Lauren pointed in the direction of the front door. "It's Judge Murphy. I—she's—I'm sure she's dead. Nine-one-one wanted me to check for a pulse. I..."

Two of the officers made their way toward the house, and one officer remained in front of Lauren. She recognized him from court. She fought the urge to collapse into this familiar man's arms and cry. Instead, she took a deep breath, then her words rushed out. "Officer Bradford, I found her—found her lying on the floor by the front door. There was blood all around her and..." Lauren's body shook at the memory.

Officer Bradford placed a hand on Lauren's elbow and escorted her away from the house toward the street. Two paramedics and firefighters, blue bags slung over their shoulders, rushed past them and up the steps.

Lauren drew in quick jagged breaths.

"You're Miss Besoner, the one who called nine-one-one?" asked Officer Bradford.

"Yes."

"Can I see some identification?"

"It's in my bag."

The officer accompanied Lauren to her car, standing close. Her hands shook as she reached into the purse, found her wallet, and produced a driver's license.

He shone his flashlight on the license, then studied her face. "Tell me what happened. What are you doing here?"

"I came to pick up Judge Murphy. We were going to ride to Casper together for a hearing this morning." Lauren added, "I'm Judge Murphy's reporter, her court reporter."

He nodded. "I thought I recognized you."

Lauren explained how she came upon her boss. When she finished, she hiccupped. "Oh, my God, I can't believe this. I just can't believe what's happened."

"Try to calm down."

She clamped her jaw tight to stop her teeth from chattering.

"Does Judge Murphy live alone?"

"Yes."

"Could there possibly be anyone else in the home?"

"I don't think so, but I'm not sure."

"We're going to need a detailed statement, but for now have a seat in my squad car." He opened the rear passenger door for her and slid his muscular frame into the front seat. After a few taps on his laptop he spoke into his shoulder mic, spewing numbers and police jargon. A female's voice crackled through the air in response.

Officer Bradford spoke over his shoulder. "Sit tight. One of us will be with you shortly."

Lauren sat in the back seat. Percy vibrated in her arms. He kept watch on her face with expectant eyes. She kissed his head and whispered, "It must have been terrifying for you, you poor little thing. It's okay. It's going to be okay." Then looking at the commotion at Judge Murphy's house, she knew one thing for sure, it was far from okay.

Chapter Three

The overhead lights of the police cruisers bounced off bare trees and nearby houses, and Lauren hooded her eyes to block out their brightness.

Headlights from behind made their way into the cruiser. Lauren turned to see who pulled up but the vehicle's bright lights kept her in the dark. A moment later someone opened the back door of Officer Bradford's cruiser. Percy barked. "Miss Besoner, if I could have you step out, please."

Still clutching the Papillon, Lauren exited the vehicle to face a tired-looking man a couple of years older than herself, dressed in plain clothes.

"I'm Detective Sam Overstreet." He flashed a badge that she couldn't read in the low lighting. "We're going to need you to come to the station and make a statement, but first I need to collect some evidence from you."

"What do you mean, collect evidence?"

"First, I need to swab your fingers. Then..." He gestured toward Lauren's chest.

Percy's paw prints had created a manic print over her coat and suit. The realization of what made the paw prints hit Lauren like a quick jab to her gut. Her first instinct was to rip off her jacket and throw it, that somehow distancing herself from the bloody coat would distance herself from this nightmare she found herself in and she would wake up. She resisted the temptation. *Pull yourself together. This man is watching you.*

"Officer Bradford will take you to the station to secure your clothes."

He walked her to the rear of his Crown Vic, where he popped the trunk and retrieved a sandwich-sized paper bag and held it open. "I'll need your phone."

With all the commotion, Lauren hadn't noticed the dark smears on the phone case. The sight brought a new wave of nausea. She tossed the phone into the bag as if it were a poisonous snake, then examined the faint red marks on her fingertips. "Do you have something I can clean my hands with?"

In answer to her question, he again reached into the trunk and pulled out two long, thin white plastic bags. "If you'll hold out your hands, palms up, please."

She complied by adjusting Percy in her arms, and then held out her hands.

He broke open the sealed packages with a quickness that came from familiarity, extracted two flat toothbrush-like objects, and swabbed the fingertips of her hands.

"Once you're at the station you'll have a chance to clean them but for now that's the best we can do."

The comment made Lauren want to rub her hands on her coat. "What about Percy?"

The dark-haired man standing before her eyed the dog. "He belongs to the victim?"

"Yes, Judge Murphy."

"Does she live with anyone, have a relative or friend we can contact?"

"I don't think she has any family in town. She's engaged though."

"His name?"

"Bradley… I'm sorry, I'm drawing a blank. But he lives in Longmont."

"We'll take care of the dog. It's not something you need to worry about."

"But he's frightened. Look at him. I want to make sure he's okay."

"We'll take care of him. One of the officers can take him over to the animal shelter when we're finished here."

"The animal shelter?" Lauren's voice rose. "You can't take him there, not after what he's been through."

"Miss Besoner, now is not the time to worry about the dog. I told you, we'll handle it." He motioned with his head to one of the firefighters coming out of the house.

The tall fireman approached.

"Can you take the dog?"

The fireman reached out for Percy, but the dog burrowed into Lauren's chest.

Before handing him over, Lauren whispered into the soft fur of his ear. "Don't worry. This nice man"—she read the name embroidered on his jacket "—Cody, will take care of you." She searched Cody's brown eyes. "You will take care of him, won't you?"

He nodded. "I'll take care of the little fella, don't you worry."

After handing Percy to Cody, Lauren went to her car, gathered her bag, and took out the key fob for her Volvo. "If you could leave it unlocked, please. We're going to need to take a look inside. If you don't mind."

"No, I don't mind."

The detective walked her to Officer Bradford's patrol car and gestured for her to sit inside. Before closing the door, he leaned in. "Just sit tight, okay?"

The overhead lights continued to illuminate the sky. Lauren looked out through the barred window and watched another police cruiser pull up to the house. After a brief conversation with Detective Overstreet the officer retrieved crime scene tape from his trunk and stretched it across the judge's front door. Lauren fidgeted on the hard plastic bench seat, unable to get comfortable.

The sky was beginning to blush by the time Officer Bradford slid behind the steering wheel. Lauren turned her attention to the neighbors gathered at the edge of Judge Murphy's driveway, huddled together in small groups, clutching at their heavy robes. Some tried to peer into the police cruiser. Lauren turned her head away.

With the flip of a switch, the display of lights was doused. Officer Bradford tapped on the keys of his laptop and again spoke into his shoulder mic. He adjusted the rearview mirror. His eyes met Lauren's and held for a beat. He pulled away from the curb, and they rode to the police station in silence.

Chapter Four

Lauren and the officer descended the stairs and entered the Crawford Police Department, which was housed in the basement of the county courthouse. Inside sat a gatekeeper, a plump woman in her mid-thirties. She acknowledged them through the glass partition with the press of a button somewhere out of sight. A buzzer sounded, followed by a click, and they made their way to the inner sanctum of the fluorescent-lit station, the large space devoid of anyone except for the woman on buzzer patrol.

"I'll be right back. Let me see what I can find in the way of a change of clothes." Officer Bradford disappeared down a long corridor. She turned to see the woman behind the gray desk openly staring at her. Her cheeks grew warm.

Officer Bradford returned.

"That's all you have?" She looked at the folded orange jumpsuit thinking he must be joking, but knowing he wasn't.

"Yep. Sorry. At least they're clean. The restroom is over there," he directed with his chin. "Heather will accompany you."

Heather came around from the metal desk and, without uttering a word, grabbed the orange bundle of clothes and white clogs from Bradford. She grabbed four brown paper bags from a cabinet and walked toward the restrooms.

Inside, the scent of faux pine made Lauren's nose wrinkle. She turned toward a mirror, then shoved open the nearest bathroom stall door and threw up. After relinquishing her breakfast to the porcelain toilet, Lauren wadded up a handful of toilet paper and wiped her mouth. She stepped out and over to the sink, turned on the faucet, cupped her hands under the cold running water, and rinsed out her mouth.

Heather looked at her in the mirror.

"Sorry," murmured Lauren.

The ashen tone of Heather's face said that she too might need to step into the bathroom stall. Until she had caught sight of her own reflection, Lauren had been unaware of just how awful she looked. Her coat and suit were streaked with dried blood, her boss's blood. With everything that had happened, she had forgotten about the blood on her clothes, then once again remembered Percy.

Heather held out the change of clothes with disdain. Lauren took them and stepped toward the stall.

"You'll need to leave the door open." Heather stood as sentry in front of the bathroom.

The cramped space made it difficult to maneuver, but Lauren managed to change out of her clothes. When she emerged, she took a quick inventory of herself. The orange pants overflowed onto the floor. The apricot colored v-neck shirt could have easily doubled as a knee-length dress.

Heather held the brown bags at arm's length, eyes focused on the sacks. Lauren dropped her dirty cream-colored suit into one bag, the coat in another, then mourning the loss of her new teal pumps, added one to each of the smaller bags. She stepped into the white scuffed clogs.

With the paper bags in hand, Heather swung around and left, leaving Lauren alone. She knelt and rolled each pant leg up, then stepped outside. Officer Bradford stood waiting. He pointed to a phone at an unoccupied desk. "If you want to call someone to bring a change of clothes, now would be a good time to do it."

"Okay." The clock on the far wall read six-fifty-five. She picked up the receiver and called the one person she knew would be awake and already on her second cup of coffee. When Claudia Martinez's voicemail came on the line Lauren left a long message, and ended with, "Claude, I'll explain everything when you get here, I promise. Just hurry."

Officer Bradford walked over to her. "Did you reach someone?"

"I left a message for my friend. She works upstairs in the county attorney's office. I'm hoping she can drop off some clothes on her way to work."

"Good. Follow me."

And so Lauren did, her orange pants swishing as she lagged behind the blond officer.

They stopped at the end of a long corridor. The officer opened a door on the right and motioned for her to enter. "Detective Overstreet should be with you in a bit."

Lauren fidgeted in the chair. She had no way to judge time but after sitting there for what felt like an hour, the words "a bit" were too generous. Just when she didn't think she could sit in the small room any longer, the door swung open. The detective who had swabbed her fingertips earlier strode in, no-nonsense air following on his heels. In the light, she took in the black slacks, gray-and-white-striped button-down shirt. The cuffs were rolled up and the sleeves tight against his biceps. Intense brown eyes peered out at her.

Lauren thought all police officers had a certain look, from their clean-shaven faces to their not-quite buzz-cut hairstyle. Not this guy. He wore his wavy dark brown hair too long for the standard police-issued 'do.

"Sorry to keep you waiting."

"That's okay."

No sign of recognition on the detective's face though Lauren recognized him from court. He had also pulled her over for speeding last spring.

He dispensed with any small talk by asking for permission to search her car. He produced a consent form.

Lauren could think of no reason not to let them look in her car and scribbled her signature on the document.

"We'll contact you when you can retrieve it." Detective Overstreet tucked the waiver in a folder. "We'd also like to swab your cheek for a DNA sample. It will help us eliminate yours as an unknown."

Lauren wanted to cooperate and nodded her agreement to the invasion of privacy.

The detective left the room, returning with a DNA kit. He leaned toward her to swab the inside of her cheek. The scent of his mint-flavored toothpaste hung between them.

He secured the sample, then began asking Lauren questions, a repeat of the preliminary questions Officer Bradford had asked—her full name, address, and phone number. His deep baritone voice was soothing and she found her muscles relaxing.

With the preliminary questions out of the way, he said, "I understand you were going to Casper this morning. What time did you arrive at Miss Murphy's home?"

"A little after six." *Don't be late.* Lauren remembered the text her boss had sent the previous evening. "I was running late. You see, my garage door wouldn't open. I don't know if it's the door or the automatic opener. I kept pressing the button and nothing happened. I thought I wasn't going to be able to get my car out until I—"

"Is driving together normal, usual?"

"I'd never traveled with Judge Murphy before but it's normal." *There are things we need to discuss.* Lauren replayed the second text from her boss in her mind.

"If you never traveled with her, why do you say it's normal?"

"Because Judge Brubaker and I did it all the time. Ride together, I mean, when we went out of town." Lauren saw the look of confusion on the man's face. "While Judge Brubaker was on the bench he'd cover hearings once in a while for other judges, you know, if they had to recuse themselves from a case."

He nodded. "Judge Murphy's been on the bench, what, six months?"

"Yes, almost six months."

"Was the plan for you to drive?"

"Yes." The short sleeves of her temporary outfit did nothing to keep Lauren warm and she found herself rubbing her arms while answering the detective's questions.

"Did you notice anything out of the ordinary as you approached Miss Murphy's house? See anyone leaving?"

She shook her head. "No, I didn't. It was still dark out."

"Who knew your schedule?"

"Susan, the judge's assistant. Liam, the law clerk. Oh, and of course the people up in Casper that the hearing was for. I don't know if Judge Murphy told Bradley."

The detective looked up from his notetaking. "Her fiancé, right?"

"Yes."

"Do you happen to know his address or phone number?"

"No, I don't, but I know he lives in Longmont. He has a practice there."

"Miss Besoner, if you would please go over how you found Miss Murphy."

She recited what she had told Officer Bradford as they stood on the sidewalk earlier that morning.

"Let me ask you, who are some of the people she had contact with, dealt with at work on a regular basis?"

"The two I just mentioned, Susan Mumford and Liam Levine. Myself of course. I'd say that's mostly who she had contact with every day."

"Anyone angry with her? Anything unusual as far as interaction with attorneys, that you saw?"

Lauren thought for a moment. "There is one person I can think of. He's a party to one of the cases that the judge has."

"What case is that?"

"It's a bunch of homeowners against a drilling company. It has to do with allowing methane drilling east of Rawlins.

The people fighting it are the surrounding homeowners but there's one homeowner in favor of the drilling, Mitchell Robbins. I don't know if you've ever heard of him, state senator, lives in Carbon County."

"How come Miss Murphy's hearing that case if it's in another county?

"The judge there had a conflict of interest."

The detective nodded. "But Robbins, he's in favor of it?"

"Yeah."

"That's a little odd. Most people have the philosophy of, 'not in my backyard.' So tell me about this Robbins guy."

"I heard he owns shares in the drilling company, High Desert Energy Services. Whenever there's a hearing in the case the tension in the courtroom is palpable. And Robbins acts odd."

"What do you mean?"

"It's the way he looks at Judge Murphy. Whenever I glance over at counsel table, Robbins would be staring at her. I mean all the time."

"Anything more than the way he looks at her?"

"I know how that sounds, but—"

"No, no. At this point I'm gathering information so whatever you can tell me is helpful."

"There's a lot at stake, on both sides. Millions, for the drilling company. The homeowners are saying their property values are going to plummet if drilling happens. Most of the homes out there are close to a million dollars. The case was scheduled to start in February. It was going to be a bench trial, you know, no jury, just the judge."

"Anyone else you can think of?"

"No, I can't."

Detective Overstreet finished jotting down notes on the pad in front of him and slid it into a blue folder. "Thank you for this information. It's early in our investigation. I'm sure you'll understand when I say that I'm going to have to ask you to come back."

"Sure. Whatever I can do to help."

The detective stood, opened the door and shook Lauren's hand, then he sat back down and reopened the folder.

Officer Bradford magically reappeared to take her to the lobby. She hoped there would be a change of clothes waiting for her.

A woman sat in a chair by Heather's desk clutching a plastic grocery bag.

"Aunt Kate? What are you doing here?"

"Claude called me. She's staying home with Sophie today. Poor thing has a cold. She asked if I could bring you some clothes."

"Thanks, but I didn't want to bother you this early. That's why I called her."

"It was no bother. I had to come to town to pick up hay for the pack and some beet pulp I ordered for Esmerelda." Alpacas, the "pack," were her aunt's latest passion.

Aunt Kate stood. "What's going on, Lauren?"

"I'll explain once we're out of here." Lauren went toward the exit.

Her aunt held out the bag to her. "Unless you'd rather go with the escaped con look." She raised her eyebrows.

"Uh, right." Lauren turned back and snatched the proffered bag and retreated once again to the restroom.

Chapter Five

The sun was out, the sky a pale blue. It should be an ordinary morning, but it wasn't. Not anymore.

The two women reached Aunt Kate's 1997 Chevy pickup truck parked at the curb. Lauren hoisted her short frame into the passenger seat and let out a loud sigh.

"Rough morning?"

"Awful. Just awful. I feel like I've been holding my breath all morning." Lauren rubbed her eyes with the palms of her hands. "I can't believe what's happened. It's just *so* unbelievable."

"Tell me what's going on. What's happened? Why were you in an orange prison outfit?"

"Judge Murphy's dead."

"*What?* Oh, my goodness. How? What happened?"

As Aunt Kate drove Lauren home, she filled her aunt in on her not-so-ordinary morning.

"Dreadful, simply dreadful." Aunt Kate pulled up to the curb, put the truck in park and turned to face her niece. "Maybe I should stay with you. Better yet, why don't you come out to the house for a while?"

"No, I'll be fine."

"Are you sure? I don't think you should be alone right now."

"I'll be okay. Besides, didn't you say you needed to get pulp for Esmerelda?"

"Oh, that's right. I forgot."

"How's she doing?"

Aunt Kate smiled, the lines on her face more pronounced at the mention of her pregnant alpaca. "She's doing great. Due in two weeks."

"I'll have to come by and see her. I've been meaning to come out and visit you and the pack but I've been really busy lately."

"I understand. You'll call me if you need anything?"

"I will." Lauren pulled on the door handle. "Wait, I just remembered, the police took my phone. I didn't think to ask when I'd get it back. That goes for my car too. Crap! What am I going to do? I have to have a phone."

The truck idled and Kate drummed her fingers on the steering wheel. "I know I have my old phone somewhere at home. And by old, I mean it's a flip phone. You can text with it and make calls but that's about it."

"That's perfect. I'll take it. I just need something temporarily. Hopefully."

"Let me see about getting it reactivated. I'll bring it over as soon as I can."

"Thank you, thank you." Lauren hopped down from her aunt's faded black pickup. "I'll text you—oh, wait, no I won't."

"I'll be over soon." Kate shifted her truck into first gear. "Be careful."

"I will. And thanks again for coming and getting me."

* * *

A little after eleven Aunt Kate stood in Lauren's living room, her old cell phone in hand. "Let me show you how this works."

"I had a flip phone in junior high, remember? You're the one that talked Dad into letting me have one."

Kate nodded, then handed Lauren a slip of paper. "Here's the phone number."

"Thanks again. I appreciate it. I'll give it back to you as soon as I get a new one."

"What do you mean? They have to give you your old one back, don't they?"

"Yeah, but the idea of touching that phone again gives me the creeps."

"I can understand that."

Do you have time for a cup of coffee?"

"I do."

Maverik nudged between the two women and stood at the back door.

"Good boy!" Lauren opened the kitchen door for him. He ran out.

Aunt Kate removed her coat and unwound the brown and white alpaca scarf from her neck and sat at the kitchen table.

"How's Maverik doing? Is he settling in?"

"He is. As you can see he lets me know when he has to go outside and do his business. No more surprises, thank goodness. But he does have a bad habit. He runs right out the front door whenever I open it. We're working on that."

"Takes time. You've had him for how long now, two months?"

"Almost. Six weeks."

As if he sensed they were talking about him, Maverik barked until Lauren let him in. He ran around the kitchen table three times, then settled himself at Kate's feet.

"People are already talking about Judge Murphy," said Aunt Kate.

"Already?"

"Yes. I was at the check-out line at the feed store and the gentleman in front of me was talking to the cashier about it."

"That's crazy." Lauren poured them coffee and joined her aunt at the small oak table.

"What's going to happen now? I mean with your job?"

"I don't know. I hadn't even thought about that." Lauren stared into her mug. "I know they'll have to replace Judge Murphy but I have no idea when the state will start to do that."

"What's going to happen to you in the meantime? Will you be out of work while this whole mess is going on?"

"I'm not sure. We were supposed to have a three-day criminal trial start tomorrow. Randall won't be too thrilled about having to reset that."

"Randall?"

"Randall Graham, the county attorney."

"Oh, right."

"Claude was telling me they've had this one expert lined up to testify for months. This was the only time he had available to testify before he leaves the country on some sort of sabbatical."

"That's not good."

"No, but nothing can be done about it now." Lauren put her cup down. "And don't worry about me. I have plenty of work to keep me busy while they search for a replacement. Judge Murphy had only been on the bench six months. That's part of why I have so much work."

"What's that got to do with your workload?"

"A new judge's decisions are challenged a lot, to see if she made the right ruling, you know, since she's new. When a case goes up on appeal that means I have to prepare a transcript of the trial proceedings. Once her rulings start getting upheld by the Supreme Court there's usually less appeals filed, which means less trial transcripts to prepare—"

"Which means less work for you to do." Aunt Kate nodded. "I think I understand."

"And right now I have plenty of trials on appeal. I can even work on them at home since there's no judge." Lauren felt a twinge of guilt for thinking that way but knew it was true. "If I was an official reporter in any other state, I'm sure some judicial administrator would assign me to another judge." She gave a shrug. "But Wyoming's so sparsely populated, we don't have judicial administrators, plus there's only one district judge in Crawford."

"You'll let me know if you need any help, financial or otherwise? You know I'm always here for you."

"I know. You're the best. But don't worry, I'll be fine." Lauren didn't know if that were true but could see no reason to worry her aunt. She felt bad for even thinking of her financial situation when her judge lay on a cold metal table in cold storage somewhere.

Before Aunt Kate left, she tried talking Lauren into coming

home with her. When that failed, she had Lauren promise to call immediately if she needed anything, anything at all.

Lauren locked the door behind her aunt and threw the deadbolt. She sat on the couch, turning the small cell phone over in her hand.

"Wow, Aunt Kate wasn't joking. This is old." She showed the phone to Maverik by way of explanation. He sniffed it. "But it'll do." She texted Claudia her temporary phone number.

Maverik nudged Lauren's leg. She scratched him behind each ear while trying to think what to do with herself. Still on edge, she inspected every window in her house, upstairs and down, including the basement, double-checking the locks. "Now what?"

Maverik followed her as she went upstairs to her bedroom and changed into a pair of well-worn brown yoga pants and an old paint-spattered long-sleeved T-shirt. Downstairs she went in search of cleaning supplies. Armed with a bucket of distraction, she dusted end tables, swept the hardwood floors, mopped the kitchen floor, and scrubbed the tile in her shower.

Maverik shadowed her from room to room, something he hadn't done since she brought him home. The first three weeks he lived with Lauren he had followed her everywhere until one day he must have realized this was now his home. Today his presence comforted her.

With no dirty surfaces left, Lauren grabbed a bottled tea out of the fridge and flopped onto her pre-divorce sofa. She patted the cushion next to her. Maverik jumped up, all seventy-five pounds, and landed on her lap. She nudged him off to her side, then put her arm around his large neck and hugged him. "Sorry, big guy, you know we've had this discussion before.

You're not quite lapdog material." With the TV remote Lauren turned the television on and flipped through the channels. She stopped on the Cheyenne news station. Judge Murphy's face filled the screen. "…District Court Judge of Albany County found dead in her home. We'll update you on this story during our evening edition." A commercial came on. Lauren leaned back into the cushions and flipped through more channels, settling on an old sitcom, hoping something familiar might put the brakes on her racing mind.

* * *

"Ar-roof, ar-roof." Maverik jumped off the couch and bounded to the front door.

Lauren sat up from the sofa. There was a knock on the door, and suddenly Lauren felt afraid. *Get ahold of yourself. It's probably some salesperson selling who knows what. Besides, killers don't usually knock first, do they?*

She reached for the phone and checked the time. Three-fifteen. She pulled back her living room curtain, peeked outside, then opened the door.

"Hi." The firefighter who had taken Percy from Lauren earlier that morning now stood on her front porch.

"Uh, hi. What can I—" Lauren stopped when she noticed the fireman cradling something against his chest with his right arm. First Percy's nose peeked out, then his whole face. He looked like a football, a furry brown and white football. Maverik came up to them and whimpered. Lauren planted herself in the doorway to prevent him from jumping on the man or running outside.

"Miss Besoner—"

"Please, call me Lauren—" She looked at his embroidered nametag again "—Cody." Too much had transpired that morning for her to remember his name.

"Lauren, my shift ended and I'm on my way home." He looked at the dog. "You told me to take good care of Percy here. I wasn't able to reach anyone that could take him. The police tried to locate a relative in town but apparently she doesn't have any family here." He looked around Lauren's living room. "The guys at the scene said to take him to the shelter. That's where I'm headed."

"Oh, no."

"Yeah. That's why I came by here first, to see if you wanted to take care of him temporarily. Officer Bradford didn't have a problem with it."

"Me? No, I couldn't possibly. I mean…" but even as she spoke she knew she couldn't let Percy go to the shelter. He had been through his own hell today. How did this man know what a pushover she was?

"It's probably only for a short time. Next of kin have been notified of her death, and I'm sure they will come get him soon enough."

Cody placed Percy in Lauren's arms. The dog, all fur, weighed six pounds max, and right now, every one of those six pounds trembled. She cradled him and sniffed him. "Mmm. Smells like someone gave him a bath."

"Yeah. Took him to the station. We didn't hose the little guy down but we cleaned him up the best we could. He definitely needed it."

"Will you let the police know he's here so they can tell her parents, next of kin or whoever, that I have him?" Saying the words "next of kin" sounded strange in her ears.

"Yeah, sure."

Lauren hesitated before speaking again. "Do you know how Judge Murphy died?"

The firefighter glanced behind him, then faced her. "Possible stabbing, but I really can't say."

Lauren suddenly had the urge for company. "Would you like to come in?"

He stuffed his hands in his coat pockets. "No, thank you. I better get going."

"Right. You've had a long day. You must want to get home."

He smiled. "Well, thanks for taking him. I was not looking forward to a trip to the shelter. And there was no way I could have taken him home. My wife would have taken one look at him and we'd have dog number three."

"Did you happen to bring any of his things? His food or his kennel?"

"No. Sorry. It was pretty hectic there when we left. He's just lucky I remembered to take him."

They said quick goodbyes, and Lauren went into the kitchen with the ball of fur in her arms. "Percy, let me show you around." She spent the remainder of the afternoon getting Percy comfortable in his new surroundings, which turned out to be no easy task. He did not sit still. He sniffed and searched Lauren's entire house and every inch of her backyard twice. She also spent part of the evening playing referee between the two dogs, afraid with Maverik's size he might hurt the Papillon. She debated whether to go to the store and pick up a kennel for Percy but talked herself out of it.

With the days getting shorter, it was soon dark outside, and the in-and-out game the dogs were playing came to an end. Before going to bed Lauren once again inspected the locks on all the doors and all the windows. At the bottom of the stairs she glanced around the living room. "Maybe I should have taken Aunt Kate up on her offer to stay with her."

Maverik bounded up the carpeted stairs and into the bedroom, Percy in the rear. Lauren rummaged through her closet, pulled out an old comforter, and lay it folded in a cushy pile next to her nightstand. She pointed to the makeshift bed. "Go to sleep, Percy." He surprised her by hopping on it, circling a few times then lying down.

Lauren climbed in bed, pulled the comforter up to her chin and tried to do the same. She concentrated on breathing in and breathing out, pushing away unwelcome images of her boss with each exhalation. But every time she inhaled, her lungs filled with air and her mind filled with the same gruesome images. The bedside clock read three-ten when Lauren's mind let go of the day's events and she drifted off to sleep.

A succession of sharp barks broke into Lauren's dream. She pushed herself up on one elbow and looked around. Morning light streamed through the partially open curtains onto her fluffy comforter. Maverik had his front paws on the edge of the bed and let out three more sharp barks. Translation, "Get up! Get up! Get up!"

"Okay, okay." Lauren threw off the covers, swung her feet onto the floor and hit Percy in the head. "I'm sorry, Percy. I forgot about you." Yesterday's events pelted her mind like sleet on a pane of glass. She slid her feet into her slippers, grabbed an oversized sweatshirt from the foot of the bed, and threw it over her T-shirt and pajama bottoms. The dogs dashed out of the room and down the stairs.

From her backdoor Lauren kept a watchful eye on the two as they ran around the backyard. She paid extra attention to Percy, worried the tiny dog would slip out under an opening in her fence and take off to who knows where.

As she spooned coffee into the coffeemaker it dawned on her she had time to drink more than a quick cup. Heck, she could drink a whole pot this morning if she wanted. It was the middle of the week, and she did not have to go to work. Two days ago this would have made Lauren feel like a kid waking up to a snow day. Today the thought made her stomach churn.

While the coffee pot came to life and gurgled, Lauren went and retrieved the newspaper from her front steps. She read the headline as she shuffled to the kitchen. "Crawford Judge Slain in Own Home." Lauren spread the paper on the kitchen table and sat down. Jane Murphy's face looked back at her, a large smile that started at her deep blue eyes and reached all the way to her full upturned lips. She was shaking hands with Wyoming Governor Mason Sterling. The photo had been taken during her swearing in ceremony. For the occasion Judge Murphy had worn her blonde hair in soft waves that cascaded down well past her shoulders. The image made her appear much younger than her forty-two years.

Lauren pored over the article searching for any new details about what happened. It did not list the cause of death, but mentioned foul play was suspected. *No kidding.* There were the usual details of her age, where she grew up, which turned out to be Rawlins, Wyoming, and how long she had been on the bench. The article mentioned the judge had been found by her court stenographer, Lauren Besoner. The story ended with the words, "The department is investigating all leads. Chief of Police Raymond L. Newell is confident the killer will be behind bars soon." Lauren lay the paper face down, hiding the photo.

Chapter Six

It was mid-afternoon before Lauren took a break from editing the latest transcript she was working on. She exited out of the file, backed it up, and went downstairs. Aunt Kate agreed to help her retrieve her car from the police station. Then her plan was to buy a new phone, and stop at the store afterwards. A shopping list sat on the kitchen table that included cleaning supplies after her marathon scouring session the day before. She added a small kennel to the list after stepping in two Percy-sized puddles of pee. Then crossed it off. He would only be a houseguest for a little while.

Maverik and Percy ran into the living room barking. She went to investigate the commotion. "Shush you two."

Lauren peered out her front window. Tony Jenkins, her ex-husband, stood on her small front porch, surveying her little patch of lawn.

"Hey." He offered her an easy smile when she opened the door.

"Hi." Lauren stuck her head out, looked left, then right, then eyed Tony. "Is everything okay?"

"Yes, sure."

Silence.

"Aren't you going to ask me in?"

"Yeah, of course. I'm just surprised to see you here." She ushered him inside. Butterflies flitted in her stomach.

The incessant barking grew louder.

"Quiet. Quiet!"

The chorus of barks continued. Lauren gave Maverik a hand signal, a raised manicured fingertip to her lips, a new technique she learned on a YouTube video. So far it had been unsuccessful.

"Just a minute." She left Tony standing by the door and went into the kitchen, grabbed a box of dog treats from the kitchen counter and shook it. The dogs raced over to her, skidding to a stop on the checkered linoleum floor in front of Lauren's feet. She opened the back door, gave Maverik a biscuit, and broke one into thirds for Percy, then closed the door and went into the living room.

"I went to your office to check on you."

"With everything that's happened I've been working from home."

"Graham's upset about that trial."

"Claude told me about his expert witness. Circumstances beyond anyone's control though."

"We've been discussing what's going to happen with the trials that were already set for this month. Anyway, I've been texting you all morning. When you didn't answer, I decided to come by and see if you were okay."

"The police have it. I'm using an old phone of Aunt Kate's. I'm thinking of getting a new one. Even if they clean it it won't be the same. I'll always see blood smears on the screen." Lauren shuddered at the memory.

"I see you got yourself a dog." Tony nodded toward the kitchen.

"That's Maverik. And...well, you know Percy."

"I do, but why is he here?"

"Because they were going to take him to the shelter. I couldn't let them do that, not after everything he's been through."

Tony shrugged. "How are you are holding up? I can only imagine how upsetting it must have been for you to find Jane."

"It was. It is." *Tony, here in her house. How odd.* "Have a seat."

Tony sat on the faux suede couch. She caught his gaze roaming the tidy living room. "You want something to drink?"

"I'll take a beer if you have one."

Lauren grabbed two beers out of the refrigerator. Before returning to the living room she looked down at her outfit—yoga pants and an old T-shirt. She shook her head.

Tony made himself at home, his left arm casually draped over the back of their marital sofa, like he just returned home from a long day at the office. She felt his gaze on her as she spread two coasters on the steamer trunk that doubled as her coffee table. Handing him an open beer she took in his familiar relaxed pose and his blue eyes that always held a mischievousness playfulness. His sandy blond hair was cut in the same style he wore when they were married, just long enough to curl over the collar of his shirt.

"Thank you." He took long a drink from the bottle. "I see you kept our old sofa."

"I have to watch my spending now that I have a mortgage."

The sound of muffled barking made its way into the living room.

Tony ignored the noise. "Don't just stand there. Come, sit down." He patted the cushion next to him.

Instead of sitting next to him Lauren perched on the far end of the couch. "When did you hear about Jane?"

"Yesterday. As soon as I got to the office. It's all anyone could talk about." He shook his head. "Man, a total shocker."

"I know. I still can't get over that she's dead." Lauren added, "And that I found her." She sipped the cold beer. "Do you know how she died? Has anyone been picked up yet?"

"No." He took another long swig of beer. "You asked me how she died. Don't you know? I mean you said you found her."

"I did, but all I remember is all that blood. Every time I close my eyes I see her lying there in that pool of..." The memory made Lauren shudder. "Makes me sick to my stomach every time I think about it. I don't know if she was shot or stabbed."

"Overstreet was in the office pow-wowing with Graham about the case. Someone must have told him I used to date her because he questioned me briefly about our relationship. He didn't bring up the cause of death."

"Graham won't be able to try the case because of you? I mean because you and Jane dated."

"Not just because of that. Every attorney in the office worked with her when she was a defense lawyer."

"That makes sense."

"He's already been in contact with the DAs in Cheyenne and Casper. Too early to know who's going to end up with the case."

"Does the detective think it was random?"

"He's keeping tightlipped about it. He did let slip Chief Newell is already on his case about finding the killer ASAP."

"Doesn't that go without saying?"

"It does but I've worked with the chief. He can be demanding." Tony glanced around the living room. "Nice little place you have here."

"I like it. I've been changing things a little at a time. I painted the living room by myself last month. I'm going to start upstairs next." Lauren reached over and placed her beer on the trunk. A few loose strands of hair fell across her cheek.

Tony set his beer on his coaster, reached out and tucked the locks behind Lauren's ear. "Are you going to be okay here all alone?"

"I—I'll be okay. I just can't believe what happened." Lauren registered his cologne, the same scent he wore when they were married. The memories of their past came rushing at her like a swift-moving current, threatening to knock her off balance.

Tony moved close, the back of his hand resting on her cheek. He took Lauren's hand and tugged gently so that she sat next to him. "I've been thinking about us lately."

"You have?" She looked up at him.

"I have." He pressed his mouth against hers, his lips rough and warm.

She leaned into the familiar kiss.

Sharp barks and incessant scratching at the back door interrupted the sparks that had ignited between them. Lauren pulled away and stood. "I better let them in, otherwise Old Lady Nash is going to be on my case."

"Old Lady who?"

Over her shoulder she said, "My neighbor. Long story." The dogs tumbled in, ignored Lauren and charged into the living room, continuing their noise-making.

"Quiet, you two. Quiet!" Lauren called after them.

Maverik let out one more bark, then sat in front of Tony. Percy, ears up and tail high, stood next to Maverik and kept on with his high-pitched yipping.

"I'm sorry. This is all new to them. Me too. Everything is new for him." She pointed to Maverik. "I haven't had him very long. And I'm sure Percy is just excited to see you. He probably remembers you from when you and Jane were, you know. . ."

Tony stood and brushed dog hairs off his black slacks. "This is one reason why I didn't want pets. But hey, there's no need to be sorry." He nodded toward Percy. "He never cared for me."

"Really? Why not?"

"I think he could sense I'm not a fan of little yappy dogs that won't shut up." He looked at Percy. "Jane sure spoiled him. Always on her lap. Slept with her too."

"He's too cute, how could you not be a fan?"

"What can I say?" He fished his car keys from his coat

pocket. "I'm going to head out. Like I said, I came over to see how you were holding up."

Lauren motioned toward the two dogs. "I've got my guard dogs here... well, one anyway, but it was nice of you to stop by and check on me."

Tony nodded his goodbye. Lauren leaned against the closed door and allowed her mind to drift to when they first met. It had been during the University of Wyoming Law School's mock trials for third-year law students. Judges, attorneys, and court reporters from around the state were invited to participate. Lauren had volunteered her services. She traveled to Laramie that morning. After the trials were over everyone stayed for a barbeque. Tony, who also volunteered, came up behind her, towering over her. They made small talk as they stood in line at the buffet, then sat at the end of a long table set up on the vast expanse of manicured lawn.

While they ate, he asked her about her steno machine. He told her how fascinated he was that court reporters typed so fast, and how could she keep up with every word. Lauren replied, "I just have a very good memory." He laughed at her attempt at humor. It had been a perfect summer evening.

Lauren looked at Maverik who sat panting softly. "What just happened? And what was that barking about, mister?"

Maverik looked at her, his mouth open, upper teeth visible. His tail swished to a rhythm all its own.

She studied him for a moment. "Is that a smile on your face?"

Chapter Seven

Branches of the aspen tree scraped against Lauren's bedroom window like an endless stream of mice scampering across tiled floor. Another sleepless night. At six-forty-five she gave up trying to go back to sleep and threw back the covers.

The memorial service was set for eleven o'clock. The pewter sky matched the somber occasion. Lauren always believed the two should sync. Sunny skies for weddings, and dark clouds, steady rain for funerals. Lauren checked the forecast the night before. The drive to Rawlins would be uneventful with no snow, no blowing snow, no black ice, no fog, all possible this time of year. While Lauren and Tony were married, there had not been enough deposition work in Crawford for Lauren to make a living. She traveled throughout Wyoming covering depositions. I-80 traversed the high plains of southern Wyoming and became a treacherous drive in winter. And in Wyoming, winter arrived late September and went as long as Mother Nature desired, not caring what the calendar read.

Maverik trotted into the bedroom.

"Hey you, where's my shoe?"

Maverik backed up, turned and ran out of the room. Lauren tossed shoes out of her closet searching for her rogue black pump. She did not know why but he always slobbered on her dress shoes, leaving her cross trainers or flip-flops untouched. "I don't have time for a scavenger hunt!"

The wet rogue shoe lay under the kitchen table. Lauren grabbed it and waved it at Maverik who sat by the refrigerator. "Stop swiping my shoes!"

Maverik lowered his head all of two seconds and then trotted out of the room, tail high.

* * *

Claude, looking professional in a charcoal gray suit, hurried down her sidewalk, turned and threw kisses to Sophie and Roberto. She slid into the passenger seat.

"Seat warmer's on just for you."

"My butt thanks you," said Claude. "Brrr, it's cold out this morning. Thanks for driving."

"Happy to. I'm glad for the company."

"You can thank Randall Graham for that. He asked if I wouldn't mind attending the funeral on behalf of our office."

"So that's why you're going."

"Yeah. I thought it was odd he asked me, but heck, it gets me out of work, at least for part of the day."

"You were her and Amanda's paralegal for a short time. Maybe that's why he asked you."

"Maybe." Claude shrugged.

They drove out of Claude's neighborhood, wound their way to Interstate 80 and settled into the rhythm of the highway.

"How's Sophie doing?"

"She's doing great. Loves pre-school. When I pick her up in the afternoon she's nonstop talking all the way home."

"And you were worried she wouldn't like it."

"I know. Silly, right?"

"And how's Roberto?"

"He's thinking of getting his real estate broker's license and opening up his own office."

"What do you think about that?"

"I told him to go for it. And if he gets busy enough maybe I'll quit my job and work as his office manager."

"Really?"

"No, not really. But sometimes I get tired of office politics. Someone is always complaining about someone or something."

"I'm guilty of that myself. You hear how I badmouth Susan."

"In your defense, she deserves it." Claude tucked a few strands of hair behind her ear. "You don't know how many times I've called down there and gotten no answer. Is the woman ever at her desk?"

"Don't get me started." Lauren steered the Volvo into the passing lane and drove around three semi tractor-trailers that were following each other. The long steep incline slowed the rigs down to fifty miles per hour. The Volvo wagon was her rock on wheels, never breaking down, its engine starting even on the most frigid mornings. She bought it while she and Tony were married. He had encouraged her to purchase it, saying how dependable they were for Wyoming's weather and terrain. Turned out the car was more dependable than Tony.

Lauren turned her attention to the highway. The wind no longer gusted but blew steady at forty-five miles per hour. Lauren clutched the steering wheel tight to keep the Volvo in its lane. Scores of tumbleweeds blew out of the borrow pit and across the highway from the north. Lauren hit one and watched in her rearview mirror as the spindly branches broke apart and scattered on the pavement.

Claude arched a perfectly shaped eyebrow. "And what are you smiling about?"

"I was thinking about the time a tumbleweed had gotten lodged on the underside of Tony's BMW and caught fire. When he told me what happened I started laughing and couldn't stop."

"You did say that was his baby."

"Yep, it was. The car was in the shop for a month."

"You never know what's going to set you off."

Lauren stifled a giggle at the memory.

With their nonstop talking, the green exit sign seemed to rise up out of thin air. Rawlins's population was a little over nine thousand, smaller than Crawford's, and Lauren found the church without the need for using her phone's GPS. The tiny parking lot overflowed with cars. Lauren drove around the block in search of a parking space.

The two women walked toward the church and commented to each other about the license plates on the parked cars, plates from counties throughout Wyoming. They entered the church and let their eyes adjust to the dark. The nave was full, standing-room only, so that's what they did, at the rear of the room. While they waited for the service to begin, the two friends surveyed the crowd. Lauren recognized several attorneys.

Governor Mason Sterling sat one row behind Mr. and Mrs. Murphy. To his left was State Senator Mitchell Robbins from Carbon County. Beside him sat Susan Mumford, who glanced out at the pews behind her.

Claude gave Lauren a nudge and a slight nod of her head to the left.

Following her nod, Lauren caught Tony in profile, in a black suit, arms down and hands clasped one over the other in front of him. All he needed was a pair of aviator sunglasses and a black coiled ear piece to complete the look of a secret service agent as he canvassed the room.

A few feet away from Tony stood Amanda Capshaw, Jane Murphy's former law partner, the woman's face a blank, emotions hidden from sight.

Behind the first pew on the right sat Bradley Schwartz, his soft middle pressing against the fabric of his tailored navy-blue suit. His thinning red hair was combed straight back, and his full red beard neatly trimmed. Lauren easily pictured Bradley as a physician, striding into an exam room wearing a white lab coat, name embroidered on the left breast pocket, and a stethoscope draped around his neck. She found it hard to picture him as Judge Murphy's fiancé. His was not a handsome face, the kind Tony possessed. Lauren assumed what he lacked in looks he made up for in personality. She watched his bespectacled gray eyes settle on Tony. Their eyes locked, their expressions mirroring one another's. Disdain. The staring contest went on until Bradley looked away, then turned his attention to the elderly pastor.

The service began and Lauren saw Tony glance at his watch.

In between the pastor's words Lauren perused the rows looking for Detective Overstreet. Not seeing him, she told herself maybe it was only on TV shows that detectives showed up at funerals hoping to see the murderer in their midst. Or maybe he plans on going to the cemetery where he'll be leaning up against a cottonwood observing the crowd from a distance.

After the service, Lauren and Claude stood in line to pay their respects to the grieving family. Jane's father, Emmet Murphy, gave Lauren a firm handshake. "You're Jane's court reporter, am I right?"

Lauren nodded, "Yes, I am—was—uh, yes."

"You're the one taking care of Percy. Thank you. Thank you very much."

"You're welcome. Maybe we can talk about him… I mean another time of course."

"Yes. I'll be in touch."

They moved away leaving the couple to shake more hands.

Claude and Lauren stepped out into the chilled air, and with heads bent, made their way to the Volvo.

As they passed the parking lot, angry voices, mixed with the wind, made the two women look up in time to see Tony walking away from Bradley.

"I want to know what was going on between you two." Bradley reached up and grabbed Tony from behind.

Tony twirled around and brushed Bradley's grip from his shoulder, like brushing off a spider. "You touch me again, asshole, and you're going to need a doctor yourself."

The two men stood facing each other, hate pulsating off Bradley, and mere annoyance in Tony's expression.

"I want to know." Bradley spat out the words.

"Fuck off." Tony straightened the lapels on his jacket, rearranged his tie, and walked away.

Bradley took a step and stopped. He did not shout his words, both women heard them loud and clear. "This isn't over."

Chapter Eight

"What do you think that was about?" Lauren turned up the heat, warm air filling the interior of the Volvo.

"Had to be about Jane, don't you think?" Claude buckled her seat belt.

"Yeah, but what?"

"Good question."

"Did you see Bradley's face?"

Claude grinned. "It matched his red hair."

Lauren put the car in gear and drove to Rose's Lariat, the two having already decided not to attend the graveside service. They spent the short drive to the restaurant speculating about the encounter they just witnessed.

They entered the old-fashioned diner and were greeted with the buzz of local conversation and the aroma of warm corn tortillas. Claude spied the last empty booth and they sat down. A silver-haired waitress approached with menus and recited the lunch specials.

The two women sipped their drinks, a Coke for Claude and an iced tea for Lauren, and observed the lunch crowd, equal parts white- and blue-collar workers.

Their food arrived. Claude bit into her deep-fried taco. "Mmm, this is delicious. Almost as good as my grandma's tacos." She wiped her mouth with her napkin. "Did you get a look at Judge Murphy's mother?"

"Yeah. That's Jane Murphy 25 years from now."

"Would have been."

"Her father remembered me from the swearing-in ceremony." Lauren dug into her pork tamale.

"When I worked for Jane I remember her mentioning that her family owned a cattle ranch on the Wyoming-Colorado border, Murphy's Land and Livestock. She said it was one of the largest ranches in Wyoming, I forgot how many head of cattle." Claude glanced over her shoulder, then turned back, and leaned forward over the table. "Oh, before I forget, Overstreet talked with Amanda Capshaw. She gave him some useful information, at least that's what Graham is saying. And now they're looking to bring in a Hector Ortiz for questioning."

"Hector Ortiz? Who is he?"

"He's a guy Jane represented ten years ago. He just got out of prison. Amanda said there was a plea agreement worked out between Jane and the county attorney for a deal of three to five in the pen followed by three years of supervised probation." Claude took a sip of soda and continued. "There were two defendants in the case. Amanda represented the other guy, James Blanco."

"Never heard of him."

"I hadn't either. It was before I worked there. It was a meth case, possession with intent to distribute, large quantities too." Claude scooped up the spicy salsa with a chip. "Judge Brubaker didn't go along with the plea agreement and gave him eight to ten."

"Wow."

"Hector was not too happy, to say the least. Amanda gave Overstreet the letters he sent from prison saying what he was going to do to Jane once he was released."

"Did he actually say he'd kill her?" asked Lauren.

"I don't know, I didn't get to read them. Apparently Amanda still has files from the partnership."

"Makes sense that she would. She's still in business, wants to keep the clients they had." Lauren looked at her friend. "Where's Hector now?"

"Don't know. Police are looking for him. He's a person of interest."

"When was he released from the pen?"

"Two weeks before Jane was killed."

"And they don't know where he's at?" Lauren spooned guacamole onto her plate.

"Nope."

"When did his parole officer last hear from him?"

Claude swallowed before answering. "He's not on parole. He killed his number."

"He did the full ten years?"

"Yeah."

"No wonder no one knows where he's at."

"Exactly." Claude put her taco down. "And I have something else to share. I know I shouldn't be speaking ill of the dead but—oh, and you can't repeat this. To anyone. Promise?"

Lauren did the universal cross-your-heart motion with her finger.

"I'm serious. If anyone found out I was spreading rumors... well, just don't say anything."

"I'm insulted." Lauren spoke with mock hurt. "You know I can keep a secret."

Their conversation ceased while the waitress placed a warm sopapilla with honey in front of Claude and left their check. "Have some."

"Maybe a bite. I need to cut back on sweets. I should be cutting back on all eating. I've put on ten pounds since Judge Murphy came on the bench."

"It doesn't look like you've put on any weight."

"Well, trust me, I have. It's all that sitting, in court and the office. It's catching up with me."

"Hey, we were just at a funeral. To me that's a sign that life is too short not to eat dessert. At least for today." Claude drizzled honey over the triangle of fried dough.

"Tell me, what's the rumor?"

Claude whispered, "That Jane Murphy slept with the governor. To clinch her nomination."

Lauren waited for Claude to laugh, to show some sign she was kidding. There was no sign. "Who did you hear that from?"

"Randall Graham."

"No way!"

Claude nodded. "Uh-huh."

"But it's a rumor, after all." Lauren cut off a piece of the warm dough.

"You know what they say about rumors though."

"Yeah, yeah. Sometimes they're true." Lauren shook her head. "Did Graham say this to you?"

"No. I overheard him talking to Bob in the break room."

County Attorney Randall Graham a gossip. "Sleeping with Governor Sterling. He's gotta be, what, ninety?"

They both giggled.

"Seriously, he has to be close to seventy-five. That is such a disturbing visual."

"I'm just repeating what I heard." Claude popped the last bite of sopapilla into her mouth.

"Thank you for waiting till I was done eating before telling me."

"I did say it was a rumor."

"She was smart enough to get that position without having to get into a compromising position with the governor. She got her clients some pretty good plea agreements, and she won more criminal cases than most defense attorneys. And whenever she tried a divorce she always did a good job."

Claude stood. "If you ask Susan, I'd bet she'd disagree. Jane represented her in her divorce and Susan complained that she didn't get her fair share of her husband's retirement."

As Claude paid the cashier for their lunch—she insisted since Lauren did the driving—Lauren leaned into her friend. "Thank you for spreading the rumor. And I know, tell no one." Then with a wry smile, "You know, since Tony and the judge dated after we split up, do you think he was tossed aside for an *older* man?"

The two friends fell into a comfortable silence on the drive back to Crawford. When they were in the parking lot they raced inside the courthouse to escape the sharp wind whipping the air.

Gunner sat at his usual post near the security scanner. He greeted them with a nod as they swiped their security badges and passed through. They reached their usual parting spot on the second-floor landing. "I'll let you know if I hear anything," said Claude.

With no one around the judge's chambers sat quiet, no calls and no visitors. Lauren worked on making a dent in the transcripts that were on appeal.

Chapter Nine

A week had passed since Jane Murphy's funeral. There had been no arrests made. Lauren made coffee and just finished pouring herself a cup when Maverik and Percy sped off and jockeyed to be the closest one to the front door. Then came a knock. She checked the time on the microwave oven. Seven-fifty. She scooped up Percy and ordered Maverik to sit, then pulled open the door.

"Good morning, Ms. Besoner." Detective Overstreet stood on her porch, his posture straight. His facial expression gave nothing away.

"Hello Detective."

"I need you to come to the station and answer a few more questions."

"Couldn't you just ask me questions here?" She moved back to open the door wider.

"No. It would be better if you came to the station. It

shouldn't take long. In fact, I can drive you there."

"No, that's okay. I'll drive myself." She had no desire to be inside a police car ever again, marked or unmarked. Lauren put Percy down, went into the kitchen, retrieved her jacket, her purse, and pulled her keys out. "You two behave." She gave the dogs a stern look. "I'll be back soon."

Lauren felt the detective's gaze on her as she pushed the button lock on the doorknob, stepped outside and jiggled the knob, rechecking the locking mechanism.

The wind blew a steady thirty miles an hour making the heavy white clouds thin out as Lauren traveled south, following the detective's Crown Vic. The pair hurried from the parking lot to the police station entrance. He held the door open for her.

Heather glanced up from her computer screen, the look of disdain no longer visible on the woman's round face, but Lauren sensed its presence nonetheless.

Detective Overstreet motioned for her to follow him down a long narrow corridor. She quickened her pace to match his stride.

They entered a small room. He removed his charcoal-colored blazer exposing a white button-down shirt tucked into navy blue slacks. Both were deeply wrinkled. He either slept in his clothes or dressed himself directly from his clothes dryer. When she had opened her front door earlier she noticed his face sported a five o'clock shadow, a feat in itself since it was not even eight o'clock.

"Before we start, I want to let you know you can leave at any time."

Lauren shrugged. "Okay."

"I have a few questions that I'd like to get cleared up. Before we get started can I get you coffee or water?"

"Some coffee, thanks. With Bailey's Irish Cream if you have it."

He arched an eyebrow, his dark eyes unreadable.

"I'm sorry, I'm a little nervous, and sometimes I say—well, you just heard what I said."

"No reason to be nervous."

The fact that the detective wanted her to come to the station and not ask his questions at her home, made her anxious.

He left the interview door open. The room screamed utilitarian, with its mourning dove gray ceiling, to the shade-darker walls and drab-gray carpeted floor. A gunmetal gray table sat in the center of the tiny room.

She sat in a straight-back metal chair with a molded seat, an identical chair on the other side of the table. She craned her neck up and behind her. The detective walked in. She answered his look of curiosity. "I'm trying to locate where the video equipment is."

"Ah. Have you been in many interview rooms before?"

"No, but I've watched interviews being replayed in the courtroom plenty of times."

"Right, right. Makes sense." He nodded toward her hands. "You're a court reporter after all." He handed her the coffee.

She wondered how she rated. Her hands wrapped around a ceramic mug, not the Styrofoam cup she half expected.

Once again, the detective asked her to retrace her movements that morning leading up to finding Judge Murphy.

She recited the events, all the while wondering why he was asking her the same questions he asked her the last time he interviewed her.

"Let me ask you, Lauren, did you like your boss? Did you like Jane?"

"Huh?" Lauren did not expect that question.

"What I mean is, what kind of relationship did you have with her? Were you friends? Did you socialize outside of work?"

"It was a working relationship. She was my boss. We didn't socialize."

"How long have you known Jane Murphy?"

"She started as the new judge in April, so..." Lauren mentally counted "... right at six months. I also knew her when she appeared in court in front of Judge Brubaker. I'm sure you know some of her background, being a police officer in Crawford. You've probably been cross-examined by her in court, haven't you?"

No reply.

"She practiced mostly defense work but she also did domestic law, you know, divorces, custody disputes," Lauren added.

"I understand you knew her previously."

It might have been her imagination but she heard emphasis placed on the word, *previously*. She stroked the single pearl on her necklace. "I see you've done your homework. I knew of her but I didn't know her, know her. I knew her from work. And before you ask, let me guess your next question and answer it for you. Yes, she dated my ex-husband, but that was before she became a judge." Lauren crossed her arms over her chest, aware it was a defensive posture but her instinct told her to be on the defense.

"I understand they were seeing one another, having an affair while you and Mr. Jenkins were still married."

The gray room closed in on Lauren and she had to tell herself not to duck her head. She blinked, and blinked again.

"It would be understandable to have animosity toward her. Hell, if someone did that to me I'd be furious. I'd want to hurt them."

"Wait a minute. You think *I* killed her? No, no, no. *I* didn't kill her." Lauren heard the shrillness in her voice. "Their relationship, that was all in the past. And I think you have your facts wrong. I don't know who told you that, but my ex and Judge Murphy started dating after we were divorced."

He leaned in, their faces inches apart, his dark eyes fixed on hers. "Heard it from Mr. Jenkins."

Chapter Ten

"That fucking—" Lauren clamped a hand over her mouth while an icepick of betrayal began to stab her repeatedly in the heart. *Tony, how could you?*

After a few seconds of silence, she withdrew her hand. "Well, he would know, wouldn't he?" Lauren clasped her fingers together until her knuckles turned white.

She stared down at her ring finger remembering the June day when Tony asked her for a divorce. Lauren had been in their bedroom packing for a week-long trip to Gillette to cover depositions. She wanted him to spend the morning with her. Instead he had gone fishing with the promise of returning before she left. And he did. Only when he came into their bedroom, it was to say, "Babe, this isn't working."

Lauren stopped packing. "What's not working?"

"Us."

She straightened. "*What*? What are you saying?"

"I'm not happy. I want out."

They exchanged words until finally Lauren asked, "Is there someone else?"

He looked her straight in the eye. "There's no one else, babe."

She returned home at the end of that week to an eerily empty apartment. The furniture was still there but Tony was not. He removed every single piece of personal belonging, removing all signs they ever shared a life together.

Lauren sensed the detective's intense gaze. At that moment what Lauren wanted to do more than anything else was to get up and run. Run out of the room, run out of the police station, run and not stop running, except for maybe stopping long enough to kick her cheating ex-husband's ass. The intensity of her anger brought hot tears to her eyes. She blinked them back. No way this smug-looking jerk-detective was going to see her cry.

His hands rested on top of the blue file. He gave her a smile that stopped long before it reached his eyes. "You're a smart young woman. Are you sure you didn't know?"

When she spoke again her voice held the newfound knowledge of her ex's betrayal. "Yes, I'm sure. I *wasn't* angry about the affair. I didn't even know about it. Besides even if I did know, I told you, that was in the past. I had moved on. I was even engaged until... well, I was engaged to someone when I lived in Denver for a short time." She straightened her shoulders. "You work closely with the county attorney's office, you must know my ex. You know he's not worth killing over."

The detective leaned back in his chair, stretched his legs out and stared at her with an unreadable expression. The quiet made Lauren run her fingers through her hair, brushing a few strands behind her right ear. She took a sip of cold coffee, and listened to the lone sound in the room, the rhythmic tap of his pen on the folder.

A trickle of sweat ran from Lauren's armpit to the inside of her elbow. She pressed her arm against her side and licked her lips. For reasons Lauren could not understand, the silence made her want to talk. "Before Judge Murphy took over as the new judge she came and talked to us, to me, the JA, Susan Mumford, who was Judge Brubaker's judicial assistant, and also Liam Beverly, the law clerk. She told all of us she had no plans to change the staff, and if we wanted to stay on, we all had a job."

Lauren wondered whether she should ask for a lawyer. Nah. She came to the station voluntarily, sort of, and she could leave any time she wanted to. At least she was semi-confident leaving was an option.

"Okay." He opened the file in front of him and read to himself.

"Judge Murphy did have me go back to her office and talk with her in private. It wasn't that same day, it was later. She asked me if I thought there would be a problem working for her, knowing her and Tony's past relationship. I told her no, it was history as far as I was concerned. She said, 'Good to know. I didn't want to have to interview another reporter.' That was it. We never spoke of Tony again. There was no need to."

"I'll be right back." The detective rose from the metal chair and pointed at her cup. "Refill on coffee? A glass of water? Anything?"

Yes, to be out of here. Now. "No, thank you."

Alone in the room Lauren concentrated on sitting still. Her right leg shook and she willed it to stop. She rubbed her face with her hands, then pulled them away. "This is crazy." She spoke the words out loud.

If she had any doubts before, none remained, there would definitely be a recording of their interview, and if for some reason it were ever to be replayed in open court she didn't want to be seen or heard talking to herself. It made her stop and wonder, how does an innocent person behave in this situation?

With no clock on the wall and no cell phone in hand, Lauren couldn't judge how long she waited in the grayness. Her hand ached for the touch of a cigarette.

The detective returned holding a piece of paper in his hand. "We've received the preliminary autopsy report back from Loveland."

Lauren knew from courtroom testimony that Wyoming didn't have a pathologist to do autopsies. In southeastern Wyoming, all autopsies were performed by a doctor in Colorado.

"Dr. Lassiter's preliminary report shows Miss Murphy died sometime between nine o'clock Monday evening and four o'clock Tuesday morning—"

"Now you're sharing information? What, is Crawford short on manpower and you have to play both good cop and bad cop today?"

The detective's brown eyes flickered with anger. "Where were you between nine o'clock Monday evening and four o'clock Tuesday morning, Lauren?" The sharp tone in his voice wiped away any smirk that had been on her face.

"I was home."

"Anyone with you that can vouch for that?"

She let out a small grunt. "I'd say Maverik but I don't think that's what you want to hear."

"Maverik?"

"My dog."

"So no one can vouch for where you were Monday evening?"

"No. I was home. Alone." Why did that fact make her feel like she was guilty of a crime? A misdemeanor offense perhaps, but still a crime.

He slid the autopsy report back in the folder. "You're free to go. But I will give you a heads up, we were able to get Judge Smith in circuit court to sign a search warrant this morning, and I have a couple of officers at your house right now executing it."

The muscles in Lauren's jaw tightened and tears of anger surfaced.

"Are they going to find something I should know about? Because now would be the time to tell me."

"No. They won't find anything linking me to her murder. I don't even know how she died." Lauren rubbed her face with her palms and spoke. "I own a gun. I keep it in my nightstand next to my bed."

"Thank you. I will let them know. What kind of gun is it?"

"A Colt Detective Special .38."

"Hmm."

The gun had belonged to her father who had won it in a poker game years ago. After attending court reporting school in Kansas, Lauren returned to Casper. Travel throughout Wyoming became a necessity to stay working full-time. Her father insisted she carry the gun with her. Too many desolate stretches of road in Wyoming for his little girl not to be prepared. Now, nestled between her driver's license and insurance ID card was her concealed weapons permit.

"My house is locked. How are they going to get in? They're not going to break in, are they?"

"If necessary. But you strike me as a hide-the-key-under-the-flowerpot kind of person. Or you can tell me where you keep a spare key and I'll give the officers the information."

Lauren's pink cheeks told him where he could find the key.

"You need to find a better hiding place. A cop isn't the only person to think to look under a flowerpot."

"*Thanks*, I'll keep that in mind." Lauren tried to control her anger. "You know, you could have *asked* to search my house. You didn't have to get a warrant. Maverik is home, and Percy's there too, and they'll be scared. I don't know how they're going to react with strangers coming in."

"I'm sure they won't have any problems. It won't be Bradford's first search warrant with animals involved."

He stood up. "That's all for now. You're free to go."

Chapter Eleven

The wind slapped at Lauren's cheeks when she emerged from the police station. It was a welcome feeling after the claustrophobic atmosphere of the interview room. She made her way to the car.

"Lauren!" Amanda Capshaw waved. She approached Lauren, arms open wide and hugged her. The gesture caught her off guard, and with Amanda being a good five inches taller than herself, the embrace awkward.

"Hi."

"I didn't get a chance to talk to you at the funeral. I still can't believe what happened to Jane." Amanda wiped at her blue eyes. She shook her head, and loose hairs fluttered across her cheeks.

"I know. It's terrible."

Jane Murphy and Amanda Capshaw had been law partners up until Jane went on the bench. The attorney reached out and touched Lauren's forearm. "And poor you. It must have been awful for you to find her."

"It was awful. It was the worst thing I'd ever seen in my life."

"I can't even imagine what it was like for you."

"It's been bad, that's all I can say." Lauren closed her eyes for a moment to block the unwanted image from entering her mind.

"I saw you leaving the police station. What were you doing there?"

"Answering questions. I should rephrase that. I was being interrogated."

"Interrogated?"

"Yeah, by Detective Overstreet."

"He doesn't think you had anything to do with it, does he?"

"With all those questions he just got done asking me, yes, he does." Lauren tugged the collar of her coat tight. "But never mind that. This must be hard for you. You lost an ex-partner and I'm sure a friend. How are you holding up?"

"I'm still in shock. I can't wrap my head around the fact she's gone." She sniffled, then reached into her mahogany leather bag. "I need to get going but here's my card. Call me if you need advice. And if that detective questions you again, tell him you want to speak to your lawyer. Then you call me."

"Uh, thanks, but you don't really think it'll come to that, do you?" Lauren held out the card to return it, but Amanda had already turned away. Impulsively Lauren held the card in the air and called out, "Maybe I'll come by and talk to you."

"Anytime. Give me a call and I'll squeeze you in," she called over her shoulder.

Amanda might have some idea why someone wanted to kill Jane. With that realization, Lauren stuck the business card into her purse.

She sat behind the steering wheel massaging her throbbing temples. Her stomach rumbled. She debated whether to go home and eat something or go to her office and throw something in the microwave. Then she remembered her house had been searched and her anger resurfaced. Maverik and Percy had better be okay.

Lauren sped out of the parking lot. Hunger pangs were replaced with a queasiness. Her head pounded in her ears as she drove home. She needed to see what the police had done to her house. She told herself it was just as well that she went home. As upset as she felt, attempting to work would have been futile. After answering the many questions Detective Overstreet had lobbed at her, she couldn't think straight. She felt as though she had worked a full day, though a full day of what was a mystery. Avoiding the courthouse would save her from being bombarded with questions by Susan and the possibility of running into Tony. Having just learned what, or *who* caused their marriage to end, she dared not come face-to-face with him now because if she did, one thing was for certain, there would be a scene and she would be the one making it. She couldn't speak to Tony in public, where people were only too happy to eavesdrop. Of course, what she had to say would come out of her mouth so loud it wouldn't be fair to characterize it as eavesdropping.

Tony had been in her home. He had comforted her. They kissed. She even allowed herself the fantasy that he wanted to get back together with her, tell her the divorce was a mistake. And now? Now she felt like a total fool. *When will I ever learn?*

As soon as Lauren turned on to Prospect Drive, she caught sight of her neighbor Jeff Henderson high up on a ladder cleaning leaves out of his gutter. On his front porch, tethered by a makeshift leash, lay Maverik, his head resting on his outstretched front legs. He sat up as soon as he saw the Volvo pull into Lauren's driveway.

Jeff climbed down the ladder, removed his work gloves, and waited for her to approach. "Hey, Lauren."

"I see you rescued Maverik again."

"It was either that or let Old Lady Nash call animal control. I heard her yelling at him to get off her lawn. You know how she is. I went and got him, brought him over here." Jeff sank his lanky six-foot frame onto the top step of his porch, arms resting on his thighs, work gloves dangling from his right hand.

"Thank you so much. I don't think I could have dealt with that today."

"Not a problem. Besides is there ever a good day to have to deal with her?" Jeff nodded in the direction of Mrs. Nash's house.

Lauren followed his gaze. Twila Nash was Lauren's neighbor to the south. Though no one knew Twila's exact age, the surrounding neighbors pegged her to be between eighty and one-foot-in-the-grave. The first time they met had been in May when Lauren set out a few patio chairs along with a fire pit she found at a garage sale. The sound of squeaky wheels made her turn to see the old woman, hunched over, making her way to the low fence separating their property. The woman pulled an oxygen tank behind her. It reminded Lauren of a child pulling a Radio Flyer wagon. Her permed hair, dyed licorice red, bobbed unsteadily when she came to a halt.

Lauren stopped arranging the chairs and went over to introduce herself. She smiled and extended her hand. "Hi, I'm Lauren Besoner, your new neighbor."

Old Lady Nash grunted. She looked past Lauren into Lauren's backyard. "Do you have any children?"

"Uh, no."

"Good," she shouted. "The last bunch that lived there," she pointed her finger at Lauren's house, "were nothin' but trouble. Never a minute's peace while they lived here."

"Oh."

Then the old woman squinted at Lauren. "You know, you kinda look like my granddaughter."

"I do?"

"Yes."

"That's nice."

"No, it ain't. She tried to rob me blind. Let her come live with me a while back till she could get on her feet again. And how does she repay me? By stealing money from me, right out of my purse. Me, on a fixed income."

"I'm sorry to hear that."

"Hmmph." She turned and shuffled toward her house, oxygen and hose trailing behind her.

"Nice to meet you, too," Lauren whispered.

Old Lady Nash whipped her head around. "I heard that, young lady. No need for sarcasm."

Jeff spoke, interrupting her thoughts. "She must not have anything better to do than spy on her neighbors all day."

Lauren looked in the direction of Twila's house.

"She's a lonely old lady." Jeff added, "In all my years living here I don't believe I've ever heard a kind word come out of her mouth. I know I've never seen her smile."

"Maybe someday she'll surprise us."

Jeff looked up at the cloudless sky. "Yeah, when pigs fly." He laughed, exposing a small gap in between his front teeth.

"Well, thanks for keeping Maverik. It's one less thing I have to agonize over." Then she turned to Maverik. "I suppose I can't be too mad at you since there were strangers in our house."

His tail thumped excitedly.

"I was up on the ladder and I saw two police cruisers pull up in front of your house. I figured you must have called nine-one-one. When I went over and asked if everything was okay, if you were okay, they said you were fine, and to go about my business."

"I think I owe you an explanation. It's been kind of—"

"No, you don't have to explain."

"Yes, I do. You must be curious. I know I would be. Besides, Tess pet sits for me, she spends time over at my house. You have a right to know what's going on."

Lauren focused her attention on Maverik. "What I'm about to say is going to sound crazy, except that it's true. I assume you heard what happened to Judge Murphy?"

Jeff nodded.

"I was the one who found her."

"Oh, wow."

"Yeah."

"Tess did tell me her pet sitting gig got canceled. She didn't say why."

"I just told her my Casper job canceled, I didn't want to go into detail with her." Lauren exhaled, then spoke. "The police—I can't believe I'm actually saying this out loud." She began to scratch Maverik behind his ears. "The police think I'm—I'm involved. That's why they were here. They were searching my house."

"No way." Jeff shook his head. "According to Tess, you're awesome. You've been good to her, taking her to see the alpacas, showing her how to put on makeup." He grinned. "She's not allowed to wear makeup yet but I appreciate you doing, you know, female stuff with her. Even baking cookies."

Lauren giggled. "Did she tell you they came from a mix?"

"It's not easy raising her by myself, especially at her age. I suppose it's going to get harder."

"You're right, it will. My dad raised me and my sister but he did have a lot of help from my aunt."

"I didn't know. That must have been tough on you."

"It was. My mother left me—us, when I was eight." Lauren hadn't said that to anyone in years. She shifted on the porch. "Anyway, I wasn't a nice person when I became a teenager and my dad took the brunt of it."

"Something I have to look forward to then."

"We're good now though. Maybe you'll get lucky. Tess is such a nice girl, maybe she'll stay that way. And she's smart. She's shown me things on my phone I didn't know I could do."

"That's Tess, my little techie. She's a good judge of character, even for her age. The way I see it, the cops must be looking at the wrong person."

"Tess is definitely a good judge of character." She rubbed her hands together. "But I'd understand if you didn't want her to come over and watch Maverik until things were a little less crazy."

"Nah, I'm not worried. Should I be?" he asked with mock concern in his voice.

"No, you shouldn't. But we haven't been neighbors all that long."

Jeff glanced at Maverik. "It's plain to see that you're kindhearted. My gut tells me you're okay."

Lauren had shared the story with Tess, how she found Maverik, thin, his fur dirty and matted, hanging around Maverik's, the convenience store on Washakie Avenue. She had, no doubt, shared the story with her father.

"As soon as the police—or at least this one detective gets his head out of his ass—I mean as soon as he realizes he's wasting valuable time looking at me as a prime suspect he'll start the real investigation."

"You know what they say, something about no stone unturned, right?"

"Yeah, I suppose."

"He's just being thorough, doing his job."

"But it's—it's so—so frustrating." Lauren unwound the leash from the rail and stood. "I should let you get back to your work up there. Thanks for keeping an eye on this one. Sometimes I wonder what I was thinking, getting a dog."

"No problem. And if you need anything, just give me a shout."

"I will." To Maverik, she said, "Let's go home and see what our house looks like, shall we?" Lauren's tone was light but her stomach tightened with the uncertainty of not knowing what she would find.

Chapter Twelve

Percy's fevered, nonstop yipping could be heard from the sidewalk. Lauren put the key in the lock and her heart beat faster. Maverik plowed in, knocking Percy over as he took on the role of drug-sniffing canine. Percy recovered and danced on his hind legs, asking to be picked up. Lauren did so. She scanned her living room. Sofa cushions still on the sofa, no end table drawers on the floor. Books neatly lined up in the bookcase.

Lauren and Percy went to the kitchen. Right away she spotted signs of the intruders, a cupboard door hung open, and a kitchen drawer pulled out to the point of dangling precariously. She closed them both, filled a large glass with water and downed two aspirin.

Maverik thudded around from room to room upstairs, continuing his drug-sniffing routine. Lauren poked her head in her office. Nothing disturbed. No signs of trespassers. She rubbed her arms and hugged herself. She stuck her head in the guest bedroom. Again, untouched.

The police no doubt had been in her bedroom and gone through her dresser drawers, even the ones with her panties and bras. "Perverts", she muttered. She sat on her bed and reached over to check her nightstand. Inside the Colt .38 lay in its usual place, under her journal. *Did they sit on my bed and read my innermost thoughts?* She fingered the journal, then pitched it against the wall. Maverik's ears flattened and Percy scurried out of the room. "Percy come back here. That wasn't meant for you." Lauren rubbed Maverik's muzzle. "I wasn't yelling at you either." Hot tears ran down her cheeks. Lauren looked at Maverik. "How can this be happening?"

She reached for a tissue from the nightstand and blew her nose. *Quit it.*

She padded into the kitchen. Her brain needed caffeine. She put on a fresh pot of coffee. While it brewed she went upstairs and took a long hot shower, wanting to wash that detective out of her hair and out of her mind.

Dressed in black sweatpants and a long-sleeved top, Lauren stared into the refrigerator. In search of comfort food, she grabbed the few ingredients needed to make a grilled cheese sandwich and added two extra slices. *Screw the calories.*

The afternoon sun streamed through the kitchen window, making the room feel cheery and bright. Lauren enjoyed its warmth on her back and began to relax. She focused on the taste and feel of the melted cheese on her tongue.

With the combination of a warm afternoon and Jeff's idea of getting outside, Lauren slipped into her favorite brown and gold hoodie, University of Wyoming colors. She put a splash of coffee in a to-go mug, and called, "Percy, Maverik." She offered each a dog biscuit from her pocket. They went to opposite ends of the backyard with their treats, and Lauren sat down at the edge of the deck, her feet resting on the top step. While the two dogs played tag and raced after one another, Lauren's thoughts went to the events of the past two weeks. So much had happened to her ordinary, safe life. Those words no longer fit. Finding Judge Murphy and being interrogated were upsetting and trumped her ability to enjoy the sunny afternoon. Added to that was learning the truth about Tony and Jane. She wondered how many people knew and never said anything. What did it matter now that he cheated on her? She moved on after her divorce. She became engaged while living in Denver. That the engagement ended badly for her was beside the point. The betrayal shouldn't matter, but it did.

She remembered the kiss. How could she have been so unbelievably stupid? Naïve? Gullible? Lauren searched her mind for the appropriate word, like shuffling through a deck of cards in search of the joker. She had believed Tony when he said there was no one else, that he just wanted out of the marriage. End of story, right? She had to ask herself, does that mean even her divorce was a lie?

"I see the cops were at your place this morning," came a raspy voice.

Startled, Lauren turned her head to see Old Lady Nash planted by the fence. She hadn't heard the squeaky wheels approach. The woman wore her usual attire, a shapeless flowery housedress from an era long ago. Over it she wore a man's faded blue cardigan, too large and too heavy for her narrow shoulders. Her feet were shoved into once pink fuzzy slippers, their fuzziness long gone.

"What's going on, young lady? The cops were at your place a long time. You doing some kinda drugs out of your house?"

"No, Mrs. Nash, nothing like that." Trying to explain the situation to Twila would have been a waste of Lauren's breath. She let her answer hang in the air without further explanation.

"Your dog was in my yard again. I was going to say something to them cops but that Jeff guy took him before I had the chance."

"Twila, Mrs. Nash, listen, I—"

"*No. You listen to me.*" Twila thrust a gnarled finger in the air in Lauren's direction. "I told you before to keep that dog of yours out of my yard. He craps here all the time."

"I know Maverik's done that once or twice in the past when I first brought him home but I keep him in the backyard now. It must be another dog in the neighborhood that—"

"No, it's him. And now I see you got another dog. You know there's a law says you can't have more than three dogs inside city limits."

"I only have the two."

"What kind of dog is that one?" Twila pointed.

"Percy's a Papillon."

Nostalgia flashed across the woman's worn eyes, brief but unmistakable.

"Between the two of them they'll bark all day long and disturb my afternoon naps."

Lauren opened her mouth to explain that Percy was a temporary houseguest but instead said nothing.

"If you don't keep them quiet, I'll call animal control. There's noise laws around here, ya know."

"Yes, I know there are laws. They won't be a problem."

Twila turned away but not before Lauren heard her mumble, "Damn good-for-nothin..."

"Come on you two." Lauren went inside, telling herself a mean old lady was the least of her worries. After their conversation—a tongue lashing better described it—Lauren needed a beer. She convinced herself another cup of coffee would be the smarter way to go. If she let herself have a drink every time she had a confrontation with her neighbor, it would only be a matter of time before she attended AA meetings regularly and had a sponsor named Wanda on speed dial. In her present state of mind, she didn't know if she could stop at one drink.

Stretched out on the couch, Lauren checked her phone. There were three text messages from Tony. She deleted all of them with a quick tap. Two missed calls, both the same number with a 303 prefix, a Denver number. Whoever it was did not leave a message. Maybe the caller was a news reporter wanting information.

She texted her aunt to let her know she was home. She did not want her aunt worrying. Ever since Jane's death Aunt Kate checked on Lauren several times a day, almost as much as she did when she was a teenager. The only difference now was it didn't irritate Lauren like it used to when she was in high school.

Lauren tapped out one more text message. "Can you meet me before work tomorrow?"

A moment later Claude replied. "Usual place?"

Lauren tapped out a quick, "Yes!" With the phone still in her hand she debated what to do, work on editing transcripts or turn on the television? She jogged up the stairs to her office to salvage what was left of the day.

Maverik nudged her leg. She glanced at him and then at her computer screen. Three hours had passed. "Hey, I'm sorry. You must need to take a potty break. Come to think of it I could use one too." She blinked slowly trying to moisten her dry eyes. Time to call it a day—or a night.

After letting the dogs out and refilling their water bowl, Lauren fixed herself a snack and retreated to the living room, plopped on the sofa, telling herself she earned the right to watch some mindless television. Percy hopped up on her lap. With remote in hand she flipped through the channels and stopped when a familiar face caught her eye. Yes, it was Susan Mumford, Judge Murphy's secretary, recognizable by the cosmetic uniform she wore every day, the thick layer of ivory foundation, rose blush, matching rose lipstick, eyes topped with shimmery blue eye shadow and outlined in black.

"It was such a shock to all of us. Everyone loved Judge Murphy. She was a wonderful person to work for. I am so, so sad. It is such a loss." Susan dabbed at her eyes with a tissue. Then with indignation in her quivering voice she said, "I hope whoever did this terrible, terrible thing is caught and brought to justice."

The camera cut back to the Cheyenne news correspondent who ended by saying, "Reporting live from Crawford, Wyoming."

Lauren pointed the remote at the TV, "Do you believe her, Percy?"

Percy yawned.

"Neither do I." She muted the TV. Feeling a little foolish for what she was about to do, she picked up a notepad and made a list of possible suspects.

Chapter Thirteen

Lauren parked the Volvo in her assigned parking space and strolled the two blocks to Dominick's Bakery. The walk made her feel less guilty about the cheese danish she planned on having for breakfast. The bakery was a weakness of Lauren's, and she found herself stopping by once a week or more to pick up a cheese danish, or her favorite this time of year, pumpkin spice muffins with cream cheese frosting. Dominick also baked the most amazing European style breads, dense and chewy inside, a crisp crust on the outside.

Several customers sat enjoying muffins and apple turnovers with their coffee when Lauren entered the restaurant. Claude's shimmering jet black hair, tied in a loose bun at the nape of her neck, made her easy to spot. She wore large jade earrings that hung from her lobes. She sat at one of the wooden tables against the wall, a cinnamon roll in front of her. Lauren tapped her on the shoulder as she made her way to the counter.

The two women met at the Law Office of Scott Thurman. Claude was his paralegal, and Lauren had gone to his office to report a deposition. They soon became good friends. At that time Claude was single, having just broken up with her boyfriend, and Lauren had just begun dating Tony. Years later Lauren was the single one, and Claude was married to Roberto.

Lauren approached the counter and saw an unfamiliar man, shaved head, bent over removing an empty tray from the pastry case. He looked up and caught Lauren eyeing him. He turned away before she had the chance to say hello.

Dominick came out from the back room carrying a large tray filled with danish. He reached in and placed the pan into the glass case, straightened and wiped his hands on his flour-dusted apron. The size of his midsection spoke of how seriously he took quality control.

"Mornin', young lady." Dominick smiled wide.

"Good morning, Dominick."

He jerked his head in the direction of the man beside him. "Have you met my new pastry apprentice?"

"No, I haven't."

"Hector, this is Lauren. One of my favorite customas."

"Nice to meet you, Hector."

The man turned to face her and gave a slight nod.

"What can I do ya for on this fine day?" asked Dominick.

"I'll take a cheese danish and a tall latte. Oh, and one pumpkin spice muffin to go, please."

While Dominick turned to the coffee maker, Lauren watched the man named Hector, his five-foot-six body, sturdy and compact, carry the empty tray to the back room. The tattoos he sported on his forearms were homemade, faded blue ink etched on mocha skin. She could not make out the calligraphy tattooed on the knuckles of his right hand.

"This must mean business is good?" She nodded in Hector's direction.

"Yep. Business has been real good. I decided I needed to hire me a helper. He's a hard worker. Doesn't mind the baker's hours. Good with his hands."

"Is he from Crawford?"

"He just moved back." Dominick held out the plate with the danish, and a paper sack with the muffin. He leaned forward into the counter and spoke. "Today it's on the house. I heard what happened, with you finding the judge lady and all." He lowered his voice, "And being questioned by the cops. Musta been rough."

"It was." Lauren let out a small laugh. "I can't believe how fast news travels around here."

"You know Crawford, news spreads faster than a grass fire on a windy day here, am I right?"

"Yes, you are." She held up the little white bag, "Thank you, Dominick." Then with a quick glance behind her, in a low voice she asked, "Would you do me a favor and keep your eyes and ears open for me, let me know if you hear anything, you know, about what's happened?"

"Sure. I can do that for my favorite customa." He winked.

Lauren squeezed past occupied tables until she reached Claude. Before she could sit her friend said, "Spill it. I want details. Leave out nothing."

"You probably know more than I do, you're the one who works in the county attorney's office. Seems like the whole town knows." In between bites of her still-warm cheese danish Lauren filled her friend in on being brought in for more questioning, the frustration of knowing her home had been searched, and her feeling like a murder suspect.

"I can't believe they'd search your place. That's crazy." Claude looked at her friend. "There's something else, isn't there?"

"What—you're right, there is." Lauren blew out a small breath. "Tony kissed me."

"What? When?"

"The day after—the day after I found Judge Murphy. I'm so mad at myself." She spoke through gritted teeth. "I feel like such a fool. That's why I didn't tell you about him coming over the other night."

"Why?"

"What do you mean why? I kissed him. Well, technically he kissed me but I kissed him back."

"You didn't sleep with him, did you?"

"No."

"Then quit beating yourself up. It was just a kiss. No big deal."

"I can't help it. What the hell was he thinking? He had to know that detective was going to tell me about him and—and Jane—I mean Judge—you know what I mean."

"Right." Claude wet her index finger and picked up the crumbs on her plate and popped them in her mouth.

"And you want to know the worst part?" Lauren focused on her danish when she spoke. "I was excited to see him. I thought he wanted to get back together with me." There.

She said out loud what she had been hoping for ever since Tony had started inviting her for coffee recently.

"My philosophy, never date an ex. Not a good idea."

"I think I finally get that, oh wise one."

"I kept my mouth shut when you told me about meeting him for coffee. You were excited." Claude wiped her hands on her napkin. "But I didn't want him to hurt you again."

Lauren set her latte on the table. "Too late for that. Did you know Tony was seeing her behind my back?"

"No way. You know me, I would have said something if I knew." Claude looked at her friend. "There were rumors, but I didn't hear them until after your divorce. By then you were living in Denver. I didn't see any reason to bring it up. You'd moved on."

"Yeah." Lauren cleared her throat. "I thought I did but I checked on him a few times on Facebook. I knew they had broken up."

Claude watched an elderly couple pass their table, then said, "You mean you didn't unfriend him?"

"No. But I wasn't planning on coming back here. After Kevin and I broke up I was going to move home to Casper."

"I remember you telling me about Kevin."

"When I saw that classified ad for an official opening here, I thought it was a sign." Lauren exhaled loudly.

"Whatever the reason, I'm glad you're here."

"If it wasn't for that *sign*, I'd be in Casper right now. With no dead boss. With no drama. With no detective on my ass." She shook her head. "And Tony keeps texting me. I'm thinking about blocking his number."

"I think you should turn your thoughts to the good-looking detective."

"Were you even listening to me? He's an idiot. In his mind I'm a suspect."

Claude waved her hand. "He can't really think that."

"No, let me rephrase that. I'm *the* suspect. I have Tony to thank for that."

"I say use it to your advantage."

"What?"

"Play along. Act like you're interested in him and pump him for information."

"I can't do that. Nope, can't do it. Right now I'd like to kill him." Lauren raised her hands, palms out. "I know, that's a terrible thing to say considering what's happened. I just can't, unh-unh."

"Sure you can. Didn't you say you took drama in high school?"

"I did. I think I was the only one in my class that got a D." Lauren took another bite of her danish.

"You, a D?"

"I had assumed it was going to be an easy class, an easy A. Turns out I assumed wrong."

"Well, the way I see it, he owes you either way. Make him keep you in the loop on what our office finds out from Detective Overstreet. I'll pass along anything I hear but Tony's going to have more information. Graham will be updating the attorneys in the office regularly."

"He won't tell me. He'll say he can't discuss it."

"But you know he can. Our office won't be able to prosecute whoever killed Jane. Another DA from another district will have to. It's not like Tony might leak some information that might jeopardize the case."

"Maybe you're right. The asshole owes me. But it means

I'll have to talk to him." Lauren finished her latte and dabbed her mouth with her napkin.

"Got to take the good with the bad." Claude fished out her phone and checked the time. "We better get going."

They made their way to the door. Lauren turned back and catching Dominick's eye, waved a quick goodbye.

Claude, who had snagged a parking spot right outside the bakery, motioned to Lauren. "Get in."

Lauren slid into the passenger seat. She snapped the seat belt on as she gripped the empty-calories-in-a-bag. "It's a good thing I didn't know about Tony and Jane's affair."

"Why is that?"

"I could never have worked for her if I knew. You know what I mean?"

Claude looked at her and nodded.

"After talking with me about staying on as her reporter, she must have known I was clueless about them. Still, I'm surprised she did."

"Maybe she kept you on because of guilt."

"She has an affair with my husband and later grows a conscience. Nah, I don't think so."

"At least now you won't have to decide what to do."

"Huh?" Lauren looked at her friend confused. "What… oh, yeah, right." She looked out the window, then turned back. She mimicked Judge Murphy's words. "Just leave it out." The words had surprised her. "How could she ask me to leave something out of the record that she said? I heard it, Brenner heard it, his client standing right next to him heard it."

"What exactly did she say to Brenner that she insisted you leave it out?"

"She actually said it to Brenner's client. It was during sentencing." Lauren cleared her throat and mimicked, "'Maybe next time you should hire a competent lawyer to defend you.'"

Claude covered her mouth before a snort could escape.

"Yep. I still can't believe she said it." Lauren shook her head in disbelief. "I was going to leave it in and hope she didn't read the transcript."

"Do you think she would have read it?"

"Don't know. I just know Judge Brubaker would never have asked me to do anything like that. Of course, he would never have said such a thing in the first place... at least not on the bench."

They both laughed.

Claude pulled into the courthouse parking lot and killed the engine.

Returning to Tony's betrayal, Lauren asked, "I know it doesn't matter but do you know, did he dump her or did she dump him?"

"She dumped him. More like kicked him to the curb when she had no more use for him."

"What do you mean?"

"This is just my take on it from the bits and pieces I've heard. She was using Tony. As long as they were dating, Tony and Jane couldn't be on opposite sides in a case, right?"

"Right."

"I know for a fact Jane had two big drug cases coming up around the time you and Tony were breaking up. She slept with Tony, ensuring he wouldn't be the one prosecuting either case. Graham had to assign another attorney to try them. You know drug cases are Tony's specialty. He rarely loses those. I think she was hedging her bets. Remember, I used to work for her. I wouldn't put it past her to do that. And as soon as those cases were over, guess who's no longer a couple?"

Lauren shook her head. "I can't believe it."

"Oh, believe it. I didn't put it together until they broke up, but I know that's what she did."

"She'd ruin someone's marriage just to win a case? I don't know who to be madder at, my dumbass ex or—God, I just—that makes me so mad. Do you really think she did that?"

"I do. I know, it sucks."

Before getting out of the car Claude asked, "Was Jane acting strange lately?"

"She seemed a little preoccupied but I didn't know her very well. I chalked it up to some of the decisions that had recently come down from the Supreme Court."

"Were her decisions getting overturned?"

"Most of them weren't, but I heard one or two had. Maybe that was it. I really don't know. And maybe I'm reading something into her mood that wasn't really there."

Claude nodded.

Lauren unbuckled her seatbelt. "Did you see Dominick's new assistant?"

"Yeah. Why?"

"His name's Hector. Do you think it's the guy the police are looking for?"

"I don't know. Probably just a coincidence."

They exited her car and jogged up the steps into the courthouse to escape the cold air.

"Hey, Gunner," said Claude. Lauren gave a small wave.

The large jailer manning the security desk nodded hello. Gunner's size might lead people to believe him slow, incapable of giving chase if the need arose. They would be wrong. More than once he demonstrated he could move his six-foot, two-hundred-twenty-pound frame with ease to chase and tackle an out-of-control defendant in the courtroom. Lauren found him attractive, in a big bear kind of way.

With Claude in front and Lauren behind her, they each in turn pulled out their retractable badges, swiped them and passed through security. They walked up the stairs. On the second floor landing they stopped. "See you later," they said in unison. Claude turned right to go up the final flight of stairs, and Lauren braced herself for Susan.

Chapter Fourteen

The second floor hosted the clerk's office, the courtroom, and the judge's chambers. Portraits of all the previous Albany District Court judges hung on the paneled walls. Their ever-watchful eyes followed Lauren into the judge's chambers. The unmistakable scent of Susan accosted her as she entered the office.

The judge's chambers consisted of a combined space that housed the judge's office along with the staff's. Susan Mumford's workspace doubled as her office and the check-in point for attorneys. Her space included an L-shaped desk which currently had shiny black and orange garland pumpkins taped to its edges.

"Oh, Lauren." Susan got up from behind her desk, came around and hugged her.

Lauren stiffened.

"How are you, dear?"

"Uh, I'm doing all right."

"How did your interview go with that detective? I hear he's a sharp one."

Did anyone in Crawford not know about the interview? "Since I'm here and not sitting in jail, I'd say it went all right," quipped Lauren, and walked to her office. She had barely sat at her desk when she heard Susan's sing-song voice. "Knock-knock".

Susan came in and sat opposite Lauren in a state-issued gray cloth chair. "I'm a little worried, you know, about having a job when they pick a new judge. I'm sure you have nothing to worry about, being young and perky. I'm sure the new judge will keep you around."

"They don't keep people around for being young and perky. I like to think I'm a good court reporter." Lauren stopped herself from saying more.

"Oh, I didn't mean it like that."

"I'm sure we'll both be fine. We were last time, right? And it's going to take some time to find a new judge to replace Judge Murphy."

Susan and Lauren were in the same situation. All judges' personnel were at will employees. The prospect of a new judge always brought the same concern, job security, or lack of it.

"I can't believe she's gone." Susan shook her head. Her monochromatic dyed black hair did not budge. She extracted a scrunched up tissue from her sleeve and dabbed at nonexistent tears.

"It is hard to believe." Lauren turned to her monitor and tapped on the keyboard, offering Susan a hint. The hint had been too subtle. Susan looked behind her toward the door and then leaned over Lauren's desk and whispered, "I never asked you, but weren't you scared that morning when you found Judge Murphy? I mean the killer could have still been in the house. They could have been hiding just around the corner."

"Of course I was scared. Anybody would be. That's kind of a—"

The distant ringing of Susan's phone cut Lauren off.

"I suppose I should answer that." She turned to go, leaving Lauren with the sight of her above-the-knee skirt, exposing a roadmap of spider veins traveling up her thighs to parts unknown. The two-inch heels she wore made Lauren fear the woman would topple over and break a hip.

Lauren clicked opened a file and began to edit.

Another "knock-knock" came at eleven-forty-five. Susan poked her head in. "I'm leaving for lunch. I have an appointment at noon so I may be late getting back."

"Okay."

"And Emmett Murphy called. He asked if we could box up the judge's personal items. I told him you'd be happy to do it."

"Why me?"

"I just *can't* go in her office. It's too upsetting. You don't mind, do you?"

She shrugged. "No, that's fine. Did he say when he might come and get them?"

"I think he said this weekend. Or maybe it was next week. He gave me his number. Why don't you call and check with him?" Susan swung around to leave. "See you later. Maybe," she called behind her.

Lauren phoned Emmett to find out when he would be in Crawford. He didn't know when, but would call her first and give her a heads up. She suggested she take the items home with her, in case he came for them on a weekend and the courthouse would be closed. He agreed.

Sunlight poured into the large corner office. It held the typical "judicial" furniture; a long, highly polished cherry wood conference table. It took up three-quarters of the length of the room, with the judge's desk placed at the head, forming a T. Thick-cushioned adjustable chairs surrounded the conference table. More than once Lauren had to stifle a burst of laughter as she watched an attorney grasping the table to keep from pitching backwards.

The empty stenographer's chair sat close to Judge Murphy's desk. Everything looked as it did the last time she sat in that chair reporting the in-chambers motions.

With three used evidence boxes she found in the evidence room, she stood in the judge's office and waited to feel some kind of emotion, a sense of loss, sadness, something. She didn't feel anything. Then she did. She felt bad for not feeling anything.

Lauren started with the large personal items. She placed the cardboard containers on Judge Murphy's desk and began gathering the judge's running shoes and workout clothes, which she often saw Judge Murphy wear as she headed out on her lunch breaks. She smiled as she remembered a time when Judge Murphy was late getting back and had thrown her robe over sweat-drenched T-shirt and running shorts. No dress code under the robe.

The framed artwork had not hung on the walls long enough to leave their impressions behind. One by one Lauren removed pictures off the walls, diplomas, and photographs off the credenza, until the office no longer held any trace of Jane

Murphy. She placed the judge's law degree from the University of Wyoming, along with her admittance to the Wyoming State Bar, in the boxes. She removed the framed photos from the credenza, one of Judge Murphy and her parents during her swearing-in ceremony, and one of Percy. From there Lauren began opening drawers of the massive desk. She found legal pads with Judge Murphy's handwritten notes on them. The top drawer on the left looked like a catch-all drawer similar to the one in Lauren's laundry room except Judge Murphy's contained a package of Double Stuf Oreos. She bit into one. "Eww." She spat the stale cookie out and tossed the rest in the trash can.

A novel sat under the cookies, bookmarked at page 195. The cover depicted two women lying intertwined on a beach blanket, a sprinkling of sand separating their naked bodies. Lauren held the book, surprised by its cover. *Should I store the book in the box? Throw it away?* After a moment she tossed it in one of the boxes. The one drawer contained too many items to sort through individually. Lauren pulled it out and emptied its contents into the second box, thinking that Mr. Murphy could sort through them.

The last large item she gathered was the laptop. Lauren assumed it to be state property but without a sticker on it stating such, she did not want to leave it in the office in case someone "accidentally" fired it up.

She carried Judge Murphy's things into her office and set them in the corner. They now sat next to exhibits that were part of an appeal she was working on. She scribbled on the boxes, "Judge M", with a thick black marker.

Lauren returned to the judge's office. There were enough personal items still in drawers to fill at least one more box, maybe two. Orders lay in a neat pile on Judge Murphy's desk, awaiting her signature that now would never come, at least not from her. Next to them sat a yellow legal pad containing the judge's handwritten notes from their last trial, a personal injury lawsuit. It seemed so long ago. Lauren picked up the legal pad and a loose sheet slid out and landed on the desk. She picked it up. A temporary order of protection.

Line five read, "Person to be included in order of protection." In blue ink, written in Judge Murphy's handwriting, the name Danielle Armstrong had been inserted. The name Danielle Armstrong teased at the inner recesses of Lauren's mind. Where had she heard that name before? A recent case perhaps?

Curiosity got the better of Lauren. With the document in hand she continued to read it as she walked toward the door. She felt a momentary flicker of guilt for taking something out of Judge Murphy's office.

She turned the corner and collided with Tony.

Chapter Fifteen

"Crap."

"Whoa there."

"You startled me."

"I've been looking for you."

"What do you want?"

"You haven't answered any of my texts. I've been worried about you, and I want to talk."

"Well, I don't."

"Lauren, cut me some slack."

"Goodbye." She started toward her office but Claude's words echoed in her ears, "He owes you." With effort, she turned and faced him, "Okay. Come on."

They walked in silence to Lauren's office.

"What have you got there?" asked Tony as he slid easily into the chair opposite Lauren's.

"Nothing." She walked around her desk and dropped

the document in the drawer to her right. She looked across at her ex-husband and noticed the bulge around his middle, something she failed to notice the other night. No longer the ultra-fit thirty-year-old man she had married seven years ago.

"I wanted to say I'm sorry." Tony's voice interrupted her thoughts.

"You're sorry? You're sorry. Hmmph. Sorry for what? For cheating on me or for telling Detective Overstreet I'm a good suspect because you were a cheating ass when we were married? And what the hell was that the other day, coming over and acting all concerned?"

"I was concerned. I am concerned. You live alone. And in case you've forgotten, there is a killer out there. And don't tell me deep down you didn't know about me and Jane. Come on, you must have put it together."

"No, I didn't."

"It doesn't matter now. That's all in the past. Let it go."

"You're such an ass."

Tony ignored the remark. "All I did was tell him the truth."

Lauren said nothing.

"Overstreet was at our office asking about Jane. He asked for a timeline of when she and I dated, if I knew of any enemies she had. I told him the truth. I'm telling you, it's not a big deal."

"*No big deal*," Lauren repeated. "How can you say that? And now you know I'm a suspect. What am I saying? Everyone in this freakin' building knows I'm a suspect. And I have *you* to thank for that." Lauren tried to swallow the anger rising inside of her. She leaned forward in her chair.

"Did you know they searched my house yesterday? *Did you?* Do you have any idea how that made me feel?"

"Yeah, I heard about the warrant. The man is just doing his job. Everybody knows you're innocent."

"Thank you for your vote of confidence. I feel *much* better."

"I told Overstreet he was wasting valuable time on the wrong person. Let it go, Lauren."

"I think you owe me."

"*What?* What the *hell* are you talking about?"

"You owe me for having my house searched and" … her voice cracked… "for cheating on me while we were married."

Tony threw his hands up. "I said I was sorry. What the hell more do you want from me?"

She pressed a finger to the outside corner of her eye to stop the tears that were forming.

He reached out to touch her hand and she jerked it back reflexively.

"Oh-kay then." His hands went up in surrender.

"I want information."

"You want *what?*"

"You heard me. I want to know who Overstreet is looking into besides me, where the investigation is headed. What he shares with your office, I want to know. And if—if he plans on arresting me, you better tell me ahead of time."

"Why? So you can abscond?" Tony laughed.

"That's not funny." Her voice rose again. "I can't take any more surprises. You have no idea how humiliated I feel. And I don't want that detective showing up here—or anyplace else for that matter—and being hauled off in handcuffs."

Tony opened his mouth to speak. Lauren knew from their past that an argument would ensue if she didn't cut him off. She held up her hand. "Don't. Don't tell me you can't. I know you can. Overstreet will be giving your office updates on his progress with the case. All you have to do is share it with me. I'm not going to divulge anything. There's no chance I'd be jeopardizing the investigation."

"I don't think—"

She cut him off again, "Your freakin' past—your running around with—with her got me into this mess, damn it! I can't just sit here not knowing."

The sound of someone clearing their throat interrupted their bickering, then came a knock at Lauren's open door.

"Excuse me for interrupting, Lauren."

"Oh, hi, Tom. No, you're not interrupting. Come on in." Lauren came around her desk.

Justice Thomas P. Matheson, Chief Justice of the Wyoming Supreme Court, stood in the doorway.

Tony stood and the two men shook hands.

"Mr. Jenkins."

"Justice, nice to see you, sir."

Justice Matheson walked over to Lauren and gave her a tight hug. "My condolences, Lauren. I'm sure it's been a shock having lost Judge Murphy."

"Shock is putting it mildly."

"And you having found her, that must have been extremely upsetting. How are you holding up?" He held her at arm's length, and studied her face.

"I'm doing okay, considering."

"I was in town visiting Brett and the family. I'm on my way home, but I couldn't leave without checking in on you first."

"Thanks, that's nice of you. How are Brett and Lindsey? I haven't seen them in a while."

"They're fine. Busy with their lives."

"And how is that grandson of yours? Any pictures?"

Tony stood off to the side and observed Lauren and the justice converse like old friends.

"Pictures?" The chief justice reached into the breast pocket of his coat and produced a cell phone. He tapped on the screen, then passed the phone to Lauren.

"Julian's adorable. And I think he has your eyes."

"You think so?" He smiled. "He's such a character."

Lauren and Thomas chatted, catching up on what each had been up to since they last saw one another. Tony, hands shoved in his pockets, looked out the window.

Chief Justice Matheson turned down an offer for coffee. He embraced Lauren again. "I want you to call me if you need my assistance. You got that?"

"I will. Thanks, Tom."

He eyed Tony, then to Lauren he said, "Say hello to Kate for me. Tell her I'm going to take her up on her offer soon and bring Julian by to see her alpacas."

"I will. She'd love that. It was good to see you again."

Lauren sat behind her desk.

"On a first name basis with Chief Justice Matheson. I'm impressed."

"You shouldn't be. Did you forget he was at our wedding?" Before he could answer Lauren asked, "Where were we?"

Tony stood in front of Lauren's desk. He ran his large fingers through his hair, another signal she remembered from their past. Exasperation and defeat.

"You have to promise not to divulge any—and I mean any information. I don't need Graham on my ass."

"I told you I won't."

"And after this is over, you can get off my ass about Jane and me. It's history. Get over it."

"I know, how about we never speak to each other again?" She knew that would be impossible, but she could always hope.

"Works for me."

"Knock-knock," came Susan's sing-song voice. "I'm back. Hi, Tony."

Neither Tony nor Lauren had heard Susan approach. They exchanged quick glances, wondering if she heard their final comments to one another.

"Susan, nice to see you as always." Tony flashed a boyish grin.

Susan smiled coyly and fluttered her eyelashes.

Lauren watched the exchange in amusement.

"Tony, can you believe what happened to Judge Murphy? I'm still in shock myself. And such a silly thing, that detective thinking our Lauren had anything to do with it."

"Our Lauren doesn't have a thing to worry about. Detective Overstreet is just being thorough."

"Oh, Tony, you're *so* smart. I'm sure you can make sense out of all this nonsense." Susan giggled, then put her fingers to her lips.

How old is this woman, thirteen? Lauren rolled her eyes.

"It's too early to say anything but the police will have some solid leads soon," said Tony.

The quiet expanded until Susan spoke. "I better get to work. Judge Brubaker has kindly agreed to cover Judge

Murphy's criminal docket for a few weeks, and I'm working on that today. I'll e-mail you the list, Lauren. I have to keep the wheels of justice moving. My work never ends." She waved like the Queen of England, turned and disappeared out of sight.

"I better get back upstairs."

"Don't forget. Information."

"I won't, I won't. I'll text you when I have something." He swaggered out of her office.

"Ass," Lauren muttered under her breath. When she heard the outer door close, she reached into her drawer and pulled out the protective order.

Chapter Sixteen

Before she could study it, the office phone rang. "District Court Chambers. This is Lauren."

"This is Detective Overstreet. I have a few more details I need you to sort out. Can you come to the station?"

"Yes. When do you want me to come down?"

"If you're not busy, I'd like you to come down now."

"I'll be down in a few minutes." Lauren placed the receiver in its cradle and stared at the phone. She opened the bottom drawer, slid the protective order in, pulled out her purse, and reached in the side pocket for her keys. She gathered one of the boxes containing the judge's personal items. *Might as well start getting these boxes home.* Susan was not at her desk. It meant no explaining where she was off to at two o'clock in the afternoon.

She walked to where her Volvo was parked and unlocked the trunk.

"Here, let me help you with that."

"Oh, thanks, Amanda."

The lawyer opened the trunk for Lauren. "I was on my way to the clerk's office when I saw you struggling with that load."

"It is just a little awkward when you have your hands full." Lauren moved her sleeping bag, a small shovel, and a pair of snow boots off to one side to make room for the box.

"I see you're all ready for winter."

"Yeah. It'll be here before we know it." Lauren adjusted the lid on the box, making sure it was secure, and closed the trunk. "Thanks, Amanda."

She walked to the north end of the courthouse, down a flight of stairs to the now-familiar police station entrance.

Detective Overstreet stood just inside the door and opened it for her. "If you'll just follow me."

He motioned for her to take a seat. The detective studied the sheet of paper in front of him, then turned his attention to Lauren.

"Just a few more questions I have since we spoke last. Now I know you found the body of Miss Murphy. You said you were alone. There was no one else there. And you didn't see anyone leaving the area?"

"No. If I saw someone I would have told Officer Bradford."

"I want you to go over again what happened upon your arrival."

"Seriously? You've asked me that question every time I've been here. I've told you everything I know."

"You might remember some new detail. Sometimes events become clearer after things have calmed down."

Lauren shook her head, but did as he asked.

"Did she know you were on your way? Had you texted her?"

"Yes. The text is still—"

"One of her neighbors remembers a car being parked in Miss Murphy's driveway sometime around nine-thirty that evening. Was that you?"

"No."

"Perhaps you dropped off a transcript the night before?"

"No, I didn't."

"If someone said they saw a Volvo in her drive, would they be mistaken?"

"Yes. Or else it was someone else's Volvo. It wasn't my car."

The detective flipped through the pages in his notebook, stopping occasionally to study a note. "Did you touch anything in the foyer?"

"I don't remember."

"You don't remember, Lauren?" The words carried a sarcastic edge.

"No, I don't." Lauren crossed her arms over her chest. It took concentration but she managed to place them back on the table. "No, I didn't touch anything else."

"Will we find your fingerprints anywhere in her house?"

"Probably. I pet sat Percy a couple of times. On an emergency basis."

"And the last time you watched him?"

"I don't remember for sure, a month maybe. She—"

"So you have been in her house before?"

Lauren moved around in her seat. "Yes. I told you, to take care of Percy. Oh, and I did search for the light switch in the entryway. That was after I had picked up Percy so..." She looked at the detective. "My prints, I'm sure my prints are on the wall around the light switch. But you already know that, don't you?"

He kept his response hidden behind a blank expression. He asked her to again go over how she found the judge, the positioning of her body on the floor. The request made Lauren uneasy. She'd heard about different tactics used during questioning. See if someone's story changes, if they add something new or leave something out.

She felt the detective's attention settle on her while she recited the story again, not quite sure if she had left something out or added a new detail.

"Thank you for clarifying those details for me. Unless you have something you'd like to share with me, that's all for now."

For now? "I've told you everything. More than once." She debated whether to mention the protective order she found. Instead she asked him, "Have you found Hector Ortiz?"

"How do you know about him?"

"Just a rumor I heard. Have you found him?"

He answered her with silence.

Chapter Seventeen

Susan left a sticky note on Lauren's locked door. "Terrible headache. Have to go home". Lauren tossed the note in the trash and sat at her desk. She opened a file on her computer, her hands poised to edit. The interview with the detective invaded her thoughts, and she replayed his questions over again in her mind. *The man thinks I killed her. Maybe I should have told him about the protective order.*

She looked back at the screen, at the transcript that she needed to finish. She had ten more days before it was due on appeal. Contested divorces ranked at the top of Lauren's least favorite things to have to listen to in court. She did not want to hear the intimate details of people's lives, their sexual proclivities now shared within the four walls of the courtroom and forever preserved on the record, and often, in her memory.

This divorce had been the worst one Lauren had to listen to, mostly because it involved Mr. Brenner, who represented the husband. He had approached Lauren's small table that held her computer, and made a big production of putting an exhibit sticker on a slim rectangle-shaped box, and placed it in front of the witness on the stand, asking the soon-to-be ex-wife if she could identify the contents. Everyone in the courtroom could see the red creep up in the soon-to-be ex-wife's neck as she explained the contents, a large purple personal vibrator she kept stashed in her nightstand. Lauren did not see the relevance of introducing the vibrator into evidence aside from the embarrassment factor. But that was Mr. Brenner's specialty, embarrassment. Many times it turned out to be his own, when he often called his client by the wrong name. The vibrator, now in a box, with a lid, and out of sight in the evidence room, was, unfortunately, not out of mind.

Lauren closed the file and went down the hall into Judge Murphy's office to see how many more boxes she needed for Judge Murphy's things. She opened the top right drawer of the judge's desk. She fingered its contents, the everyday assortment of pens, pink sticky notes, paper clips, a tin of mints, a bottle of Tylenol. Tucked in the back of the drawer was a medicine bottle, a prescription for Vicodin. Lauren shook the amber container and heard the rattle of pills.

In the bottom right drawer was a brown file folder. Inside were letters of congratulation to Judge Murphy on her newly appointed position. Underneath the file were outdated copies of the local bar's newsletters. Lauren lifted these up and rifled through more papers. At the bottom of the drawer lay a sheet of lined white paper. In the judge's handwriting was the word, *Confirm.* Underneath were three names. Lauren took the list of names to her office, jotted them down on a sticky note, and returned the paper where she found it.

Lauren got on her computer and logged into the court's database. She typed the first name on the list. Duane Cochran. The name appeared along with a criminal docket number. Clicking on the information tab she saw he had been charged with possession of a controlled substance with intent to deliver and found guilty of the charge.

The second name on the list was Calvin Merck. The information on the screen indicated Mr. Merck was a plaintiff in a divorce action. The action had been filed the previous January.

The last name Lauren typed in was Melanie R. Schneider. A civil docket number popped up by Miss Schneider's name, another plaintiff in a divorce proceeding. The status of her case showed that the divorce decree had been signed by Judge Childers in May.

The same firm name, Murphy and Capshaw, appeared on all the files. Lauren swiveled in the chair pondering what, if anything, this meant. Maybe nothing but Amanda might know the answer. They could either be her old cases or old cases of the judge's or both. Maybe the judge wrote the names out to help her remember them in case they appeared before her and she could remember to recuse herself and let another judge hear their case.

Lauren picked up the receiver and dialed Detective Overstreet's cell number, then hung up the phone. The names probably meant nothing. He would look at her like she was stupid. Besides, she did not want to talk to him.

Long shadows cast on the wall told Lauren it was quitting time. She massaged her temples. Before leaving, she went online and checked to see if Susan had scheduled any hearings in the coming days. Now that Judge Brubaker agreed to fill in for Judge Murphy, it meant criminal cases kept moving through the system and they would not run the risk of going beyond a defendant's right to a speedy trial, one hundred and eighty days. If that had happened, their case could get dismissed, the equivalent of playing Monopoly and picking up a get-out-of-jail-free card.

Susan calendared a full day for Friday. The first hearing was a motion to suppress evidence, starting at nine o'clock. At eleven o'clock a motion in another criminal case, where the defense attorney sought to disqualify an expert witness. Arraignments, sentencings, and bond revocations were set for the afternoon to start at one-thirty. The criminal list was a long one, which made sense. There had been no hearings of any kind in the last two weeks, and criminal cases were piling up.

Lauren backed up her files, shut down her computer, tidied her desk, putting away stray paper clips and sticky notepads. She found herself looking forward to working with Judge Brubaker again. He spoke loudly, clearly, and slowly, a court reporter's dream judge.

With her hand on the light switch Lauren glanced around, checking to see if she forgot anything. The office phone rang, and she picked up the receiver. "Good afternoon, District—"

"It's me," said Claude.

"Hi. What's up?"

"We just scheduled a shelter care hearing for eight o'clock Friday morning. Thought you should know."

"Thanks. Has Judge Brubaker been notified?"

"Yep. FYI, it's Tony's case."

"That's just how I want to start my day. Thanks for the heads up."

"No problem. I'll talk to you tomorrow."

Lauren walked along the empty corridor and tried not to think about having to face her ex. The thought of seeing him Friday made her want to put punch something.

Chapter Eighteen

At seven-fifteen Friday morning Lauren passed through the security station of the county courthouse. The building had the distinction of being the oldest functioning courthouse in Wyoming. Though retrofitted with modern amenities, air conditioning and closed-circuit security cameras throughout, the structure's facade remained the same for over one hundred years. Lauren always felt a sense of awe upon entering the imposing structure.

In the courtroom, Lauren hooked up her computer to her writer and turned on the iPad she placed on the bench for the judge. He liked the ability to follow the proceedings, and could review what someone just testified to on the spot by reading the live feed from her steno machine to the small screen in front of him.

While waiting for the judge and Tony to arrive, Lauren enjoyed the view out the large windows to her left, where amber leaves hung precariously from the cottonwood trees.

Tony entered the courtroom, breaking the serene moment. He ignored Lauren. Officer Bradford accompanied him. The sight of the officer brought back the image of Judge Murphy's body. She wondered how long it would take to stop equating seeing Officer Bradford with that image. Lauren had no answer to that question.

Tony set his leather satchel on the table and removed a brown file folder. The two men leaned into each other, poring over documents between them.

The judge stuck his bald head into the courtroom. "Come and get me when everyone is ready, Lauren." He smiled at her, his green eyes sparkling with youthfulness that belied his seventy years.

At seven-fifty-five, Lauren unlocked the rear door that led into the hallway of the judge's chambers. She found Judge Brubaker standing by Susan's desk, his frame impressive, both in height and weight. Whoever said black was slimming hadn't seen the judge in his robe.

"Everyone's ready, Your Honor."

"Well, let's get started then."

The first and only witness called to testify was Officer Bradford. Judge Brubaker placed him under oath and the questioning began. The pace of the questions and answers were easy for Lauren to write and keep up with.

Tony paused and searched for a document to show the officer. The large room fell silent. Lauren heard the courtroom door open. Detective Overstreet stepped in and stood just beyond the double doors, arms down and hands crossed in front of him.

The questions and answers resumed. Lauren's fingers fumbled on the keys of her writer. *Was he coming to arrest me? Here?* From listening to past criminal trials Lauren knew that happened; the police showed up where a person worked and cuffed them in front of their coworkers.

When Overstreet didn't produce handcuffs, Lauren breathed a sigh of relief and settled back in the rhythm of writing on her machine. The hearing ended at eight-forty-five. Detective Overstreet went over and spoke with Officer Bradford.

With fifteen minutes to spare before the nine o'clock matter began, Lauren went to her office, retrieved the information she printed out earlier for the next two hearings.

Susan was at her desk when Lauren came out of her office. "Hi Lauren. How are you today?"

"Good. And you?"

"I could be better. I'm coming down with a cold."

"Oh." Lauren passed Susan's desk without saying more, and went into the break room.

Judge Brubaker motioned with his hand toward the bakery box next to the coffee maker. "I think there's time for a muffin before our nine o'clock starts. Help yourself. Please."

She reached for a pumpkin spice muffin, swiping a little frosting off with her finger, all the while telling herself, you will go to the gym tomorrow.

"Lauren, how are you holding up? It's such a terrible thing that's happened."

Not knowing how much he knew of her being questioned and being a suspect, she replied, "It's been strange. Everything's sort of up in the air."

Judge Brubaker nodded. "I just cannot understand how someone could do that to Jane. Are you aware of any new developments in the case?"

"No."

He took a sip of coffee. "Have you been busy? I mean before this thing with Jane happened?"

"Very. I think you retired at the right time. The docket's been crazy."

"I timed it that way you know." He laughed.

Lauren popped the last bite of muffin into her mouth, wiped her fingers on a napkin, and tossed it in the trash can. "I've been looking forward to working with you again. With you back on the bench things feel normal. And right now, normal feels good."

"I'm happy to help out. And I'm sure my wife is happy I'm out of the house for a while." He set his coffee cup in the sink. "If you are ready, we better get to work and see what the attorneys have to say for themselves this morning… or for their clients rather." He winked.

A man in an orange jumpsuit sat at the defense table, Amanda Capshaw at his side. Randall Graham sat at the other table, representing the state. The proceedings went by fast. Lauren had not glanced at the clock on the wall until it was twelve-forty-five.

She hurried to place a frozen meal in the microwave, and while the timer counted down she went to see if Amanda was still in the courtroom. The attorney sat with her client. They spoke in hushed tones until two jailers approached, then they stood. After the man in the orange jumpsuit was escorted out a side door, Lauren said, "Do you have a minute?"

Amanda closed the red file folder in front of her and set it in her briefcase. "Yes. As a matter of fact, I was just coming to see you."

"I'll meet you in my office. I just need to grab my lunch from the break room."

A few minutes later Lauren waved Amanda in and motioned for her to have a seat.

"Hope you don't mind if I eat while we talk." Lauren gestured to the little rectangle in front of her.

"No, no."

"If I don't I'm no fun to be around in the afternoon."

"Full docket?"

"Yeah. I'll be lucky if I get out of here by five o'clock." Lauren looked around her desk. "I forgot my tea. Would you like something to drink? A cup of coffee?"

"Do you mind? I have a caffeine withdrawal headache. But I can get it myself."

"No, no. I'll be right back."

Lauren returned to find Amanda behind Lauren's desk looking out the window. She handed the attorney the mug of coffee and placed packets of cream and sugar on her desk. "Wasn't sure how you take it."

"Thank you. Nice view." Amanda took a sip of the hot coffee. "I wanted to stop in and see how you were doing."

Lauren sat at her desk. "I'm doing okay."

"You look a little stressed out. Has that detective been bothering you still? Any more questioning?"

"He keeps having me come down to the station and asking the same questions over again. I'm not sure why."

"He's more than likely just being very thorough. Have you learned of any details about Jane's death?" Amanda asked.

"No. I'm hoping to get some information from Tony but it hasn't happened yet."

"Getting information from an ex; good luck there."

"Do you have one of those too?" Lauren asked jokingly.

"No, I don't but I have dealt with my fair share of them in my career."

"I'm sure you have."

"Did Overstreet say what they found in Jane's home? Anything to give them an idea who was there that night? Do they think it was a burglary gone wrong?"

"I don't know." Lauren took a long drink of the bottled tea.

"I thought he might have mentioned something. You really need to start pumping that ex of yours for information. He must know details of the investigation, and who the detective has turned his sights on."

"Like I said, Tony should be sharing some information, I just don't know when."

"I did have a talk with Detective Overstreet about one of Jane's old clients."

"Oh?"

"Hector Ortiz. I did a little digging into Jane's old files. I represented his codefendant at the same time Jane represented Ortiz."

Although Lauren already knew this she wanted to hear if Amanda had more to add.

"Thankfully she didn't throw away those letters he sent her. I gave them to Overstreet. I gave him a rundown of the original case, the charges against him, and the sentence he received."

"What did Overstreet say? Did he seem interested?"

"He was. I'm sure he's going to follow up on the information."

"Did Overstreet share anything with you?"

"No. Not that he would. I don't imagine he's a big fan of defense lawyers."

"But that reminds me..." Lauren opened her desk drawer, pulled out a slip of paper and slid it over to Amanda. "I found these names in Jane's desk drawer. I don't know if they mean anything but they were stuck under a bunch of papers. I thought you might know why she wrote them down."

"Doing a little sleuthing of your own?" Amanda arched an eyebrow. She studied the names, then looked up. "Cochran, Merck, Schneider. They don't ring a bell. If you don't mind, let me hold onto this and I'll check them out." She put the slip of paper in her briefcase. "If they turn out to be important or might have something to do with Jane's death, I'll give them to the detective."

Lauren glanced at the clock on the wall. "Oh crap, I have to get going." She got up so fast her chair rolled and banged into the shelf behind her desk.

"It's not like they can start without you."

"Technically they're not supposed to but it has happened before." Lauren hurried out the door.

"I'll put this back in the break room for you." Amanda held up the empty coffee mug.

"Thanks." Lauren jogged down the hall.

* * *

The words "court is adjourned" didn't come soon enough for Lauren. She closed shop in the courtroom and carried her writer to her office. Sitting and writing on her machine for a full day after not having written on it for two weeks felt like doing dozens of leg squats after being in couch-potato mode for two months. Her neck and shoulders ached. She left the house that morning with good intentions, bringing her workout clothes, and catching the five-thirty yoga class at the gym. The clock on the wall read five-forty-five, too late to make the class. Secretly relieved, she tried to convince herself that stretching in front of the TV would count as some exercise.

"Have a minute, Lauren. I won't keep you. I know it's late." Judge Brubaker stood in the doorway.

Lauren waved him in.

He lowered his large frame into the chair opposite hers.

"How did it feel being back on the bench? Are you ready to come out of retirement?"

"Ah, now I remember what I missed about this place, it was that sense of humor of yours." He offered her a warm smile. "But, no, I don't miss being on the bench. I thought I might at first. I even worried I would get on Julia's nerves being home all the time but she insists she loves having me around. I don't know how true that is." He laughed out loud. "But I told the powers that be I can hear cases until Thanksgiving. Julia and I have plans to go south for the winter, south as in Prescott, Arizona. We plan on doing some cycling."

"That sounds like fun. I'll be thinking of you in all that sunshine and warm weather when we have our first blizzard."

"They have put hiring a new judge on a fast track. They would like to have Jane's replacement by early December."

"Oh."

"The committee has received several applications and they plan to start interviewing in a week or so."

Lauren's curiosity piqued. "That is fast. Do you know who any of the applicants are?"

"No, I didn't even think to ask. I just know winter will be here before you know it. Most of us judges don't mind traveling in the winter... well, I should only speak for myself. I did not mind the traveling, but it's a smart idea to have a new judge in place before winter has us firmly in its clutches."

Lauren nodded.

"I wanted to let you know what was in the works. Keep you in the loop such as it is."

"I appreciate it. Susan and I were wondering when they were going to start the process."

He pushed himself out of the chair. "Have a good evening. I am sure I'll be back again before the missus and I make like snowbirds."

"I look forward to working with you again," said Lauren, and meant it. Before leaving her office she checked her cell phone for messages. Tony left a text at four-thirty. "Drinks? Have information." She texted him, "Just got out of court. You still upstairs?" While waiting for a reply Lauren backed up the files from her writer onto her office computer, and indexed all the cases heard that day. When she finished she checked her phone. Six-twenty. *Info or no info, having a drink with my ex on a Friday night? I'd rather have a root canal.*

She pulled her purse out of the drawer and reached into the side pocket for her keys. They were not in there. She patted the side of her purse. When they were married, Tony had accused her of being obsessive compulsive. Lauren liked to think of it as organized, everything in its place. No searching for keys or cell phone. Only now she had to search for her keys. She shook her purse. It jingled. Digging into the center compartment her fingers found the keys. She looked up toward the ceiling. "See, I've lost my compulsive ways, asshole."

She locked her office door, jiggled the doorknob, then took the stairs leading to the rear of the courthouse. She walked out into the brisk night air wondering what information Tony had to share.

Chapter Nineteen

A blast of cold air greeted Lauren when she entered her kitchen. She flipped the light switch on. The door leading to the backyard stood partially open. She stepped over, closed it, then noticed the dogs had not been there to greet her, something they always did. "Maverik? Percy?"

No answer.

She tightened the collar of her coat and stepped out onto her deck. It was dark and she could only make out the shapes of the trees and shrubs. A rustling sound came from the bushes to her left. "Maverik?"

Percy and Maverik ran up to her, both dogs panting.

"How did you get out?" Lauren retrieved a flashlight from the laundry room, stepped outside and swept the beam of light around the yard. Nothing to see.

She examined the doorknob and the doorjamb. No scratches. No forced entry.

Maverik and Percy went to their water bowl and between the two of them, drank it dry. Lauren patted the dogs. Maverik's fur felt cold, and Percy's body shivered. She picked him up and held him in the folds of her arms. She looked around her kitchen. Nothing looked out of place. With Maverik by her side, they inspected every room, upstairs and down. After checking all the windows to make sure they were secure, she put out kibble for the dogs.

She thought about calling the police but thought, *And tell them, what? Come quick, I found my backdoor open?*

Lauren lay tucked under the covers, listening for any unusual sounds and thinking about the open door. The last time she checked the clock on the bedside table, it read three-thirty.

It was midmorning when she woke, and it was to the feeling that she had not slept at all. She wanted to get to the gym early and now it was too late. The place would be packed with people, all who tried to cram a week's worth of exercise into a Saturday morning.

In the shower, her mind went once again to what she found when she walked into her kitchen. There was a slim chance she didn't close it well enough when she let the dogs back in before going to work. She just wasn't sure.

Downstairs, Lauren secured Maverik's leash and the two went into the backyard, through the gate, and out into the alley. From this vantage point she studied the rear of her house. Nothing gave her a clue as to how Maverik and Percy ended up outside. She didn't know what she expected to find.

"Are you going to fill me in on what happened?"

Maverik stopped sniffing the ground long enough to look at her, then turned his attention back to the damp leaves.

"Might as well take a walk since we're out."

Maverik wagged his tail and trotted alongside Lauren. She liked her neighborhood, with its mix of families with small children combined with empty-nesters. Bicycles and skateboards were in driveways, and the windows of those homes were adorned with Halloween decorations. Lauren needed Maverik to become familiar with the area. He still dashed out the front door, and she wanted him to be smart enough to find his way home before getting picked up by animal control. That extra expense did not fit into her already tight budget.

The route they took led them past Crawford Elementary School. Maverik stopped and marked a tree. Lauren watched two mothers sitting on a bench, chatting while their children played on the playground equipment. Lauren lingered, smiling to herself at the shrieks of laughter the children let out as they chased one another. After a few minutes Maverik tugged on the lead. She pulled herself out of her thoughts. "Right. We're supposed to be on a walk."

❋ ❋ ❋

Lauren poured herself a large glass of water, and leaned against the sink planning what to do next. Having Saturdays free still felt like a novelty. She shouldered her purse and pulled the keys out of the side pocket, locked up, and drove downtown.

Dominick stood behind the counter talking with a customer. The aroma of baked goods, mingled with fresh brewed coffee, made Lauren's stomach rumble with anticipation. She passed the seated customers on her way to the front, greeted with "hello" nods and quick smiles. It made her appreciate being in Crawford, where making eye contact with strangers was still the norm.

The only customer at the counter paid for his purchase and stepped aside. The baker turned around and his lips widened into a warm smile. "Lauren, how is my favorite customa today?"

"I know you say that to everyone, but I'm doing good. How are you?"

"Nevva better. Hector is working out. He's a natural with the pastries. I'm gonna show him how to make bread next."

"I'm glad he's working out for you."

Hector came out of the back room, a sweet potato pecan pie in each hand. He placed them in the pie case.

"I could never be a baker. I hate getting up early. I don't even think I'd last a week. Plus, I'd eat all the profits."

Dominick laughed. "I have some fresh-out-of-the-oven pumpkin spice muffins with your name on them."

"I think I'll just take a loaf of seven-grain bread today and a medium latte. And could you slice the bread for me?"

"Sure. No muffin today? How about a fresh cinnamon roll?"

"Not today, thanks."

He reached for a loaf of bread on the top shelf.

"What I always wanted to know is what's your secret for baking bread at this altitude?"

"Well, you start with everything your mom and grandma taught you, and, voila, you've got bread. It did take a while getting used to baking at seven-thousand feet. A little different than New York."

"All my attempts at baking bread ended up with a loaf so heavy it could be classified as a deadly weapon, or a choking hazard."

He laughed. "Dangerous."

"I finally gave up. Much easier to come here and buy a loaf instead."

"It just takes practice, but in the meantime I'm more than happy to send you home with one of my fresh loaves." He turned back to the bread slicer.

While Lauren waited she became aware of a woman behind her talking on a cell phone.

"I am exhausted. And I'm too old for this shit… You and me both. I did my time."

Lauren glanced past the woman, pretending to look for the arrival of a friend.

"Thanks. I might take you up on the offer… Yeah, she started Monday… Me too. I have been run'n on no sleep since I brought her home from the hospital… And I forgot how expensive babies are. I'm going to go broke buying damned diapers… Yeah, I should've sent that bitch a bill for them while she was still alive." The woman turned away making listening difficult.

The conversation continued and Lauren continued to eavesdrop. The woman was all sharp angles; her chin, her elbows, and the prominent wrist bone that held the phone to her ear. She had dark close-set eyes. The sound of her voice held notes of a longtime smoker mingled with regular drinking, deep and husky. Lauren often recognized people just by their voice but not today.

"Call me later. Bye." The woman ended the call and put her phone in her large red bag.

Dominick handed her the loaf of bread. "That'll be seven-fifty."

Lauren paid, then moved to the right. The angular woman approached the counter. Lauren lingered, pretending to study the different flavored creamers, and checking out all the colorful sugar packets.

"A dozen assorted, Dominick," said the woman.

"You got it, Dani. How's my favorite customa today?"

Lauren smiled to herself. How many favorite customers did Dominick have?

The woman let out a sigh and shook her head, her dyed blonde hair swaying. "I'm hanging in there."

While Dominick filled a white box with muffins and danish, Lauren flipped through a Rolodex of voices in her head. She did not want to outright stare at the woman—well, she did but had better manners. Instead she tried to glance nonchalantly in the woman's direction as she made her way toward the door.

Lauren turned to Dominick. "Do you know her?" She pointed at the woman who just left.

"Who, Dani? Sure, I know her."

"Dani?"

"Dani Armstrong."

"Danielle Armstrong?"

"Yep. I call her Dani. Sort of a regular. But not lately. I think she's got herself some personal… you know, issues." Dominick wiped nonexistent crumbs out of the display case. "What's going through that head of yours, young lady? I can see them wheels turnin'."

"It just dawned on me where I've seen her before. I didn't recognize her at first. I didn't know she went by Dani. That and the last time I saw her she was a redhead." Lauren inwardly beamed. "I'm glad I came in today, Dominick."

⁂ ⁂ ⁂

"Down Maverik." Lauren nudged the dog with her hip, put her keys in her purse and put it on the kitchen counter, along with the fresh bread. She plopped on the sofa, then got up, and paced between the living room to the kitchen, a mental tug-of-war battling inside her. She pulled her cell phone from her purse along with the business card Detective Overstreet had given her. Staring at them in her hands she laid them both on the kitchen counter. "What should I do?" In answer to her question, Maverik cocked his head to the left. Percy scratched behind his ear.

Detective Overstreet picked up on the second ring. After speaking with him, Lauren looked around her living room. He had offered to come to her house rather than have her come to the station. She did not know why he made the offer but since she had no desire to see the inside of the police station ever again, she took him up on his offer.

While she waited for the detective she gathered up old newspapers and took them to the basement, and reflected on Danielle Armstrong, the mother of Tyfanee Hutchins.

"Thanks for coming over." Lauren gestured for Detective Overstreet to come in while giving Maverik a hand gesture to stay, which amazingly he did. Percy barked from the safety of the sofa. She cleared her throat. "Have a seat." She had flirted with the idea of checking out Tyfanee Hutchins's file and tracking down Danielle Armstrong and asking her questions, but a real-life Nancy Drew she was not. Besides, any information that pointed the detective to another suspect, or the real killer, was a good thing.

Detective Overstreet sat on the sofa and Lauren in her overstuffed chair. Maverik lay on the wool rug between them, and Percy moved to the sofa arm opposite the detective.

He plucked a notebook and pen from the inside pocket of his dark blue jacket. "You said you had something to tell me, something you thought might be important?"

"Yes. It has to do with Danielle Armstrong."

"Danielle Armstrong?"

She nodded and straightened in the chair.

"Who's she?"

"She's a—you see I was—" Lauren stopped herself. *Oh, hell, so what if he thinks I've been snooping around where I shouldn't? He already thinks of me as a killer.* "Let me sort of start from the beginning. Oh, would you like some water or a soda?"

He answered with a wave of his pen. "No thanks. You were saying."

"I was in Judge Murphy's office the other day and I happened to pick up a legal pad on her desk and—"

"You were in her office?" he asked, his voice remaining even.

"I just—I went in, was looking around and—"

"Why?"

"No particular reason." Before he could ask another question, she went on. "Anyway, I found a protection order against a Danielle Armstrong. Until this morning I couldn't remember where I'd heard the name before. I've been racking my brain about it but it wouldn't come to me."

"And?"

"Today it clicked. Danielle Armstrong is the mother of Tyfanee Hutchins. Judge Murphy sentenced Tyfanee to prison. It was one of the first sentencings she ever did." She watched as the detective's pen scribbled furiously.

"Tyfanee and her boyfriend… what was his name? Oh, yeah, Drew, Drew Stiles, were charged with a string of convenience store robberies. There was another guy involved too, I can't think of his name. They robbed convenience stores here in town, Rawlins, Torrington, and in Cheyenne. I'm sure you remember the robberies."

"I do. Wasn't my case but I remember them well."

"At the time of the robberies Tyfanee was sixteen. She turned seventeen sitting in jail waiting for her case to be tried. The county attorney charged her as an adult. Her attorney filed motions to have her tried as a juvenile. Judge Murphy denied them."

She studied Detective Overstreet hunched over his notepad. The story had his full attention.

"If you remember the case you probably know Tyfanee eventually plead guilty so there was no trial. But here's where it gets interesting. Danielle Armstrong got up and spoke on Tyfanee's behalf. She gave this long spiel to the judge about how her daughter is a good girl, and this would never have happened if it weren't for Drew Stiles, that she was just following her boyfriend. She'd never been in trouble before. She never touched a gun before in her life."

"Do you know what Judge Murphy said?" She paused. "'Such a good girl she got herself pregnant I see.' Well, Tyfanee started wailing and Armstrong glared at Judge Murphy. I mean it was no secret the girl was pregnant. She must have been, I don't know, seven, eight months pregnant the day she was sentenced."

"Interesting."

"Matt Christensen, Tyfanee's attorney, argued for first offender treatment. You know, if you complete five years of probation you can have the record expunged. No one would know you ever committed a crime."

"I'm vaguely aware of the Wyoming statutes."

She ignored the sarcasm in his voice. "And if not first offender, straight probation. The state remained silent on the matter. So Judge Murphy could have given her probation if she wanted to, but she said after reading the victim impact statements, prison time was warranted."

"Did Tyfanee actually brandish a gun?"

"No. She went in the stores with the two guys, her hands in her pockets pretending she had a weapon but it was the guys who did the brandishing."

"How much time did she get?"

"Four to six years."

The detective filled three pages with his scribbles and Lauren had to resist telling him, *Yes, go get the real killer.*

"When Tyfanee heard the sentence, she doubled over and let out this, this sort of guttural cry. I thought she was going into labor right there at the podium. So she's sobbing, the judge is telling her she has the right to appeal the sentence within thirty days, and Armstrong is shouting over Tyfanee's wails, 'Oh, we will appeal! This is bullshit. My grandchild will not be born in a prison!'" Lauren stopped for air.

"Anything else?"

"The jailers had to escort her from the courtroom. As she was leaving she turned to the judge and started shouting, 'This ain't over. This ain't over. You'll be sorry.'"

"Is that in the record?"

"Oh, yeah. Judge Murphy said she was going to say something but decided to let it go." Lauren relaxed a little in her chair. "Tyfanee appealed the sentence but it was upheld. The decision came just before Judge Murphy was killed. Until I saw—rather, until I heard Danielle Armstrong this morning I had forgotten about her—I mean I forgot her name. It was Tyfanee's name I remembered."

"And you think Miss Armstrong was mad enough to kill Judge Murphy?"

"Maybe. Her words could be taken as a threat, don't you think? And you didn't see the look in her eyes that day. Pure hate." Lauren added, "I get the impression she's raising her grandchild on her own. At least that's what I got from what I overheard this morning."

He stopped writing. "And what did you overhear?"

"This morning I was at Dominick's—"

"Dominick's?"

"Yep. I'm surprised I've never seen you there. I thought it was a requirement of the job, like a quota you have to fill, you know, you have to issue X number of speeding tickets and you have to eat X number of donuts each week."

The detective opened his mouth to say something, changed his mind, and shook his head instead.

"I'm sorry. It's not like—"

"We don't all eat donuts twenty-four-seven."

She eyed his muscular forearms as he wrote, and heard herself saying, "It's obvious you don't. I'll bet nothing unhealthy passes those lips of yours." Lauren stopped herself but not before her cheeks grew warm.

"What did you overhear?"

Before answering, Lauren looked at Maverik. He had scooted over and now rested his head on Detective Overstreet's left thigh. She mouthed the word, *traitor*. "She was talking to someone on her cell phone about finding day care or a baby-sitter or something and how exhausted she was. I'm pretty sure she mentioned something about a judge. I tried getting closer to her but I couldn't hear what she was saying."

"And it just came to you who she was?"

"Actually, I asked Dominick. He knows everybody, everybody who frequents his bakery. And then it clicked." Lauren gave him a look of smug satisfaction.

The detective stood. "I'll look into this. It would've been helpful if you had told me about the protective order the day you came across it, Miss Besoner, not wait until you put two and two together and then decide to share."

The smug expression on Lauren's face vanished.

"They call it interference. Working in the judicial system I presume you're aware of that concept?" He snapped his notebook shut and tucked it into his shirt pocket.

The warmth once again crept into Lauren's cheeks. Maverik repositioned himself next to her.

"I don't know if I've said this before but if I did, let me repeat myself. There is a killer out there, and *everyone* is a suspect. I repeat, *everyone*. If you come across anything else you think might be important, I want to know immediately. Not a day later, not two days later. Do I make myself clear?"

Lauren cleared her throat and tilted her chin up. "Yes."

Detective Overstreet strode to the front door. Lauren followed. Maverik trotted over and stood between them. He reached down and scratched behind the dog's black ears.

Lauren recovered enough from Detective Overstreet's verbal slap to the face to ask, "Is there anyone else you're looking into besides me? Any new developments?"

He shook his head and made his way down the steps. Lauren didn't know what to make of the head shake. Maybe it meant, no, I'm not looking at anyone else, or maybe, this one doesn't give up with the questions.

She closed the door and eyed Maverik. "That went well—not. And what was that all about, sitting next to him? Whose side are you on?"

Maverik leaned all his weight into Lauren's thigh.

Chapter Twenty

Lauren opened the kitchen curtains to let the morning light filter in. Since finding her backdoor open, not only had she checked every window to make sure they were secure, she went and closed all her curtains and blinds when the sun went down. She had felt safe in her home, until that night.

The two dogs ran out to do their business. She watched them for a few minutes, scanning her backyard for what she didn't know. If anyone hid in the bushes, the dogs would no doubt alert her. Still, she couldn't shake the notion that someone let the dogs out of the house on purpose. The idea of someone lurking in her yard creeped her out.

The two came inside and she topped off their water bowl and set out kibble. She went into the laundry room, pulled out yoga pants and a T-shirt from the dryer.

With the dogs inside she set out for the gym, feeling guilty for missing yesterday's workout. She wanted to get there before it filled up with early morning regulars, thereby forcing her to wait in line to use one of the elliptical machines, her favorite piece of equipment.

She pulled into the parking lot and had to search for an open spot. She toyed with the idea of driving straight through the lot and going to High Altitude Roast for coffee instead but resisted the urge.

Inside Lauren headed for one of several unoccupied elliptical machines. She looked through the window at the far end of the room where an instructor-led spinning class was in progress, which explained all the cars. She had made the mistake once of attending a spinning class. Her thighs had never quite forgiven her.

She stepped up on the elliptical, set her phone in the holder, popped in her pink earbuds, and with the help of tunes from Avenge Sevenfold and Five Finger Death Punch, began her workout. An hour later, heart rate raised, sweating and feeling good about her decision to stay, Lauren pulled the buds from her ears. A tap on her shoulder made her jump.

"Didn't mean to startle you."

Standing on the elliptical she reached Tony's height. "What's the information you have?"

"I'm surprised you didn't jump all over me and bug me about it."

"I had—stuff came up." Lauren didn't want to explain about Maverik's getting out of the house. "But you're here, I'm here, just tell me what you have."

Tony looked around. "Not here. Too many ears."

Unfortunately Tony was right. There were plenty of sweaty bodies in various stages of working out, and several familiar faces from the courthouse. With the latest pop tunes being piped into the large industrial room, they would have to raise their voices to be heard.

"Did you just get here or are you done?"

Tony looked past her, his eyes glazed over. "Tony?"

"Hmm? What did you say?" He continued to look at something or someone.

Lauren turned around and saw a blonde-haired woman, her ample chest high, toned abs exposed, doing triceps extensions in front of a wall of mirrors. She wondered what Tony ever saw in her. His tastes obviously ran to tall blondes. Lauren was neither tall nor blonde, though she had been blonde for a brief time when she lived in Denver, wanting to see if the old saying about blondes having more fun was true. Turned out she had not had more fun.

"I said, did you just get here?"

"Uh, yes."

Lauren wanted to walk away, leaving Tony with his mouth open but she also wanted information. "What if we meet later?"

He returned his attention to her. "Sure." He looked at his watch. "You can stop by my place later."

"Yeah, right."

"I can come by your place."

"Yeah, right again."

Tony exhaled with exaggeration. "How about lunch at the Slice It Up then?"

"I guess."

"Don't sound so excited. Noon?"

"Sure. Hey, did you come by my house the other night?"

"No."

She started to say something else but Tony had already left, heading in the direction of the tall blonde.

The only good thing about having lunch with Tony, I don't have to dress to impress. That included putting on makeup. She took a quick shower, put on a pair of old but comfortable jeans, a short-sleeved black T-shirt, and a UW hoodie. Downstairs she took Maverik's leash off its hook in the laundry room and called to him. "Come on. You need to get used to riding in a car. Plus, the two of you won't be able to get into any mischief."

Percy came scurrying off the couch and sat in front of Lauren. She gave him a small rawhide chew with instructions. "You stay here and behave."

The sidewalks of downtown Crawford were filled with people taking advantage of the warm day. People strolled past storefront windows displaying colorful leaves, pumpkins, and corn stalks. The decorations made Lauren miss summer less.

Slice It Up was located on Fourth Avenue. Lauren found a tight parking spot at the curb in front of the restaurant, and parallel-parked in one swift movement. Inside, the aroma of pizzas baking enveloped Lauren. Tony stood in line with the other customers, and Lauren walked up to him, told him what she wanted on her pizza, then went in search of an open table, finding one by the window facing the street. From where she sat she had a good view of Maverik, who, at the moment, was behaving himself, content with looking out the passenger window.

The lunch crowd consisted of several groups of men sitting on tall stools at tall tables sharing pizza and pitchers of beer. Two different college football games played on large flat screen TVs at opposite ends of the dining area. The collection of mismatched chairs and tables, scarred oak flooring, and exposed brick walls gave the room an urban chicness.

Tony joined her, handing her a bottle of beer. He sat across from her and glanced at the other tables, then checked the score of the game on the TV screen behind Lauren. He pulled out his phone and tapped away. They looked like a couple on a bad date. Tony glanced out the window. "What or who is in your car?"

"That's Maverik. You met him the other night, remember?"

"Right." Tony looked at his screen.

"I've been taking him on short rides so he gets used to being in the car."

"Why?"

"So we can go on hikes to Vedawoo or Snowy Range next summer. I'd feel safer having him with me."

"Uh-huh."

"What were you and Bradley arguing about?"

"What are you talking about?"

"After the funeral. Claude and I saw Bradley grab you."

"Nothing. I don't know what the hell his problem is."

"What did he say to you?"

"I told you, nothing."

"It had to be something."

The arrival of their food put a stop to the bickering.

One bite of her slice of pizza and Lauren forgot about Tony and instead savored the combined flavors of food nirvana—rich tomato sauce, melted mozzarella, and onions and peppers. After concentrating on the slice of heaven in her hand, she asked, "Did Detective Overstreet or Graham ever tell you how Jane died?"

Tony swallowed. "She was stabbed. Once. Most likely with a knife used to gut fish."

"How could they tell what kind of knife?"

"By the size of the opening, the edges of the skin and how deep it went. It was thrust upward and punctured one of her lungs. According to the pathologist, not a quick death. She must have laid there for—"

"I've heard enough."

Tony picked up his beer and took a swig. He set it next to his plate and wiped the sweat from the bottle on his jeans. "Oh, that's right. I forgot what a weak stomach you have."

"I just don't need details, that's all."

"You did just ask."

"Whatever." She swallowed another bite of pizza. "What's the information you have?"

"I know you'll want to hear this. Should make you happy. I spent over an hour with Overstreet the other day. He was questioning me."

"Really?"

"Yes, really. Did you say something to him about me?" Tony asked.

"No. What would I say about you?"

"I don't know, but I was surprised he wanted to talk to me again."

Lauren set her pizza down and looked around the room. All the tables were now occupied. She leaned over and spoke above the noise, "I never did ask you, what were you doing that night, you know, the night she—"

Tony raised his voice, "What the *hell* are you asking me?" He shook his head. "Are you serious?"

"I'm sure Overstreet asked that same question. Just curious what you told him, that's all. You don't need to get upset."

"I was working on Miss Demeanor if you must know, Nancy Drew." He watched irritation spread across her face. "You were always jealous of her. Admit it."

The picture of Tony's boat came to mind, with its name that he thought clever and she thought lame. Maybe she had been jealous of the boat and all the time Tony spent on it fishing.

"I was working on her engine before dry docking her."

She helped herself to a second slice of pizza. "So you don't have an alibi."

"I don't *need* an alibi. Geez, quit being annoying."

"Doesn't feel so good when someone asks questions like that, does it?"

"*You asking* is what's annoying, otherwise it would be no big deal."

"What other questions did he ask you?"

"Mostly questions about the relationship Jane and I had, how long it lasted, who ended it, were there any bad feelings between us after it was over. You know, what you'd expect him to ask. Just a formality."

"And when did it start?"

He shook his head and turned his attention to the TV.

"Well? When did it start?"

"What difference does it make now?"

"I want to know. And don't look at me like that."

"Like *what*?"

"Like I'm asking a dumb question. When did you start cheating on me?" Asking the question was like staring at a car wreck on the highway. She did not really want to know but could not stop herself from asking.

"Is this how all our conversations are going to sound like from now on? Because if they are, I'm done here."

The chatter from the dining area filled the space between them. She waited for him to speak.

He answered with exasperation in his voice. "Maybe three months before I moved out."

Lauren put the slice of pizza on her plate and pushed it away. She stared into her lap. She had a sudden urge to stand and heave the table at Tony, imagining drinks and food spilling onto his pants. She twisted the napkin in her lap.

"Happy now?"

The sarcasm went unanswered. "And how did it end?"

"It ended. That's all that matters."

"Did she end it or did you?" Had he heard the rumors, that she dumped him?

"It was mutual. Or maybe she did. I don't remember." He checked his phone, then pretended to concentrate on the people occupying the tables around them.

Lauren broke the silence. "So, what's the information you have?"

"For starters Graham said Jane's home had been searched. Whoever killed her must have been looking for something and they tried to make it look like a burglary. Oh, and you might be off the hook as a suspect."

"Might be? That sounds comforting."

"At least he didn't say Overstreet had an arrest warrant for you. Take that as a good sign, will you?"

Lauren shrugged.

"Bradley's been interviewed. According to him they were going through a rough patch, but also according to Bradley, the wedding was back on."

"I didn't know anything about it being off, but she didn't discuss her personal life with me." A very true statement, Lauren realized. "Did he say what the rough patch was? Personal, professional?" Lauren pulled a napkin out of the metal dispenser and set her uneaten pizza on it.

"According to Bradley, Jane needed time to think."

"Where have I heard that line before?" Lauren remembered Tony saying the exact same thing to her before she left for Gillette, before he abandoned her.

Tony ignored the comment. "Jane said something about being tired of always commuting back and forth to Longmont, or wherever he lives, especially after long days on the bench. He chalked it up to a case of cold feet."

"Now that I think about it, she hadn't mentioned going to Colorado the last couple of weeks before…" Lauren still found it difficult to say the words death or murder. "I assumed he had been coming here. That means it's just his word that they were back together."

"Think, Lauren. If that were true he could just as easily have not mentioned a rough patch. He could have lied about it, said they were doing fine. Jane's not here to contradict him."

"Maybe he's not a seasoned liar like some people."

Tony shook his head. "You're so damned annoying."

Lauren scratched at the label on the beer bottle with her thumbnail.

"There was a mini trial separation, but that lasted a week

or so. On the night of her murder Bradley said he had grabbed a quick bite after work with his physician assistant. Overstreet has a call in to her." Tony straightened up in his chair. "According to the good doctor he was with patients all day. He didn't leave his office until five-thirty. He's a pain management doctor, isn't he?"

"He is."

Tony glanced up at the big screen to check the score, then returned his attention to her. "The cops found something interesting at Jane's house."

"What?"

"I'm getting there. A little patience, please." He bit into his slice of pizza.

Lauren sat quiet, hiding her impatience.

"The cops found several pill bottles in her medicine cabinet at home. Prescriptions for OxyContin and Percocet. They were all written by the *good doctor*."

Lauren sensed Tony had been jealous of Bradley.

"What does that mean exactly? Did Overstreet ask Bradley about the pills?"

"He did. The *good doctor* had written her the prescriptions for a ski injury she had."

"I didn't know she skied."

"Yes. She and I used to go skiing up at Breckenridge."

"You ski?"

"Yes, I ski. Don't sound so surprised."

"You never told me you skied."

"It was something I did during college. I took it up again after we split up." He leaned against his seat. "Now you know what I know. And remember, no sharing."

"I remember."

Tony shook his now empty bottle of beer, his cue for, I'm ready to go.

They walked out and stopped at Lauren's car. She went around to the driver's side and unlocked her door.

He looked at her over the roof of the Volvo. "What, I don't even get a thank you?"

"Thanks for the pizza."

"You don't change, do you?"

"Thanks for the information."

"I'd say it's been a pleasure but we both know that would be a lie," said Tony.

Maverik barked

They bent their heads and looked in the car. Tony straightened, shook his head, and strode off.

Maverik sat in the driver's seat. Lauren nudged him over to the passenger side, then rubbed his face, scratched behind his ears, and praised him for not chewing on the seats, and for not barking at passersby, except for Tony, which she told him did not count. In response, he swooshed his tail and sniffed the air. Lauren pulled a napkin out of her coat pocket and gave her companion the pizza. "Just the pizza, not the napkin."

The treat disappeared in one bite. Maverik circled once and curled up in the seat.

"Shall we go home?" She put the car in gear and pulled away from the curb. "And don't tell Percy about the pizza."

Maverik lifted his head and panted.

"You're right, he'll smell it on your breath."

Chapter Twenty-One

Detective Overstreet leaned against the door of the judge's chambers, arms folded across his chest. "Ms. Besoner, can I have a word with you?"

"Sure." Lauren unlocked the office door, stepped inside and gestured for him to follow.

"If you don't mind, we'll just go down to the station."

She did mind but didn't think that would matter to him. "It must be important to come get me first thing in the morning."

The detective didn't answer.

Lauren locked the door and jiggled the knob. She hugged her purse as she walked down the stairs alongside the detective.

They were settled in the interview room and the familiar blue file folder lay on the table.

"We finally got your phone records from Verizon."

No offer of coffee today

"There are a few text messages I'd like to ask you about. I'm particularly interested in the one that mentions Miss Murphy."

"Judge Murphy?"

The detective reached in the blue folder, pulled out a sheet of paper and slid it around so it faced Lauren.

By the time she read to the bottom of the page her cheeks burned. "I was blowing off a little steam to my friend. That's all."

He turned the paper toward him and read out loud. "'I have to find a way to shut her up'. Care to explain?"

Lauren did not. "You're—you're taking it out of context. I sent this after a really long day in court. Judge Murphy took forever during a sentencing. I was just thinking of all the unnecessary pages she was creating by talking so much. Her way of doing things was a lot different from Judge Brubaker."

"Maybe you wanted to shut her up permanently."

"No. That's not what I meant."

"And this one?" He pointed to the next text on the page. "'Can't take it. Have to do something.' Remember that one?" Detective Overstreet turned the sheet toward Lauren. He watched her eyes scan the paper.

"That? I just meant that I was going to talk to her. See, during arraignments the judge has to read every defendant their rights. The rights are the same for every defendant, and after being on the bench for a while she began to read the rights fast, I mean really fast. So fast I don't think any defendant understood half of what she was saying, and I wasn't able to get every word down."

The detective studied Lauren as she explained herself.

"I was going to talk to her about that, ask her to slow down."

"That must have made you mad."

"Not mad enough to kill her." Lauren's voice rose. "You don't kill someone because they talk fast. There would be a lot fewer lawyers around if that were the case." Lauren meant the last comment as a joke but the detective didn't smile.

"You are twisting my words around. What you're suggesting is ridiculous, total…" Lauren shook her head and sank back further in her chair.

"What about Judge Murphy's last text to you Monday evening? 'There are things we need to discuss.' What did she want to discuss with you?"

Lauren was confident she knew what was to be discussed. It was the comment she had said in open court in front of Mr. Brenner, and regretted saying, and instructed Lauren to delete from the transcript. If I try to explain this, she thought, it's just one more thing he's going to twist around to where I look bad.

"I don't know. We obviously didn't get a chance to talk."

"You have no clue what she wanted to speak with you about?" The question hung there a beat, then he added, "She didn't say anything at work that day?"

"No. No, she didn't." And that much was true. Lauren hadn't started work on that particular transcript, putting off the decision of whether to follow the judge's orders or not.

The only sound in the room came from a vent in the ceiling as it blew in warm air.

"Just a few more questions. Tell me, do you feel like you were overworked by Miss Murphy?"

Lauren considered the question. If she told him the truth it would be one more reason for the detective to think she killed her boss, because, hell yeah, she felt overworked. Judge Murphy took on a heavy caseload when she started on the bench six months earlier and worked long hours. Albany County's population had been steadily growing, which translated into an increase in crime. It meant nonstop trials, either civil or criminal, every week. Throw in the mix of half-day hearings, motions, and, Lauren would have to say yes, I'm overworked, overworked and exhausted. Working every Saturday and half a day on Sunday preparing transcripts had become the new norm for her. Thinking about it made her want to lay her head on the table, close her eyes, and take a nap.

It dawned on her that sometime in the last six months she quit having a life outside of work. "Judge Murphy worked hard which meant I worked hard too. Came with the territory." Holding his gaze, she added, "Kind of like you."

He arched an eyebrow.

"From the looks of it you must be putting in long hours yourself or do you always wake up with a five o'clock shadow?"

"A murder in Crawford is very unusual as you know, Miss Besoner." He scribbled a few notes on the folder in front of him, then glanced up at her. His tone softened. "Lauren, I feel you're not telling me the whole story. Trust me, I would feel stressed out if I were you. Here she is, she's your boss. She's working you hard. You're a professional yet she has you pet-sitting for her like you're some kind of domestic help, and making you her chauffeur, driving to Casper and who knows where else. And the icing on the cake," he said with mock anger, "she had been sleeping with your husband behind your back. I mean surely you must have been angry, very angry. I know you have more to tell me."

Lauren pressed her lips together and told herself to keep her anger in check, not lose her temper, then promptly ignored her own advice. "Oh, yes, detective, the answer to being overworked is to kill your boss. Makes perfect sense to me. Go from overworked to unemployed." While Lauren talked, Detective Overstreet sat with his forearms resting on the folder, his expression letting her know he was indulging her venting.

Anger punctuated her words when she spoke again. "I cannot believe you think I had anything to do with her death. This is just so—so unbelievable. And please, don't insult me. I know what you're trying to do. You become Mr. Sympathetic, Mr. Nice Guy, and then I'm supposed to confess. The only problem with that tactic is I have *nothing* to confess." Lauren once again folded her arms over her chest.

The baritone voice returned. "I see you know a little about the process but there's no reason to get defensive unless, of course, you have something to hide. I'm just doing my job. I have to look at every bit of evidence."

"You're accusing me of murder," Lauren snorted. "How can I not be defensive? I consider myself an officer of the court. How can you possibly think I could do such a thing?"

The detective let out his own snort. "What you're telling me, Miss Besoner, is because you work in the court system you're above reproach?" He leaned forward in his seat. "In my experience killers come from all walks of life and every profession known to man."

His remarks made Lauren's cheeks burn.

"I'm not accusing you of murder. I'm looking at the facts. I'm searching for the truth. Miss Murphy deserves that."

"I agree, she does." Lauren shifted in the chair. A headache was forming behind her right eye. She glanced at the half open door, her hands clasped together on the desk.

"If there's nothing else you think I should know, that's all the questions I have for now."

* * *

Lauren wasted no time. Outside the station she dug her phone out of her bag and texted Claude. By the time she made it upstairs to her office, her friend was standing by the door waiting.

"Thanks for coming down."

"That is what your text said to do, 'Come down now'. What's up?"

"I just finished another round of questioning with that jerk-detective." Lauren unlocked her office and collapsed in her chair. "Claude, he really thinks I killed Judge Murphy. He even had the texts I sent you printed out."

"What texts?" Claude sat opposite Lauren.

"Where I was complaining about her talking so fast."

"Oh, yeah. You were just venting."

"I know that and you know that but he's taking them out of context."

"He's just grasping at straws."

"If he grasps at enough of them he's going to have a nice bundle of circumstantial evidence against me, and then… then he'll arrest me." Lauren's voice rose. "And Tony told me yesterday I might be off the hook. He's such a liar."

"Maybe you should talk to an attorney. Maybe Amanda?"

"You think I should?"

"Try and get some free advice first. Work the angle that they were partners, and you were Jane's stenographer and how wonderful a defense attorney she is. You know, lie a little."

"She's not a bad attorney."

"I didn't mean it like that. Besides, I can't be running down here every time you see Overstreet. I mean I could, but I'd have to start bringing my cross trainers to work. And you know how I feel about exercising, especially at work."

"Yeah. I will call Amanda." Lauren leaned back in her chair, hands over her face. "When is this freak'n nightmare going to end?"

Chapter Twenty-Two

The gold letters on the door read, Capshaw Law Offices. The reception area housed a large desk with a petite woman in her mid-twenties behind it. She held up a black lacquered index finger and mouthed, "Be right with you."

Lauren stood inside the door and waited for Lydia, according to the nameplate on the desk, to finish her call.

"Can I help you?"

"Yes. I'm Lauren Besoner. I'm here to see Amanda."

"Yes, Ms. Capshaw is expecting you. Please, have a seat. She'll be with you in a moment. Can I offer you coffee or a soda while you wait?"

"No thanks." Lauren sat in one of two paisley-patterned wingback chairs against the wall by the door. The small table between the chairs held a few law-related brochures. There were several dated law journals fanned out, *The Trial*

Lawyers Association and *The Wyoming Lawyer*. She opted for *The Wyoming Lawyer* and flipped mindlessly through the pages.

A door on the right opened and Amanda stuck her head out. "Lauren, hello. Come on in." She motioned to a chair. "Please, sit."

"Thanks for seeing me on such short notice." Lauren sat in one of two chairs that faced Amanda's desk. She clasped and unclasped her hands and took in the office décor. On the wall to Lauren's right hung Amanda Capshaw's law degree from the University of Wyoming. On the opposite wall hung botanic-themed generic prints.

If office furniture could talk, her furniture would be saying, you will be represented by competent counsel with no frills. No fancy rugs on the floor, no bronze statues adorning a corner shelf, no expensive paintings hanging on the walls. The leaves of the perfunctory fichus in the corner needed dusting.

Two framed photographs sat on the credenza. One of a teenaged Amanda, long hair braided, standing on a pier, jade waters in the background. She stood between a man and woman, probably her parents, and held a fishing rod in one hand and a fish in the other.

In the second photo Amanda was dressed in a brown and gold cap and gown. The tassel, along with her long dark blonde hair, fluttered from a breeze. She stood between the same man and woman in the previous photograph. They all wore large smiles.

Today Amanda's hair came just past her shoulders, more a business woman's hairdo, but other than the hairstyle, and a few lines at the corners of her eyes, she had not changed much from the younger version of herself in the photographs.

"Tell me what's happened. You said it was important, and I can see you're upset."

Lauren shared the details of her recent meeting with Detective Overstreet.

"I don't say this to alarm you, Lauren, but it sounds to me as though you are their number one suspect."

"This is—" Lauren shook her head. "This can't be happening. It's crazy. Freak'n insane."

"Try and calm down. I know you're upset."

"Of course I'm upset."

Amanda reached into the desk drawer, pulled out a legal-size document and handed it to Lauren. "I think you're going to need representation, and soon."

The paper in Lauren's hands was an agreement for retaining counsel. She could not focus on the words.

"This just explains my fee schedule, what you can expect from me and what I will expect from you should you decide to hire me to represent you."

"I–I don't know. I guess I'm just in shock, like this really can't be happening, even as it's happening."

"I understand. Trust me, that is a natural reaction. I can offer you a little free advice but I'm afraid it is starting to look like you're going to need more than that."

Lauren sat straighter in the chair, crossed her legs and tried to concentrate on the form.

"Why don't you take that with you, look it over and get back with me. If you have any questions, call me. Or if you want, I can come by your place in the next day or two and pick it up."

"A lawyer who makes house calls." Lauren gave a small laugh. "No, I can return it to you." She folded the paper in half. "Amanda, do you know of any enemies Judge Murphy had, anyone that hated her, hated her enough to kill her?"

Amanda arranged a large stack of papers on her desk. "I did share some information about an old client of Jane's with Detective Overstreet."

"That's good, right? I mean for me? I mean for Judge Murphy?"

"It could be. I don't want to get your hopes up but I think it is something he will look into."

"I was—"

Amanda stood up. "I'm sorry but my four o'clock is surely waiting outside."

"Oh, no, don't be sorry. I appreciate you seeing me on such short notice—actually no notice."

Amanda reached across her desk and gripped Lauren's hand in a firm handshake. "Try not to worry, Lauren. I know that's easier said than done but try."

The brief meeting only heightened Lauren's unease. She had hoped Amanda would tell her she had nothing to worry about. *Even with his threats Detective Overstreet wouldn't, couldn't arrest me. I'm innocent.* A disturbing realization hit her. How many people thought that very same thing as they were being handcuffed?

Rain fell as Lauren drove the short distance to the courthouse. Susan was still MIA. Lauren backed up the job she had been working on to the cloud, then locked her office and drove home.

The clock on the car's dash read four-forty-five when she

pulled into her driveway. Her cell phone rang. By the time she retrieved it from her bag the ringing stopped.

Inside, Lauren placed her purse on the kitchen counter and let Percy and Maverik out in the backyard. The rain pelted the ground hard. She called the dogs in as soon as they had done their business, wanting to keep muddy paw prints on her kitchen floor to a minimum. They followed Lauren into the living room. She sank onto the couch, leaned forward, buried her head in her hands. "What the hell is happening?"

Percy, apparently not used to such questions, sat, lifted his back leg and licked himself. Maverik nudged Lauren's hand with his wet nose, his way of saying, pet me, it will make you feel better, so Lauren did.

Retrieving her cell phone, she saw the missed call came from her aunt, who left a message inviting her to dinner. She texted her aunt, thanking her but saying she was tired and would stay home. Less than a minute passed before her cell phone rang.

"Hi Aunt Kate… I don't think I'd be very good company, that's all… No, but… Six-thirty? Okay. Yeah, I'll be there." She hung up and looked at the dogs. "Sometimes it's just easier to say yes."

Lauren pulled into Aunt Kate's long gravel driveway, the Volvo bouncing in the puddles. An unfamiliar Dodge pickup sat parked in front of the garage. Lauren got out of her car, pulled her UW hoodie across her chest to keep out the cold night air, trotted to the front door, and knocked.

"Door's open," came a chorus. The aroma of something cheesy filled the house. Lauren's stomach growled. Passing through the living room Lauren spotted a dark blue jacket lying on the arm of the sofa. Jack's black leather recliner held the day's newspaper folded open to the sports page. Stacked neatly on the coffee table were several back issues of *Alpaca Culture*.

Making her way to the kitchen, Lauren saw the dining room table set with four place settings. She frowned. Voices wafted out from the kitchen. Aunt Kate's, Jack's, and a familiar voice.

No. It can't be.

Chapter Twenty-Three

Aunt Kate called out, "We're in here."

Lauren entered the spacious kitchen, the warmth inviting.

"Hi, dear. I'm happy you decided to come."

"Uh, thanks for the invite." Lauren looked around.

Kate stood next to Jack, and next to Jack stood a man with his back to Lauren. He turned.

"Lauren, I'd like you to meet our new neighbor, Sam Overstreet." Jack patted Sam's shoulder.

The look of surprise on Detective Overstreet's face mirrored Lauren's own look of surprise. She backed up. "I'm sorry, Aunt Kate, Jack, I can't stay."

"What? You just walked in the door. What do you mean you can't stay?" said Aunt Kate.

"No. You don't have to leave. I will." Sam set his half empty beer can on the kitchen counter.

"No, you were here first. I'll go." Lauren practically shouted the words.

"Don't be ridiculous. I didn't realize Kate and Jack were expecting company. I'll leave."

"What, did you just drop in uninvited?"

"*Lauren.*"

"Sorry." Though Lauren was almost thirty years old, her aunt still had the ability to make her feel like a ten-year-old when she spoke in that tone of voice.

"Before anyone leaves will one of you mind explaining what's going on," asked Jack.

"Go ahead, Detective. Explain." Lauren folded her arms across her chest.

"Your niece—who I did not know was your niece until this moment—is a person of interest."

"Hmmph," mumbled Lauren.

"*Lauren*? You can't be serious," Kate said.

He cleared his throat. "Miss Besoner—Lauren was in my office earlier today going over the events surrounding Miss Murphy's death."

"Don't you mean you had me in your office trying to get me to confess to her murder?"

"I'm sorry, Lauren. I didn't know you were being questioned by Sam here." Aunt Kate gave a nervous laugh. "We knew you worked for the Crawford Police Department, but," she turned and faced him, "I didn't know you were a detective."

He shifted his weight. "Listen, I need to get going. I can't stay. Thank you for inviting me over."

"Are you sure you have to leave?" said Jack.

"Yes."

"Aunt Kate, he can't be having dinner with a killer."

Kate shot Lauren a disapproving look. "Why don't you at least let me fix you a plate to take home with you. It won't take but a minute."

"No, I'm fine. But thank you, Kate." Sam strode to the front door, picking his jacket up on his way.

Jack followed him. "Thank you again for helping with the fence, Sam. We'll do this another time."

"Glad to help. You folks have a good evening."

A moment later they heard the deep rumble of a truck engine come to life.

"I could have left. I didn't mean to interrupt your dinner plans."

"No, you didn't interrupt anything, except maybe a little matchmaking attempt." Jack winked, the lines around his brown eyes deepening.

Lauren turned to face her aunt, "Is that true? Is that why you invited me over?"

"No, sweetie. Would I do that?"

"Uh, yeah, I think you just did," said Lauren.

Piping up, Jack said, "Sam came home and found Arnie and Josephine in his driveway. He offered to help us find out how them two managed to get through the fence. Your aunt just wanted to repay him by having him stay for a home-cooked meal, didn't ya, honey?" He scratched his mostly salty beard, sprinkled with pepper, which he started to grow in September in anticipation of hunting season. Lauren used to think sporting a beard had been a prerequisite to get a hunting license.

"You would think Arnie and Josephine were two teenagers, not alpacas, the way they're always getting into mischief." Kate laughed.

Jack stood by the dining room table. "I'm starving. Is dinner almost ready?"

"Go. Sit. Both of you."

They both sat. Kate joined them at the table with a casserole in hand. "Tell us about these interviews with Sam."

In between warm and comforting bites of chicken enchiladas, Lauren detailed the accusations Sam Overstreet had levied against her, and ended by telling them of the search warrant of her home. She could not resist throwing in a few adjectives of what she thought of their neighbor Sam Overstreet, none flattering.

"Surely he was just doing his job," Aunt Kate said.

"So I keep hearing but if he is he's doing a lousy job. I think he truly believes I killed Judge Murphy."

Jack wiped his mouth. "He's a pretty sharp guy. He'll realize you had nothing to do with it."

"I hope it's soon. It's ridiculous he thinks I did it."

They finished the meal talking about alpacas. After dinner Kate and Lauren gathered the dirty plates and set them in the sink. Lauren handed her the dishes to load in the dishwasher. "So dinner had nothing to do with you trying to fix me up with your neighbor?"

"No, no." Then holding up her index finger and thumb, "Maybe a tiny bit. You haven't been on a date since you moved back here. That's way too long for someone your age."

"I've been—"

"I know, you were too busy getting settled into your new house to go out and have fun. And lately you've been working such long hours we hardly see you. I didn't see the harm in introducing you to Sam."

"You saw how that turned out."

Jack joined in the conversation. "You know your aunt, minding her own business has never been one of her strong suits."

"I know." Lauren nodded in agreement.

"He seems like such a nice young man. And he reminds me of a young Tom Selleck." Kate flashed a sly grin.

"Who?" asked Lauren.

"Tom Selleck. He played *Magnum P.I.* on television. We had a date every Thursday night." She laughed out loud. "That's what I called it. My date with Tom."

The blank look on Lauren's face made Kate smile. "I suppose he was before your time. But trust me, if Sam had a mustache and lighter colored eyes they could pass for twins. I think it's those dimples of his." Kate let out a little sigh, then bent and put the last plate in the dishwasher, her long salt and pepper braid falling to the side. When she spoke again her tone was serious, "You be extra careful until whoever killed your judge is caught. Do you hear me?"

"Yes, *mom*."

"I'm serious, Lauren."

"Listen to your aunt. She's right. You can't be too careful."

"Maybe you should reconsider and stay here for a while," her aunt said.

"No. I'll be okay. I have the dogs. I appreciate the offer though. Don't worry, I'll be careful." Careful of what, she wasn't sure. "I just wish I knew if it was random."

"If it was random or a stranger, then everyone in Crawford should be worried," said Kate.

"To me that's the scary part, not knowing." Lauren rubbed her arms. "If it's random that means there is some whack-job killer running around loose in Crawford and Judge Murphy was just the first victim."

"Why don't you get that ex of yours to give you some information," Jack said.

Lauren half grinned. Jack always gave off vibes that he didn't care for Tony.

"I'm trying."

"I wonder if Sam questioned Tony," said Jack.

"Tony's spoken with him a couple times already."

Jack nodded. "Sam strikes me as being thorough."

"I know I said it before when you two broke up, but I always thought you could do better," said Kate. Then added, "And you will."

"Thanks for your vote of confidence but let's not go down the Tony-was-a-mistake path. I know that now."

"No, no. That's not what I mean." Aunt Kate walked into the living room to join Jack on the sofa.

"I know you mean well but I don't want any more surprises like tonight," Lauren said. Then to Jack, "If you have any influence over your wife, please tell her to stop playing matchmaker."

"I'll try but I can't guarantee anything." With his arm around Kate, he gave her a playful squeeze.

"I want you to be happy." Kate tapped Jack's chest playfully. "I found this one. And he loves me just as I am, don't you, honey?"

"You betcha." He kissed her cheek. Husband and wife laughed, their affection for each other commingling in the air.

Aunt Kate often told Lauren there was someone out there for everyone. "You just have to keep looking until you find the right one." She spoke from experience. Lauren remembered laughing to herself when her aunt told her she had signed up on Country Love, an online dating site. And when her aunt told her she met this wonderful man and they were engaged, Lauren thought of Jack simply as husband number four, meaning it was only a matter of time before there would be a husband number five. That had been eight years ago. Snuggling on the sofa together, they could have passed for high school sweethearts.

"I know you want me to be happy. Both you and Claude. You two must get together and critique my love life, or lack of one I should say."

"Love life. I think this is my cue to go check on the pack, see if that fence mending did the trick." Jack walked into the kitchen and grabbed a flashlight off the counter.

Lauren sat opposite her aunt and told herself that maybe it was time to be more open with her. *Maybe, just maybe that will get her to stop with the matchmaking.*

"You remember Kevin?"

"Your ex-fiancé in Denver?"

"I didn't tell very many people the real reason I broke off the engagement. I caught him cheating on me." Lauren proceeded to share the details, of catching him, literally, with his pants down in their living room, with his very naked legal secretary. She also told her aunt of the many, many men she dated afterwards, using the word "dating" loosely.

"I haven't been with a guy since I left Denver. And now I can't even think of going out and having a good time, not with everything that's been happening. So no more talk about dating. Deal?"

"Deal." Kate cocked her head to the side. "But Denver was such a long time ago. I think you need to get out more. Maybe you should try one of those online dating sites."

"That *deal* didn't last long, did it?"

Kate walked Lauren to the door, and handed her a container with leftovers. Before releasing Lauren from her goodbye hug, Aunt Kate once again had her promise she would be careful.

Lauren weaved around the ruts as she drove out of her aunt's driveway. She was comforted by the thought Maverik and Percy would be waiting for her when she arrived home.

Chapter Twenty-Four

Lauren lay snuggled under her fluffy comforter not wanting to emerge from its warmth. She heard a soft snoring and stuck her head out of the covers. Maverik's large bulk lay beside her. She felt a lump at the foot of the bed, Percy curled up in a ball.

She rolled over and spoke into the covers, "Why did I agree to do this? Why can't I ever say no?" Lauren braced herself for the chilly room as she unfolded herself from the warm bed. She reached for an oversized sweatshirt and pulled it over her long-sleeve T-shirt and fleece bottoms adorned with sleeping cats, shoved her feet into her slippers and trudged downstairs.

Emmett Murphy phoned her two days ago and she grudgingly agreed to meet at Jane's house at ten o'clock this morning. She tried to coax him to come to her house. After all, she had some of Jane's belongings stored there.

He told her it was too soon to bring her things home. The sight of them would be too much for his wife to handle at the moment.

For Lauren, it meant a return to the murder scene but it also meant Percy would be going to his new home with Emmett.

"Hurry up, it's cold outside," came Lauren's warning as she let the dogs out. "And no barking." She didn't know why she bothered to say that. They were, after all, dogs, but she did not want to disturb Old Lady Nash and have her make good on her many threats to call animal control.

Ever since moving into her home, Lauren offered to help her elderly neighbor with yard work, rake leaves. She even offered to trim her lilac bushes that had grown so tall they blocked her windows and any sunlight that might come through. She was trying to be neighborly, with the added possible bonus of getting on Twila's good side. Every attempt proved unsuccessful. The final time Lauren offered to help, Twila told her if she stepped foot in her yard she would call the cops. It turned out the old woman did not have a good side.

With Percy and Maverik inside, Lauren marched herself upstairs. Twenty minutes later, showered, dressed in jeans and a sweatshirt, she rummaged through her refrigerator for breakfast, settling on a raspberry-flavored yogurt seven days past its expiration date. She peeled the lone banana on the counter, overripe but edible, and dipped it into the yogurt. She stood with her back against the sink eating her breakfast. Her mind settled on the feeling of unease that now followed her everywhere. The image of Judge Murphy's unblinking stare, the blood on the floor, the blood on her own clothes popped into her mind unannounced and uninvited, most often when she began to drift off to sleep. Last night had been no exception.

The memories caused her to toss the half empty yogurt container in the trash.

She went to work gathering what was left of Percy's toys. Maverik managed to get ahold of most of them and devour almost every single one. Percy's favorite, thankfully, had been spared. It was the first one she bought for him after he came to stay with them. Lauren found it jammed under her sofa. She dropped the damp matted frog into a plastic storage bag, thinking Percy needed to have something for the ride to his new home.

Percy followed her, or rather, his frog. "Well, Percy, shall we?" He trotted to the door, his tail high and fanned out. Lauren scooped him up, still amazed at what a little-ball-of-nothing he was compared to Maverik.

Maverik wagged his tail. "No, you stay here." He sat and cocked his head to the right and watched them leave.

Percy hopped out of her arm and into the passenger seat. Lauren backed out of the garage and gauged the weather. Heavy gray clouds were gathering in the west. She glanced at him. "Hope the snow holds off until you get to Rawlins."

When Jane Murphy's house came into view, Lauren's stomach tightened. In the daylight hours the home appeared innocuous, another well-maintained Victorian style home in a row of the same. The old house had a wraparound porch. Mature pines flanked the west side of the house, juniper bushes bordering the front porch. Three flowerpots, one on each step leading to the front door, contained the remains of dried chrysanthemums. If one had been unaware of what terrible event transpired here just weeks earlier, they would think dried flowers were part of a planned fall decorating scheme, and the only thing missing, a few strategically placed pumpkins.

A white 2016 Ford 350 pickup truck sat in the driveway.

Percy scratched at the passenger window. Reaching one hand over to pick him up, his body vibrated in her hand. "Are you excited? Well, let's do this."

The broken pane of glass had been replaced. Lauren knocked on the door. The silhouette of a man approaching grew large and tall. Mr. Murphy opened the door and ushered them in.

"Hello, Lauren. Come in."

Reaching out, Mr. Murphy took her hand in a strong handshake. Lauren remembered the feel of the rough and calloused hand from the funeral.

"Thank you for coming over." He smiled down at her. He looked comfortable in a faded red-flannel shirt with a white triangle of T-shirt exposed underneath.

Lauren stepped onto the spotless oak floor, all signs of brutality and death removed, but the memory of that morning made her sidestep into the living room.

"Hi, Mr. Murphy."

"Call me Emmett. Please."

"Emmett."

Percy squirmed in Lauren's arms. She set him down, and he sniffed around him, then shot up the carpeted staircase.

"How was the drive over? Did your wife come too?" Lauren looked toward the kitchen.

He shook his head. "Margaret couldn't bring herself to come."

Lauren nodded. "That's understandable."

"My son Chris is here. He's upstairs packing Jane's things."

"I'm sure your wife is going to love Percy. You too. He's a loveable little dog."

"Lauren, about Percy," Mr. Murphy kept his gaze on his worn cowboy boots. "We were hoping you could keep him, at least a little while longer. Margaret and I talked it over and we don't think it's a good idea to have Percy come live with us."

"Keep him?" Lauren couldn't keep the surprise out of her voice. "You mean Mrs. Murphy doesn't want him?"

Mr. Murphy shook his head.

"But he is such a sweet dog. Judge—Jane spoke about Percy like he was her child. I know she loved him. I don't understand why you wouldn't want him."

"I told you, we can't."

"I have a dog, Mr. Murphy. I thought that's why you wanted me to come over this morning. I—I assumed from our conversation on the phone you were taking him with you. Me keeping Percy was temporary until you came back to get him." Lauren heard the whininess in her voice as she spoke.

"It's not that we don't want him but we can't have such a small dog on the ranch. I know if he were outside he would be snatched up by a hawk or a fox in no time and we'd feel terrible if that happened."

"You could keep him inside. He's so little it's only natural for him to be an inside dog."

"Margaret is against the idea."

"But Mr. Murphy, couldn't you keep him while you look for a new home for him?"

The man's hooded blue eyes searched Lauren's for understanding. "This has simply been too much for my wife. Please understand, we just can't take him. It's perfectly understandable if you can't care for him any longer and need to take him to the pound."

"I can't do that."

"That's why I had you come here, I didn't want to just show up at your house with Percy's things. I wanted to explain the situation first."

For the first time, Lauren noticed the small canvas kennel in the center of the living room, all of Percy's worldly possessions tucked inside; a plaid dog bed with his name embroidered on one end, two ceramic bowls, a lead, a tiny harness, and a half empty bag of kibble.

"I'll take him back home with me, of course, but can you check around, find someone that's willing to take him? He is such a good dog. He wouldn't be any trouble for anyone."

"I can ask around. And, Lauren, I do know this is asking a lot, but this has been a helluva nightmare for us. We've lost Jane. The police haven't arrested anyone. They don't seem to have any clear idea who did this to her. They're not any closer to finding her killer than they were two weeks ago. All I get is, we're following up on all leads."

Lauren didn't know what to say, so said nothing.

"Chris and I even looked around here ourselves this morning. Looking for anything they might have missed." His voice rose. "If I find the son-of-a-bitch who did this to my daughter they won't have to worry about arresting anyone or having a trial." His expression turned to granite. "That is one thing Jane and I disagreed on. I know she was good at her job and was proud of the work she did. We were proud of her too, but her mother and I were not crazy about the people she represented. We were relieved and excited for her when she became a judge." He shook his head. "Do you have children?"

"No."

"You bring them into this world, and they bring you joy, a little heartache along the way, but this..." his voice trailed off. He let out a ragged breath, "Anyway..."

Lauren shifted her gaze away from Emmett and his grief-stricken face. They stood there in awkward silence.

The floorboards above them creaked breaking the quiet.

He walked over to the kennel. "Let me carry this out for you." He gathered it up, moving toward the front door.

"Percy. Percy come," Lauren called out. The dog stood at the top of the stairs, then scampered into the living room. Lauren bent to pick him up and noticed a stack of papers on the end table by the blue chintz sofa. It was the transcript Lauren had given to Judge Murphy on that Monday afternoon. Across the top in bold font were the words *Confidential/Blackburn.* Most everyone in Wyoming's small legal community knew about the Blackburn case. The actual record itself was confidential. Albert T. Blackburn was one of three district court judges in Casper. The judge and his wife were in the midst of an epic, nasty divorce, fighting over their Rhode Island-sized working ranch. Jane Murphy, new to her role as judge, had little interaction with Judge Blackburn, making her the perfect choice to preside over the case.

A few of the pages were dog-eared. She flipped through a few sheets and saw the familiar handwriting in the margins. There were sentences highlighted in pink.

Lauren decided she could not just leave the transcript behind. Who knows where it would end up if she did? She folded the booklet and tucked it under her arm. With her free hand, she scooped up Percy and walked out.

Emmett stood at the rear of her car. "What have you got there?" He motioned to the papers.

Lauren explained the confidentiality of the document and her need to take it. "I'm going to take it back to the courthouse."

"Good idea."

She unlocked her car. "If there's anything I can do, Emmett, please let me know."

Mr. Murphy opened the rear of the Volvo, moved Lauren's sleeping bag to make room for Percy's kennel, and closed the cargo area. "Have you removed Jane's things from her office yet?"

"Yeah."

"Thank you. I was contacted by the county attorney. The selection committee is going to be using Jane's office, to start the interview process to replace Jane..." He looked over his shoulder at his daughter's house and then at Lauren. "They didn't say it outright, but I understand it makes sense not to have any of her personal items there."

"Did Mr. Graham say when the interviews were scheduled?"

"Tomorrow morning at nine o'clock."

"Okay." No one had told her about the interviews, but Lauren reminded herself there was no reason for her to be informed.

He ran a hand through his thick gray hair. "I don't know when I'll be back. There's still so much to do. We're going to put the house up on the market of course. That'll take time." He glanced behind him again and shook his head. "I'll contact you."

After a quick goodbye, Lauren got in the Volvo and drove home. The season's first snowflakes were falling by the time Lauren pulled into her garage. She killed the engine, turned to the Papillon curled up in the passenger seat. "I tried, little guy."

Percy got up, stretched, and walked onto Lauren's lap.

"On the bright side, we can go straight into the house from the garage. I have a garage. No more scraping snow off my windshield. Yay for me."

Percy wagged his tail.

Chapter Twenty-Five

Snow blanketed the town of Crawford. Lauren left home early to give herself extra time to stop at Dominick's before going to work. She stomped her feet trying to remove the snow that filled the thick treads of her waterproof boots before entering the store. The bell above the door sounded loud in the quiet bakery. She walked up to the counter and removed her gloves.

"Morning, young lady."

"Hi, Dominick. I need an assortment of your finest. I think a dozen should be good."

Dominick reached behind him, grabbed a white bakery box, and, bending slightly, reached in the case for the still-warm pastries. His usual banter with her was absent.

"Looks like you might have a slow day with this weather."

He straightened. "Just as well. Hector didn't show this morning. He don't call, no nothin'."

"That's not good. Maybe he had car trouble?"

"He coulda at least called and let me know." Dominick folded the flaps of the box and added tape on each end. "A little extra precaution for that wind out there."

"Thanks."

He handed Lauren the box. "Is this for your big meeting today?"

"Huh? Big meeting?"

"Yeah. Amanda was in here yesterday. She told me she had a real important meeting today at the courthouse."

"Hmm. Amanda said that? They're doing interviews today for a new judge."

"I was going to ask her what the important meeting was but she was in and out pretty quick. Didn't get a chance."

"Was Hector working yesterday?"

"Yeah. Why do you ask?"

"No reason. Just asking. So, are you going to call him later, ask him why he didn't show?"

"Nah. Not my place to call him. He oughta be callin' me. I'll wait and see if he shows up tomorrow."

She handed Dominick her credit card. "Did you know about Hector's past before you hired him?"

"Like any kinda trouble he'd been in before I hired him?"

"Yeah." Lauren admired the pumpkin spice cream cheese muffins in the case while she waited for her card to process.

"I knew he'd been in some kinda trouble before. He told me he did jail time but who hasn't been in trouble when they were younger, am I right? I myself was no choir boy, let me tell you. Joining the service turned my life around." He handed her the card. "Enjoy."

Lauren put her gloves on, thanked him, and turned to leave.

He called out to her, "Watch out for idiot drivers out there. First snowfall and everyone acts like they never drove in the stuff before."

"I will." As she reached the door, Detective Overstreet entered the bakery with Chief of Police Raymond Newell at his side. The detective brushed snow off his shoulders, nodded a curt hello to Lauren and continued past her.

She turned and caught the chief's hard gaze on her.

The men walked up to the counter. Dominick did not reach for a bakery box or a bag. Lauren wanted to stay and find out the reason for their visit, but she needed to get to the courthouse before the committee arrived. With a final glance at the two men, she made her way into the frigid air.

Inside the courthouse, Lauren did more foot-stomping to rid her boots of snow, her purse balanced on the bakery box, which she held with a firm grip. Gunner sat in his usual spot. Lauren unzipped her coat, took out her badge, and swiped it.

Gunner nodded toward the pastries and wriggled his eyebrows. "I'll be up in a few minutes to help you with that."

"Okay, but you better hurry. There's going to be interviews going on for the new judge. They're supposed to start at nine in chambers."

"Who are you expecting?"

"I have no idea other than there will be at least three attorneys and two lay people, nonprofessionals. I found out about it by accident myself. I'm sure we'll both know soon enough." Lauren pressed the button for the elevator.

The main office was locked. She used her key to let herself in, turned on lights as she made her way to the break room where she deposited the sweets, then went to her office and put her bag away.

Stale air permeated Judge Murphy's office. She left the door open for a little fresh air infusion, then hurried to the break room to make coffee and put out clean cups. In her office, she took the Blackburn transcript out of her bag and put it in a file folder marked *Confidential.* The brown folder housed the exhibits from the Blackburn case. With the matter now on temporary hold, Lauren made a note to herself to store the documents in the evidence room.

With the computer up and running, Lauren logged in to the state system and checked her email. Susan sent one the prior evening, explaining she hoped to be well enough to come in by lunchtime.

There were two emails from attorneys informing her of appeals they were filing and requesting she prepare transcripts in their respective cases. The rest of the emails she deleted without the need to open them.

A knock on her door made Lauren look up.

"Excuse me. There was no one at the desk out front. Am I in the right place? I'm Jessica Lancaster. I'm on the nominating committee."

"Yes, you're in the right place." Lauren stood, walked around her desk, and extended her hand to the woman with short spiky blonde hair and tortoise shell-framed glasses. "Hi. I'm Lauren Besoner, the judge's—I'm the court reporter. Let me show you where I think you're going to be today."

"The information I was provided said we would be in the judge's chambers. Does that sound right?"

"Yes. This whole area is the judge's chambers. Let me show you to the judge's office." Lauren escorted the petite woman into Judge Murphy's office. On the way, Lauren pointed out the break room. "There's fresh coffee and fresh muffins so, please, help yourself." Before going back to her office Lauren asked, "How many interviews are you doing today?"

"We have six prospective candidates."

"Are they all from Crawford?"

"Three are from Crawford, one is from Cheyenne, one from Lander, and one from Casper. I hope everybody is able to make it despite the snow. I haven't heard of any road closures but you never know."

"True, and how quickly it can change from one minute to the next, especially up on the summit."

Miss Lancaster nodded.

"Are you from Crawford?" Lauren asked.

"Yes, I'm an accountant at Brady and Lancaster."

"Your offices are right across the street then."

"They are. Thank you for your help… Lauren, is it?

"Yes. You're welcome."

"You said you're a court reporter?"

"I am."

"How do those little machines work? They look so small."

"It's all based on phonetics. That way we should be able to take down everything that someone says, even if we've never heard of the word before, or if it's a medical term that we haven't heard before, like spondylolysis."

"Interesting."

"There aren't twenty-six keys on the machine, like the alphabet, so a combination of keys makes up for the letters that aren't there. For instance when I hit the T-P-H together, that's an N. When I hit the P-W together, that stands for the letter B."

"Oh."

"And then we also have briefs, one keystroke for phrases that come up a lot, like, 'I don't know.'" Lauren stopped her explanation when she noticed Miss Lancaster's look of confusion. "It's hard to explain. If you need anything I'll be in my office."

Within a minute of sitting in her chair, muffled voices could be heard outside. The other committee members had arrived. Curious to see who they were, she walked out to the outer office. Attorneys Sylvia Horst, William Danville, and Scott Thurman were walking into the judge's office. Scott Thurman, in his early sixties, unwrapped a camel-colored wool scarf from around his neck revealing his signature accessory, a striped bowtie. He offered Miss Lancaster one of his many smiles as they shook hands.

The word dapper always came to Lauren's mind when Scott entered a room. The man exuded a quiet intelligence and possessed a dry sense of humor. She enjoyed working with him.

Once the introductions were over, Lauren approached the group. "Hi, Scott. You're part of the committee too, huh?"

"Yes. Seems like we just went through this process." He shook his head. "Terrible thing, what happened to Jane. Have you heard if the police are making any progress with the case?"

She shook her head. "I have no idea what's going on."

"Jane was smart, capable. Such a shame." Mr. Thurman hung his coat on the coat rack, and they walked to the break room together. He took the cup of hot coffee Lauren offered. "The first candidate should be showing up any minute."

"Who is the first candidate?"

"Amanda Capshaw."

After talking with Dominick earlier, Lauren wasn't as surprised as she might otherwise have been. She was, however, ambivalent whether Amanda had what it took to make a good judge. She didn't win most of her criminal cases, but Lauren chalked it up to the fact that most of her clients were guilty of doing what they were charged with and shouldn't necessarily reflect on her talents as a lawyer.

"Well, have fun." Lauren returned to her office. With a potential new boss being interviewed down the hall, she found it hard to concentrate on editing. She texted Claude and asked if she wanted to come down and have lunch. A moment later Claude texted back, "Yes. See you at twelve."

Lauren pulled out a fresh pack of sticky notes. On each pastel-colored square she wrote the name of a possible suspect. Her scribblings included Hector Ortiz, Bradley Schwartz, Danielle Armstrong, Susan Mumford, and Tony. She jotted down motives.

Hector blamed Judge Murphy for the harsh sentence he ended up with. She did not have a strong one for Susan other than the woman complained about having to work harder. The judge did represent her in her divorce, and Susan was unhappy with the outcome. Danielle Armstrong's daughter was now a felon and Danielle was stuck raising her grandchild. She blamed both of those things on Judge Murphy. That's a strong motive.

Bradley. Being Jane's fiancé, maybe something happened in their relationship and he lost his temper and killed her. Husbands and wives were always the first suspect. Fiancés would fall in that category.

Tony. Could it be Tony found out she used him, only went to bed with him so he wouldn't be able to prosecute some of the cases she had? His ego would not like that.

Last, Lauren added the name Senator Robbins. He had a case being heard in their court. She put question marks on two other sticky notes, one for Randall Graham and one for Nina Thornton. They were the other two attorneys in the running with Jane to become judge. She held the sticky note with Albany County Prosecutor Randall Graham's name, debating whether to toss it in the trash. *Everyone is a suspect.* Detective Overstreet's exact words.

Tony did not have an alibi for that night. The idea of him being capable of murder made Lauren uneasy. He could get mad, something she witnessed a few times during their marriage, but he had never been violent with her. *Nah. I'm just angry at him. Asshole, yes. Killer? No, he wasn't capable of that. Or was he?*

After finishing making the notes, she studied the blue, yellow and pink squares all over her desk. She gathered them up and placed them on their own yellow legal sized sheet of paper, and in blue Sharpie at the top of each sheet wrote, S-PS. She tacked the three pages to her corkboard that hung from a hook on the wall by the door. It was where she kept a running list of appeals that were due. Stepping back, she appraised her ideas. Eight suspects.

A half hour later Lauren sensed the presence of someone and looked up from her computer. "Hi, Amanda."

The attorney stood in the doorway, her face flush. She sat down opposite Lauren and let out a loud sigh. "I'm relieved that's over. I was interviewing with the selection committee."

"Dominick sort of mentioned that this morning."

"Dominick?"

"Yeah. I was at the bakery this morning. He said you were there yesterday, and told him about having a very important meeting today at the courthouse. My math skills aren't the greatest but I put two and two together."

"That's right, I was there. He is an incredible baker."

"I know. I can gain five pounds just on the smell alone. How did your interview go?"

"It went very well. I have a good feeling about it."

"Way to go. Do you have time for a cup of coffee? I'm getting ready to fix myself one. Or a soda?"

"I need to stop at the clerk's office but I have time for a cup. I couldn't relax in there. I can get it myself."

"No, let me. I'll be right back." No time like the present to start sucking up just in case Amanda becomes the next judge. She returned with two mugs of coffee and set them on her desk. Amanda's back was to her.

"I couldn't remember how you took your coffee." Lauren placed sugar and creamer packets in a small pile and sat in her chair.

Amanda turned away from the window. She held Judge Murphy's framed law degree in her hand. "Packing up Jane's things?"

"Yeah. Emmett Murphy asked me to."

"I still have a hard time believing she's gone." Amanda slowly shook her head.

"Me too. How long had you known her?"

"Sixteen years. God, I feel old. We met in our second year of law school. Seems like yesterday." She sniffled and placed the degree back in the box.

Lauren set her mug down. "When I went to Jane's house to meet with Emmett yesterday I thought he was going to take Percy. I don't know if you've heard but I've been taking care of him since… since this all happened. And yesterday he told me he wouldn't be able to take him."

"That's too bad."

"You've met him before, haven't you?"

"Who, Mr. Murphy or the dog?"

"Percy. I assume you had met her father before, since you were partners."

"Right. I have met Mr. and Mrs. Murphy. And I've met the dog. Jane brought him to the office a few times."

"Any chance you'd be interested in taking him?" Lauren offered a small grin. "If you've been around him you know what a sweetheart he is."

"He is cute but I travel too much to have a pet. I had a cat once. Even that didn't work out."

"You won't be traveling much at all if you get the job."

"True." Amanda seemed to be thinking. "Maybe I can come by your place and meet him—or re-meet him."

"Yes, you should." Not wanting to lose the momentum, Lauren wrote her address and cell number on one of the notepads on her desk, ripped off the little square of paper, and handed it to Amanda.

"I'll think it over and let you know." She folded the paper in half and placed it in her bag. "I need to get going. I have clients coming in this afternoon and I still have to stop at the clerk's office. Thanks for the coffee."

The bright spot of Amanda stopping by, Lauren told herself, was that Percy might have a new home.

Chapter Twenty-Six

At noon Lauren went to the break room to check on the coffee. She made another pot, the third one of the day. While it brewed, she heated up her lunch in the microwave.

"Where are you, Lauren?" called a voice.

Lauren stuck her head out of the break room. "In here."

Claude walked in holding a plastic container with a blue lid. "Hey, do you mind if I heat this up?"

"Go ahead."

"I see Susan is here today." Claude hit a few buttons on the microwave.

"Yeah, I smelled her come in about ten minutes ago." She shook her head. "Sorry, I'm being mean. I just think it would be nice if she was here for more than thirty minutes a day. Seems like she's taking advantage of the situation."

"You have to admit, it's a pretty nice gig if you can get it. A paycheck whether you show up for work or not."

"It irritates me." Lauren grabbed a bottled tea from the refrigerator.

Three beeps sounded from the microwave.

Claude removed the container.

"Smells good. Is it chili?"

"Yeah. Roberto made it last night. Want some?"

"No thanks. I've got my own amazing lunch. Not that I've had much of an appetite lately."

"He's a better cook than I am, but that's not saying much. Cooking was never my strong suit. Eating, yes. Cooking, no." Claude reached for some napkins.

Had Tony ever cooked me dinner? Lauren knew the answer, Not once. A man who cared enough to cook her a meal. Wouldn't that be nice? "Let's go eat in my office."

They walked to Lauren's office and she closed the door behind them. The small room held stack upon stack of documents. Exhibits from various trials had begun to make their way all over her normally neat desk, and some were piled on the floor. The office became claustrophobic. She made a mental note to organize the space before leaving for the day. In the meantime, she grabbed the confidential file folder from the corner of her desk and put it on a box marked *State versus Howard.* She did not want to spill any food on the folder or worse, on the exhibits themselves. Food stains were frowned upon by the Wyoming Supreme Court. She gathered up handwritten notes she scribbled for herself and put them into a neat pile, making room for Claude to eat her lunch.

"The committee is here interviewing."

"Who's been interviewed so far?"

"Steven Whitaker. He's from Lander."

"Don't know him." Claude gave a dismissive wave with her spoon.

"I've worked with him a few times. He's pretty sharp and a nice guy. Sonja Espinoza interviewed."

"Don't know her either."

"You'll know the next name. Amanda interviewed."

"Amanda Capshaw?

"Yeah."

"Interesting."

"Did you like working for her?" Lauren asked.

Claude tore off a piece of flour tortilla and dipped it into the green chili. "She was okay. But I never once regretted my decision to leave. The atmosphere in that office was too intense for me. They were so serious *all* the time."

"Defending the innocent is serious business." Lauren smiled.

"I'm convinced those two shared joint custody of a sense of humor."

Lauren laughed.

"No, it's true." Claude wiped her mouth. "I understand defense work is important and can't be taken lightly, freedoms are at stake, blah, blah, blah, but would it kill them to crack a joke or a smile once in a while? But Jane was definitely harder to work for. Didn't you think she was a bit of a perfectionist?"

"I don't know what to think about her anymore. Wait, what am I saying? She slept with my husband. Used him. At least if Amanda gets selected, I can be pretty sure she hasn't slept with Tony." She surprised herself that she was able to joke about the relationship.

Lauren used her fork to push the food around on the

little tray. "I think someone was trying to get in my house the other night."

"What?" Claude stopped eating and looked at her.

She pushed the food away, and told Claude how she found the dogs outside and her backdoor open.

"Did you call the police?"

"No. I wasn't sure. It's possible I didn't close it hard enough."

"Well, I think you should have. Just as a precaution."

Lauren wadded up her napkin and tossed it in the trash. "This whole thing with the judge has got me on edge. Overstreet keeps questioning me. After he came over to my house the other day I started to relax a little, but then, bam, he shows up at the office and escorts me to the station. I mean, what the hell is with him?"

"I don't know." Claude had a sly grin on her face. "You have to admit, he is good looking."

"No, I don't. Not whenever I turn around he's in my face, trying to get me to confess."

"Oh, come on. You know that'll never happen. And you mean to tell me you haven't pictured him in a pair of faded blue jeans, cowboy boots, and a T-shirt stretched across those shoulders of his?"

"No, but I know who has. Should Roberto be worried?"

"Nope. But Overstreet's been in our office a lot. I think he's cute."

"If you say so."

"Oh, that's right, I forgot, you're attracted to someone with a sense of humor. And their voice. Don't forget the voice."

"He does have a deep voice. Too bad it's drowned out by the stupid things he says."

"I don't get how you can be attracted to a voice."

"I just like the sound, you know, the deepness, richness."

"Give me something solid, something I can feel, touch." Claude flashed a wolfish grin.

"I did share something with him the other day."

"Oh? And what did you have to share with him?"

Lauren ignored the teasing in Claude's voice and told her about the protective order she came across in the judge's desk.

"I know Overstreet had Armstrong come down to the station. She swears she had nothing to do with Judge Murphy's death." Claude took a drink of her tea.

"Of course she's not going to admit it." *He's finally looking at other people as suspects. It's about time.*

"And she has no alibi."

"I don't have an alibi either."

"She swears she was at her salon. She owns one of those hairstyling franchises. Family Cuts."

"I've never been there."

"She claims she was going over inventory."

"You hire a sitter to do inventory at night?" Lauren gave her friend a questioning look. "Did you know she was raising her grandchild?"

"I'd heard that. Overstreet confirmed she had hired a baby-sitter but he hasn't been able to confirm where she went."

"What time did she get home?"

"Sitter said she got home at eleven."

"Falls within the window of what Overstreet said about time of death."

"She also told him if he had any other questions he could direct them to her lawyer."

"Can't say as I blame her. She must have been harassing Judge Murphy a lot for her to decide to get a protective order against her."

"Yeah," Claude agreed. "When I worked for Jane she dealt with some nasty clients. She didn't scare easily."

They spent the rest of their lunch hour talking about what Sophie wanted to be for Halloween, and segued into what they used to dress up as when they were kids and how much "loot" they used to bring home from trick-or-treating.

Claude got up to leave and spotted the corkboard adorned with colored sticky notes. Moving closer to them she read the letters out loud. "S P-S?"

"Suspects."

"Tony? Seriously? And Susan? I need to get you away from all this craziness. What about a shopping trip to Loveland this weekend?"

"I've got the time, I'm not sure I have the money though. But I could use a distraction from everything."

"We should go. I'll text you."

Two hours into editing, Lauren got up, stretched and made her way to the evidence room. Using her key, she unlocked the door and flipped on the light switch. One long fluorescent bulb ran the length of the small windowless room.

Along two of the walls were floor-to-ceiling metal shelving. On every surface, except the top shelves, were cardboard banker boxes, filled with assorted exhibits from various cases, mostly paper documents. An open area against the far wall housed larger exhibits, including a skeleton. There were crime scene photographs blown up to disturbing proportions, and even a poster-sized photo of a botched colonoscopy used in a medical malpractice suit. Lauren remembered that case. The jurors and everyone in the courtroom became rubberneckers on a freeway as they collectively gaped at the filled colostomy bag attached to the plaintiff's side.

The small room needed to be cleaned out and reorganized. She told herself after she got caught up on appeals, she would sort through everything, contact the attorneys involved in the civil cases and tell them to come get their exhibits, their skeleton, and especially the colonoscopy photos.

Lauren went straight to the box marked Bolton, in search of exhibits that the attorneys had quoted from. She often double checked to confirm she had gotten every word down.

With the bulky box balanced on her left hip, she locked up the evidence room. She saw Tony at the end of the hall heading in her direction. "I'm just going to my office. Do you have some more information for me?"

"No, I'm here for my interview."

Lauren stopped. "Interview?"

He walked up to her and nodded. "Yes, my interview. Wish me luck?" He grinned.

Lauren pushed past him, bumping him with the box but said nothing.

Tony walked down the hallway. Over his shoulder he said, "Does that mean you're not going to wish me luck?"

She kicked her office door shut and dropped the banker's box on the chair. "Fuck, fuck, fuck! This cannot be happening. If Tony gets this job—"

Susan entered Lauren's office. "Oh, I thought maybe you were on the phone. I just saw Tony. Did you know—"

"*Yes, I know.*"

"Well, you don't have to bite my head off. I came to say I'm leaving, so you need to answer my phone."

Lauren glanced at the clock on the wall. Three o'clock.

"Don't you think you should stay and lock up after the committee members leave? You know, do your job for a change?"

"Somebody's in a bad mood." Susan backed up toward the doorway. "You know I would but I have this awful headache."

"Well, I have a headache too and I'm not going home early." Lauren sat at her desk.

"Then you know how I feel. I knew I could count on you." With that, Susan spun around and disappeared down the hall, her perfume lingering in the air.

"*Shit.*" Lauren opened the large drawer of her desk and slammed it shut. She wanted to do it again but told herself to calm down. Tony should be done with his interview soon. Then she could lock up, go home and slam every drawer in her house if she wanted, even twice. Ignore him and get some work done. Don't even think about the asshole, but Lauren didn't listen to her inner voice. She reached for her cell phone, tapped out a message to Claude. "Did you know Tony was interviewing?" She hit the send button, then stood looking out her window and massaged her temples.

Thirty minutes later Mr. Thurman knocked on Lauren's open door. "The committee is all done. I want to thank you for your hospitality."

"You're welcome. How soon do you have to have a decision on the final three?"

"I think we'll be ready by Friday to give Governor Sterling our choices."

"Pretty quick then. That's good. Any chance you'd share who you're leaning toward? Never mind, I shouldn't ask."

Scott smiled. "Always good to see you, Lauren." He buttoned up his coat and left.

Lauren's cell phone pinged. A text from Claude. "Tony silent about applying." Before she could reply she heard voices in the hallway.

Chapter Twenty-Seven

The sound of the detective's voice made Lauren's mouth go dry. A moment later, there he stood, poised to knock on her door frame.

"If you're not busy, I'd like to go over a few more things."

"Down at the station, right?"

"Yes, please."

She jiggled the doorknob, turned to follow the detective, and braced herself for what he had to ask her this time.

When they reached the inner sanctum of the police station, Lauren followed the detective along the narrow hallway, resisting the urge to turn and run away. Her heart beat fast as she sat.

The detective clasped his hands and rested them on the table. "Lauren, did you leave anything out when we talked the other day?"

"I don't think so." She heard the hesitancy in her own voice.

"Are you sure?"

"I'm pretty sure. But all these *interviews* are beginning to run together in my mind. Why don't you just tell me what you brought me down here for."

"Sure, I can do that. We're both busy people."

Detective Overstreet pulled a sheet of paper out of the folder and slid it in front of her.

She read the document. She took in a breath and then another, desperate for air. She had never hyperventilated but wondered if this is what was happening to her. "This isn't true."

"What's not true?"

"This!" Lauren waved the paper at him. "Judge Murphy didn't tell me my job was in jeopardy. Ever. We never had a conversation like that." She reread the words. "This doesn't make any sense, Detective."

He leaned forward. "You can't give me any explanation for this?"

"I—"

"Let me tell you how I think it went. Judge Murphy calls you into her office and tells you you're on thin ice. You're not showing up on time, you have a poor attitude about your work."

It was her turn to interrupt. "That's not true. I was late one or two times at the most."

"She tells you how sloppy your work has become. She tells you that you have one month to straighten up or you can kiss your job goodbye. Am I getting close?" The detective leaned in. "You had bought your first home—"

What else does this man know about me?

"—You can't lose your job now. This woman, how dare she fire you. She has no damn right to treat you this way. It was then, wasn't it, Lauren, that you decided, no more? It was then, wasn't it, Lauren, that you decided to kill her? *Wasn't it?*"

The accusations flowed until they reached a crescendo. Lauren wanted to cover her ears. "*No*! No, you've got it all wrong. This whole thing is... is wrong. She never told me these things." Lauren shook the sheet of paper, then let it fall onto the table. "She never said anything to me about sloppy work. *Never*. My work isn't sloppy. I take pride in my work. And I already admitted I was late a time or two."

"So you admit you have been late?"

"Yes. All right, I admit it. I. Was. Late. Call out the tardy patrol and arrest me for God's sake."

"No need to raise your voice." The detective picked up the piece of paper. "It's all right here, Lauren. Right down to the last bullet point. 'Miss Besoner's attitude toward me has become hostile.'"

"That's *not* true." She snatched the paper from his hand. "Where did you get this anyway?"

"Does it matter?"

"Yes." Wanting to say something, anything, she blurted out, "You probably typed it up yourself."

"Yes, and then I signed Judge Murphy's name on the bottom." He sat back. "Why would I do that?"

"To trick me. To... so you can tell the chief what a good little detective you are by solving the case so quick." Lauren angered, continued. "You're just looking for a scapegoat. And here I am. We're practically in the same building. You don't even have to get in your car and track me down. Saves on gas too, doesn't it? How freak'n convenient." She had to stop for air.

His dark eyes bore into her. "Sometimes the answers are right in front of us. But I'll tell you where I got this. It was found in Miss Murphy's home office by her printer."

Lauren processed this information. "That doesn't even make sense. Why would it be at her house? If she supposedly gave this to me, wouldn't it be in her office at the courthouse?" She looked at him. "None of this makes sense. Why would I kill her? I'm telling you, it doesn't make sense." Lauren kept her hands clasped in front of her on the table, pressed her lips together, and concentrated on the sheet of paper.

The detective studied something in his file, and the room began to fill with an awkward silence of two strangers sharing an elevator ride.

He looked up from the paperwork. When he spoke again his words held notes of false concern. "Lauren, talk to me. Tell me what really happened. I'll understand. I've worked for some very demanding people. I know what you're going through."

She looked at him and slowly shook her head. "Now we're back to Mr. Nice Cop."

Detective Overstreet blew out a long breath.

Not daring to meet his gaze, Lauren concentrated on the milky white buttons on his shirt.

"I want to make this easy for you, Lauren."

With her hands still clasped together, Lauren fought to keep her mouth shut.

"I can see you aren't ready to cooperate." He picked up the piece of paper and returned it to the blue folder. He leaned back in his seat, folded his arms over his chest and stared across the small table.

Lauren moved in her chair, made an attempt at eye contact, but looked away.

The detective broke the silence. "You're free to go. Once we find the weapon—and we will find the weapon—we will be talking again." He rose abruptly, opened the door, and motioned for Lauren to leave.

Dismissed. She was being dismissed, a mere student leaving the principal's office after being given a stern warning.

Lauren stood on the top step taking in gulps of fresh air to calm herself. She could not go to her office. If she did she would just replay the interrogation over and over again in her mind until it sounded like a worn-out vinyl record. Instead, she made her way to her car and sank into the driver's seat. She pulled the pack of cigarettes out of the glovebox, held it in her hand for a moment, then tossed it on the passenger seat. She thrust her hand in her purse and pulled out Amanda's business card.

Capshaw Law Office accepted credit cards. Lauren had to use two to cover the retainer the lawyer charged. She would be paying legal fees for years to come, assuming Amanda did a good job and kept her out of prison. It made her want to cry.

Chapter Twenty-Eight

The moment Lauren flipped the light switch in her kitchen she knew something was wrong. It took a moment, then recognition set in what lay all over the floor. Bits and pieces of foam were scattered on the black-and-white checkered linoleum flooring. "What is this!" The foam pieces, like a trail of snickerdoodle cookie crumbs, led straight to a deflated sofa cushion now on the living room floor, a corner ripped open.

"*Who did this?*"

Maverik, who had been trotting toward her, stopped and sat. Percy stopped dancing on his hind legs, turned and dashed upstairs but not before Lauren saw a tiny piece of cushion sticking out of the side of his muzzle. While it did not tell her who the guilty party was, it did tell her that to be on the safe side Percy needed to be kenneled. Since Maverik chewed up the mesh one that belonged to Percy the day after she brought it home, she needed to replace it, fast.

With a plastic trash bag in her hand, Lauren alternated between muttering to herself and gathering up the damp pieces of foam. She hoped neither dog had eaten the foam or soon there would be a new mess to clean up. She set the full bag in the garage and went into the living room. Percy stood at the top of the staircase.

"You're coming to the office with me tomorrow, you little train wreck."

His body quivered, his large brown eyes full of fear.

"I'm mad at you." Lauren sat on the remaining intact cushion.

Percy eyed her.

"Come here." The anger had drained from Lauren's voice.

He slowly made his way down the stairs and sat by the chair.

"Up." She patted the intact sofa cushion.

He jumped and sat next to her.

"I just don't have the energy for this." Lauren set him on her lap. She stroked his fur and whispered in his ear, "Between you and me, I was ready for a new couch."

❋ ❋ ❋

Lauren remembered her plan to take Percy with her that morning. She hauled out a large canvas tote from the hall closet, tucked a towel in the bottom for comfort, picked up Percy and placed him inside. "That's not so bad. Let's go, you." She placed Percy on the passenger seat of the Volvo.

His furry ears along with his brown and white nose peeked out from the bag.

Gunner manned the security desk. Lauren approached, hoisted the bag onto her right shoulder, swiped her badge, and passed through the metal detector.

"I didn't see anything," said Gunner.

Percy yipped.

"I didn't hear anything," he added.

"Thanks." Lauren's plan was to spend a couple hours at the office, then make a quick stop at the store and pick up a kennel on her way home.

Lauren entered the judge's chambers. Percy barked. Susan craned her neck to see around Amanda who stood in front of her desk. They both stared at Lauren and the large bag she shouldered.

"What are you doing bringing a dog to the office?" asked Susan.

Lauren raised her voice over Percy's yip-yip-yipping. "He's only staying for the morning. You won't even know he's here." To Percy she said, "Ssh."

Percy growled as Lauren hurried past the two women.

"I'm allergic to dogs. I told you that. He can't be here or I'll break out in hives."

"He's been destroying my house," Lauren called over her shoulder, "But I have a plan." She slipped into her office and closed the door behind her. Lifting Percy out of the tote, she held him at eye level. "What was that all about? I told you to be on your best behavior. Was that really your best?"

Percy licked Lauren's cheek.

Lauren had checked the calendar the day before. With nothing scheduled, she didn't expect to see Susan at the office. "Okay. This wasn't such a good idea." She placed the little dog on the floor and went out to Susan's desk, which sat empty. Amanda stood nearby checking her phone.

"Where did Susan go?"

"To the clerk's office. She rushed out of here."

"Oh. Amanda, did you want to come and visit with Percy since you're here?"

Amanda looked up from her phone. "I can't. I have a client waiting for me at the office." She opened the door to leave. "Let's do it another time."

"Sure."

Back in her office Lauren spoke to Percy. "I don't ever remember Susan telling me she was allergic to dogs but I have to get you out of here, otherwise she'll just use you as an excuse to go home, if she hasn't already left."

Before leaving Lauren left Susan a note, asking her to email her if she put anything on the calendar.

The feed and ranch supply store was on the way home. Lauren purchased a small wire kennel, then dropped Percy off at home. Determined to not waste the whole day, she returned to the courthouse. Susan was gone but had left a note. "I have set a hearing on Thursday. Judge Childers will be covering it. I've set the usual for Friday. Judge Brubaker will be here. Thank you for removing that dog."

After an hour, Lauren's stomach growled. She looked at the clock. One-fifteen. The thought of another frozen meal left her wanting, like wanting something else for lunch. She gathered her jacket off the coat rack thinking something from Dominick's sounded much better. If his chicken tortilla soup was on the chalkboard menu Lauren would be in food nirvana.

On the sidewalk, Lauren slipped on her sunglasses and tilted her face toward the blue sky. The sun warmed her cheeks. No wind. A perfect autumn day. The first snowfall was already history, every last flake melting the day before. Lauren breathed in the earthy scent of damp leaves gathered on the sidewalk and against the curb. She often wished, irrationally so, that the feeling it provoked could be stored in a jar, to be opened when her spirits were low.

The old-fashioned bell above the door tinkled. Lauren entered Dominick's Bakery, removed her sunglasses and let her eyes adjust. They settled on Tony, alone at a table, an empty plate in front of him. He was hunched over his cell phone.

He glanced up as Lauren strode past him. "What, no hello?"

"Hey." She continued to the counter. Ever since learning of the betrayal, whenever she saw Tony it took concentration to keep her feelings to herself, feelings that ran from feeling the total fool and wanting to burst into tears, to suppressing a hot rage that made her want to punch Tony where it would hurt most. She knew she shouldn't dwell on something in the past but in her mind it was as if the affair just happened. She spent many sleepless nights asking herself, how does a person become so blind, so blind not to see the signs? Surely there must have been signs. She shook off the negativity.

The handwritten menu confirmed what her nose suspected. This was turning out to be a good day, except for Tony's presence. She told herself not to let that bring down her good mood. Crawford was big enough for the two of them. At least it had been until recently.

Dominick took her order and Lauren waited for his usual follow-up question trying to get her to order something sweet. Today he didn't. He ladled the soup into a deep bowl without speaking, and his brown eyes lacked their usual spark.

Tony removed his jacket from his chair and walked over to Lauren. "I've got some more information. I'll catch up with you when I've got some time."

"Okay." She didn't bother to make eye contact with him.

Lauren took a table near the door and gazed out into the bright afternoon. The soup lived up to her expectations. Spicy. Thick. Delicious. Lauren had a tissue at the ready just in case. It was the first time in weeks since she enjoyed a meal.

She crushed more lime-infused tortilla chips into her soup. Dominick came over to her table, a damp towel dangled from his hand. "How's that soup tasting?"

"Delicious. Maybe someday you'll let me have the recipe?"

"I'm not sure I can do that."

"Not even for your favorite customer?"

"Not even for my favorite customa." He smiled apologetically, then asked, "Do you mind if I sit? I want to ask you something."

"Of course not. Sit."

He pulled out the chair opposite Lauren, the legs scraping along the floor, and lowered his stocky frame into the wooden seat. He spoke just above a whisper, "You were in here the other day when Chief Newell came in with that detective, right?"

Lauren nodded.

"They ordered coffee and sat over there." Dominick pointed toward a table by the register. They was acting like they come in all the time and was just shooting the breeze with one another. But they finally come out and said they was looking for Hector. They wanted to ask him some questions. I said, 'What kinda questions?' It had to do with the murder of Judge Murphy. I told the truth, that he was a no-show that day. I couldn't help them."

"I remember you told me about Hector."

"Yeah. I kinda got used to having him here." He looked toward the back room. "Anyway, Hector called me way early this morning. The cops picked him up for questioning. That's why he never showed up the other morning."

"Picked him up? Where did they find him?"

"Traffic stop, on the interstate."

"Did they arrest him or just take him in for questioning, did he say?"

Dominick rubbed his chin. "Just asked questions. He apologized like a dozen times and wanted to know if he still had a job here."

"What did you tell him?"

"Nothing yet. I don't know what to do. He's been a heck of a good worker but this whole business with the judge...That's what I want to talk to you about. What do you think?"

Lauren thought a moment. "Gee, I don't know what to tell you."

"I'm a good judge of character but I keep asking myself, what if I'm wrong and I let a killer come back and work for me. He told me he was scared. Amanda told him the police were looking for him." He scratched at his chin again. "Do you know anything about him?"

"I know a little about his past from what others have told me." She pushed her empty bowl aside and wiped her mouth. "Judge Murphy represented him a long time ago on a drug possession charge. He blamed her for the long prison sentence he ended up with. I didn't know any of this when you hired him."

Two customers walked toward the door. Dominick gave them a two-fingered salute goodbye. "Thanks, folks, for coming in. Enjoy that fine weather we're having."

The pair nodded and went out into the afternoon sunshine.

He turned his attention back to Lauren. "I told him I'd think about it."

"One thing I do know, if the police had enough evidence to charge him with her murder, he'd be sitting in jail right now. His fingerprints are already in the system. If they let him go that could only mean they didn't find his prints at her place."

"I see what you're saying."

"But if he's scared, he might run again."

Dominick nodded.

"It doesn't make sense to me that he'd kill Judge Murphy and then go looking for a job in town."

"What you say makes sense, young lady." He pushed back his chair, stood, and tucked the bar towel into the pocket of his white apron. "One more thing. It probably don't mean nothin' but I overheard the chief telling the detective that he still—I'm pretty sure he said he likes you for the crime. Whatever that means."

"Are you sure that's what he said?"

"Yep."

"It means he thinks *I* killed Judge Murphy."

"*No way.* He's gotta be nuts if he thinks that." Dominick looked around at the empty tables before he spoke again. "I don't think the detective agrees. He was shaking his head pretty hard."

"I'm not sure I'd agree with you. He's been questioning me a lot."

"Trust me. I know what I saw." He tapped the table with his hand. "I didn't mean to bother you while you was eating, Lauren. Or to make you worry. I probably shouldn't have said nothin' about the chief. I hope I haven't chased away my favorite customa."

"You weren't bothering me at all, and I appreciate the information. I just wish this whole thing was over and the killer behind bars already. It gives me the creeps every time I think about it," then added, "which is a lot." Lauren shrugged into her coat.

Dominick wiped down the table. "Have a good one, young lady."

She smiled at Dominick. "Thanks for having my favorite soup on the menu."

The still air had been replaced by a strong breeze, and Lauren walked the two blocks to the courthouse at a brisk pace, the words Dominick spoke filling her mind. *The chief likes me for the crime. Why the hell would he think I killed Judge Murphy?*

She reached the steps leading up to the courthouse and saw two men, both in dark suits, exiting the police station. The shorter man did all the talking, his face animated and his arms moving about as he spoke.

"Hello, Bradley."

Jane Murphy's fiancé stopped and looked at her. It took him a moment, then recognition set in. "Hello. It's Lauren, isn't it?"

"Yes. I didn't get a chance to talk to you at the funeral and I wanted to tell you how sorry I am for your loss."

"Thank you."

"What brings you to Crawford?" *Did I just ask that?*

"I had business that needed attending to. The detective needed my help with some information."

She tried to think of something else to say, but Bradley gave her no chance. "Nice seeing you again."

"Same here." Lauren gave herself a mental kick for lacking the ability to think quick on her feet. She stood on the first step and watched the two men scurry down the sidewalk.

Before they reached a silver Mercedes-Benz S-Class sedan, it chirped and the doors unlocked. Bradley slid into the driver's seat. The taller gentleman folded himself into the passenger side, his door not quite closed. The Mercedes shot away from the curb and raced down the street.

The wind acted like a lasso, and she rushed up the courthouse steps to free herself of the cold air. In her office, she pulled out her phone and texted Claude. "Just saw Bradley leave PD. Know anything?" She laid her cell phone on her desk, then picked it up again and sent her friend another text. "Heard why Newell thinks I killed Jane?"

Lauren opened the *Howard* file to edit it, and two hours later had the first day's proceedings finished and ready for proofreading. While it printed, she backed up the edited file.

As she was leaving she glanced in the small mirror by her door. Gathering the ends of her hair between her fingers, she examined the long strands. "I think it's time for a trim."

Chapter Twenty-Nine

The yellow neon sign pulsed, Walk-ins Welcome. Lauren stepped into the salon. The odor of hair-processing chemicals assaulted her senses and she wrinkled her nose. It always took Lauren a few moments to get used to the smell.

Three of the four stations were occupied. A hair stylist looked up from the bangs she was snipping. "Someone will be right with you."

"Thanks."

A large board on the wall behind the register explained the services Family Cuts provided, along with their "family friendly" prices. Lauren didn't see Danielle Armstrong. She browsed an open cabinet whose shelves were filled with a variety of hair products, each colorful bottle proclaiming its unique virtues. One for shine, one for curl, one for volume, and one for moisturizing. Where, wondered Lauren, was the one for making all your troubles disappear?

"Sorry to keep you waiting."

Lauren turned in the direction of the husky voice. "Oh, no problem."

In the afternoon light Danielle Armstrong looked tired. Foundation had settled into every line on her face, and her mascara-smudged eyes added to the weary look.

"Your sign says, walk-ins welcome. I just need a trim if you have time."

"Sure. Follow me."

Lauren trailed behind the woman dressed all in black, from her cross-trainers, her leggings, and short-sleeved polo shirt. The only pop of color came from the yellow scissors embroidered on the sleeve with the words Family Cuts underneath.

Danielle gestured with a sweep of her arm to the empty chair, and Lauren sat and faced the mirror.

"How much are you wanting to take off?"

"About an inch."

With a snap of her wrists, Danielle unfurled a black cape and draped it over Lauren. She examined a few strands of Lauren's brown hair, then ran warm water through Lauren's hair and massaged shampoo into her scalp with her long fingernails. Lauren closed her eyes and enjoyed the mini massage.

"You said about an inch?"

"Yes."

Danielle held her comb in one hand, scissors in the other, parted Lauren's hair and began cutting the ends.

With pleasantries out of the way Lauren launched into a series of questions about the salon, how long Danielle had been cutting hair, if she liked what she did, if she owned the shop, which Danielle did.

It was Danielle's turn to ask questions, the first being, "What do you do for a living?" She tipped Lauren's head forward.

"I'm a court reporter."

The scissors in Danielle's hand stopped mid-snip.

"I used to work for Judge Murphy." Lauren sat, head still down, in the heavy silence. *Maybe a trim wasn't such a good idea.*

Danielle's eyes narrowed. "That bitch sent my daughter to prison."

The older woman in the chair next to them, her hair swathed in tinfoil, cocked her head but kept her eyes focused on the magazine in her lap.

"I know. I thought the sentence was harsh," The lie rolled off Lauren's tongue with ease.

"It was total BS." Danielle combed a section of hair out to the side and resumed snipping away at the ends. "I read in the paper that her body was found by her court stenographer. That was you?"

"Yeah. It was pretty awful. And on top of that I was brought in for questioning."

"Oh yeah?"

"Wanted to know if I had an alibi for that night, which I didn't."

The tinfoiled woman no longer attempted to hide her curiosity.

"They must be hard up for suspects because I had some detective come and ask me a bunch of stupid questions too."

"Really? Why would they question you?" She hoped the question sounded innocently inquisitive.

"He said they were questioning everyone that the judge recently sentenced." Danielle swiveled the chair around with more force than necessary. Holding a razor, she sliced through Lauren's bangs, then picked up a straightener and pulled it through her hair.

"I was upset about my daughter's sentence, sure. But I didn't kill her." Danielle pulled on two sections of hair, checking her work. "I followed her home one day, tried talking to her when she got out of her car but she wouldn't speak to me. She told me it would be inappropriate to be speaking about the case outside of the courtroom."

Danielle shook her head. "It wasn't a *case*. It's my *daughter*."

"What did you tell the detective when he asked where you were that night?"

"*Me*? You're asking me where I was?" Danielle's hand tightened around the straightener.

"No, no. I was just wondering what you told the detective."

"Did he put you up to this? Come in here—"

"No. I—"

"—asking me all kinds of questions?"

"I didn't mean—"

"You can tell him, nice try." With that, Danielle whipped off Lauren's cape sending pieces of hair scattering. A few landed on the tinfoiled woman's lap. "You can pay up front."

"I'm sorry, I was—"

Danielle stormed off.

Lauren caught the stares from the other customers and hairstylists. If there had been bouncers in the salon they would have been at her side right about now to escort her out. She paid quickly, dashed to her car where she waited for her breathing to return to normal.

Chapter Thirty

Lauren hoisted her messenger bag out of the Volvo's backseat and kicked through the colorful leaves underfoot until she reached the courthouse steps. For a moment she felt like a kid. All troubles abandoned.

Two pink sticky notes, one on top of another, were stuck to Lauren's office door. Susan had scribbled the basic information for the hearing Judge Childers was coming over for the next day. The second note said Susan may not make it in Thursday, her sinuses were acting up. "Poor Susan," muttered Lauren, her sarcasm wasted since she was alone.

She logged in to the court's computer system, getting the complete case name and file number, then phoned Vincent Gladstone, Judge Childers's court reporter, and offered to cover the hearing for him. Vincent accepted her offer. He was working on an appeal due at the end of the week. Their conversation centered around their respective workloads, then turned to any plans they had for the upcoming holidays, and inevitably segued into the circumstances surrounding Jane's death. Lauren gave him a condensed version of what happened to her judge, even though she sensed he wanted to hear more detail.

⁂ ⁂ ⁂

There was a knock on the open door and Claude walked in.

"You look cute," said Lauren.

"Thanks." Claude wore a turquoise jacket over a black ankle-length skirt. "I was on my break and needed to get out of the office for a few minutes. Are you busy?"

"No. Want some coffee?"

"No, I'm good, thanks." Claude sank into the chair and ran her fingers through her hair, sweeping her bangs to the side. She looked at Lauren. "Did you get your hair cut?"

"Yeah. Yesterday."

"I like it."

"Guess who cut my hair?" Lauren shook her head, her hair still shiny from the straightener Danielle used on it yesterday. It fell neatly into place.

"Who?"

"Danielle Armstrong."

"Seriously?"

"I needed a trim."

Claude raised an eyebrow. "Of course you did."

"I wanted to get a sense of what she was like."

"And what is she like when she's not acting like a total psycho?"

"Angry. When I asked her if she had an alibi for that night she practically threw me out of the salon." Lauren shook her head. "Good thing she was finished cutting my hair, or today could have definitely been a bad hair day."

"That sounds like her. Were you expecting her to confess?"

"I don't know what I was expecting." Susan's phone rang but Lauren did not answer it. "I won't be going back there again. Which is too bad."

"Why is that?"

"I like the way she cut my hair." She did another toss of her head.

"That is too bad. And look at you. Casual Friday in the middle of the week. I'm jealous."

Lauren glanced at her outfit, then hiked her foot up on her desk, revealing her dark-wash jeans and running shoes. "I could get used to casual Friday every day." She put her foot down. "What's going on upstairs that you need to escape?"

"Your new hair stylist just left our offices. She was in with Graham, talking to him… more like shouting at him. Maybe you heard her from down here?"

"No. But is that why you called her psycho?"

"Yep. She was in the reception area, yelling that she was going to sue the county if he dared to bring murder charges or any other charges against her. And that she was done answering any more questions from that, and I quote, 'don't-know-his-ass-from-his-elbow detective.'"

Lauren put her hand over her mouth to silence a snort.

"I know. Who says stuff like that? I don't know if she's just wired different than the rest of us or what, but she actually jabbed Graham in the chest with her finger." Claude mimicked Danielle Armstrong with her own jabbing motions in the air in front of her. "Took him by surprise. But it was a little funny."

"Funny?"

"Sort of. Here's this big teddy bear of a man and this anorexic woman standing face-to-face. I mean if he had sneezed she'd have been history. He told her if she didn't stop right this minute he would have her charged with assault."

"Wow."

"I thought she was going to spit on him she was so mad."

"I miss out on all the excitement here in my little office."

"You do. And I did hear her tell him, or I should say yell, that she had taken a polygraph and was done cooperating with the police. If you call that cooperating."

"She didn't have to agree to one. I suppose that's cooperating. Does Graham have the results from the polygraph?"

"No. That's where she had been right before she came to see him." Claude checked the time on her phone. "I wanted to share."

"Glad you did. "

Claude's voice grew serious. "How are you holding up with everything that's been going on?"

"I'm doing all right." Lauren reached for the pearl hanging from the gold chain around her neck and rubbed it between her fingers.

"You look tired."

Lauren covered her eyes with the palms of her hands. "I haven't been able to sleep since I found Jane. But I'll be fine. Judge Childers is coming tomorrow so I'll be in court the whole day." Lauren caught Claude's expression. "No, that's a good thing. Take my mind off the investigation. Working is my new therapy."

"Speaking of which, I need to get back upstairs."

* * *

"Lauren? Mind if I come in?"

The detective's familiar baritone voice startled her and she flinched.

"Uh, no." She did mind but he would probably waltz on in anyway.

"I came by to see what personal effects Judge Murphy has in her office but everything's gone."

"You're in luck then, sort of." Lauren pointed to the box in the corner. "Some of it's still here."

"Where's the rest of it?"

"At my house?"

"Why is it there?"

"Because..." Lauren glared at him... "Emmet Murphy asked me to box up her personal belongings. Sorry I didn't call you first and get your permission."

The detective stared at her.

"Anyway, I thought you would have come over or sent someone over a long time ago to check her office."

He shook his head. "Turns out they forgot."

"I saw you in the bakery the other day." Lauren wanted to change the direction of the conversation. She knew she had no reason to feel guilty for removing the judge's belongings but his asking made her feel guilty all the same. "Did you try one of the pumpkin spice muffins?"

"No."

"You should next time. They're awesome. I heard you were questioning Hector Ortiz."

The detective looked at her but said nothing.

"If you're questioning him can I assume you're actually looking for the *real* killer and I'm no longer a suspect?" Her words were sharp, even to her own ears, but since he was in her office, on her turf, she didn't apologize for them.

"You work in the court system, you should know I can't rule anyone out."

Lauren opened the top drawer, putting away pens and sticky notes, then slammed it shut. "There's a difference between ruling me out and treating me like a suspect, like a killer."

He walked over to the box marked Judge M. "Just doing my job. But I will tell you I'm looking at all leads. And, yes, one of them is Hector Ortiz."

"Detective, think about it. If Hector killed Judge Murphy he wouldn't stay in town and apply for a job at a bakery where everybody could see him, would he? He'd leave town. It doesn't make any sense to me."

"Sometimes you can't outrun stupid." He lifted the lid on the box.

"What?"

"Maybe the man is dumb, plain and simple as that."

"*Oh.*"

The detective knelt and opened the box. "Do you remember what's in the boxes you took home already?"

"Her workout clothes, and the contents of one of her desk drawers."

He lifted out the photograph of Percy. The dog lay on a white fluffy pillow, front paws crossed in front of him. He looked expectantly into the camera.

"That's an, I-see-a-treat look."

"You're speaking from experience, I presume?"

"Yeah. He's cute, don't you think?"

With a half-smile he said, "If you say so." He moved aside the framed diplomas. His eyes lingered on the novel Lauren had found. He tossed it in the box. He thrust his hand deep into the jumble of items at the bottom, pulled out a flash drive, and held it in the palm of his hand.

"I don't remember seeing that." Lauren shrugged. "It probably came from her junk drawer. I pulled it out and dumped it all in the box."

His eyebrow went up a notch.

"I was in a hurry. I didn't have time to sort through everything."

"You shouldn't have been sorting through anything." He pocketed the flash drive and continued the search. His hand wrapped around a small cellophane package. He lifted it out. "Know anything about this?"

Chapter Thirty-One

Lauren leaned in close to see what he was holding.

The detective opened his hand, revealing a pregnancy test.

"Un-uh." She continued to stare at his open hand. "By now you know we weren't close. There's no way she would have shared something like that with me."

He pulled out his notebook, scribbled in it, then placed the pregnancy test back in the box.

Before he returned to his inspection of the contents, he caught sight of all the sticky notes on the corkboard. He walked over and studied the names. "S-PS"?

"Suspects." Lauren's face grew warm.

"This better be the only investigation you're doing, Miss Besoner, little thoughts on little pieces of paper."

"Little thoughts? That sounds insulting, but if you look closer you'll see I don't have a clue what's going on. They're just pieces of paper with names."

"I'm warning you, you better not be playing detective. That's how people get hurt." He pulled off two of the sticky notes. "Why is this person on your list?"

She stood next to him and read the name. "Nina Thornton was one of the finalists competing with Judge Murphy when she was selected as the new judge." She tapped her finger on the sticky note with Randall Graham's name. "And so was he."

He studied the other comments on the colorful squares. "Jane was using Tony. Where did you learn that from?"

"It's my friend Claude's theory." Wanting to change the subject to anything, anything where she did not come across as pathetic and silly for making a list of suspects, she asked, "Did you know Tony applied?"

"Hmm?" Overstreet had tucked his notebook away and gone back to rummaging through Judge Murphy's belongings.

"For the judge's position."

"No, I didn't."

"Yep. I might be out of work soon."

With his focus still on the contents of the box, he asked, "Why?"

"I couldn't work for him, not after finding out about him and Jane."

"Oh."

"Are there any new developments in the case? Any that you can share?"

"Seriously? I'm not going to discuss the case with you."

"Why not? I won't repeat a word to anyone. I promise."

The detective, still kneeling, looked up at her.

Sunlight filtered through the window. Lauren turned a tired face to him. "It's not about my silly attempt to list suspects on little sticky notes, Detective. For the past couple of weeks I've felt—I don't know how to describe it." Lauren hugged herself. "Not scared—well, a little scared but more uneasy. I've had this feeling in the pit of my stomach."

Detective Overstreet didn't comment, and so Lauren continued, "Look, I know I'm not explaining myself very well. I'm good at listening. That's what I do for a living, right?" Lauren gave him a small smile. "But I've had this gnawing in my stomach and it won't go away. Ever since I found Jane, that's the first thing I see when I wake up. I have no control over what's been happening, the whole situation, and I hate that feeling. And to top it all off I found my backdoor open when I came home the other night–"

"You found your backdoor open?"

"Yes. The dogs were outside."

"Did you contact the police?"

"No. Nothing was taken. I thought maybe I didn't close the door hard enough and the wind blew it open."

"If that happens again, or you even feel someone's been at your house, you need to contact the police. He studied Lauren for a long moment. "I'm sorry, I can't discuss specifics about the case." He walked over to the window and peered out at the courtyard below. Cotoneaster shrubs lined the sidewalk, delicate red and yellow leaves clinging to the branches in the breeze. "I'm envious. This is a great view."

"It is." Lauren went over and stood next to him, his strong presence like a magnetic field around him. "I love this time of year. The cottonwoods are beautiful."

"It certainly beats what's outside my window."

"You really don't have much of a view from the basement, do you?"

"Trash swirling around, that's what I get to see. That and shoes, lots of shoes, scuffed shoes mostly. And if I'm lucky, I'll see a pair of red high heels walk by."

He glanced at her and she saw something in his eyes that she had not seen before. Playfulness.

"Red high heels. Interesting. You probably have a way of sizing up people just by their footwear."

"I'm good at what I do but even I need more to go on than a pair of shoes. Though they can and often do say a lot about a person."

"What about if someone doesn't have an alibi? It must happen a lot. Take me, for instance."

"Just makes it more of a challenge. And I'm *always* up for a challenge."

She caught a Cheshire-cat expression on his face.

"Maybe you should be more suspicious of the people *with* alibis."

"We check everything out."

"Do you ever get a gut feeling about someone," Lauren asked, "that you just know they're not telling you the truth?"

"Sure." He sat and stretched out his legs, and rested his clasped hands in his lap. "Like when people won't look me in the eye." He stared at Lauren. "But some people will look me straight in the eye and I still know they're lying."

Lauren held his gaze. "I hear you," and added, "Is that what you think when you're questioning me?"

"I told you before I can't rule anyone out." He motioned with his chin. "And what about you?"

"What about me?" Lauren pretended to inspect her arms and hands.

"Listening to people testify every day, you must learn a lot about body language. Are you able to tell when someone's being untruthful?"

"Oh, yeah." Lauren twirled a lock of hair around her finger.

"The first sign is where they look when they're sworn in. If they don't look the judge or the courtroom clerk in the eye, to me that means it's not a matter of *if* they're going to lie, only what they're going to lie about. And if a witness talks fast, and I don't mean somebody that's naturally a fast talker. Those people are just annoying. I mean someone who gets to a certain part of their testimony and all of a sudden they ramp up the speed. Hard to keep up." Lauren pondered the question. "And then the ones that keep adding to their answer, adding things that have nothing to do with the question. Or they repeat the question before they answer. When they do that I think they're stalling for extra time, time to think up a lie."

"I think that too when I'm questioning someone. Interesting. Sounds like you pay attention."

"I do. That is when I'm not thinking about what to have for lunch." She smiled, then ran her fingers through her shiny hair. Her phone pinged. She turned it over to check the caller I.D. It was Claude.

"I need to get going." The detective pushed back his chair.

"I wanted to ask you, did Amanda Capshaw ever give any names, names of clients of Judge Murphy?"

"No. Why?"

"I gave her a list of names I came across." Lauren added quickly, "When I was boxing up her things. I didn't know if they meant anything. Amanda said she would check."

"Who are they?"

Lauren reached in the top drawer and searched for a slip of paper. "I kept a copy. But they probably don't mean anything since Amanda didn't get in touch with you."

He read the names, then placed the piece of paper in his shirt pocket. "Well, I don't want to keep you from any plans you might have." Detective Overstreet nodded at the phone on her desk.

"No, no plans. Just going to curl up with a good dog… I mean a good book." Lauren laughed to let him know she was making a joke, and caught the corners of his mouth turn up.

As soon as the detective was out of sight, Lauren texted Claude. "Check autopsy report. Was Jane pregnant?"

Chapter Thirty-Two

"*Pregnant?*"

Lauren looked up from her Google search to see her friend standing in the doorway, hands on hips.

"Yeah. Look." She dug into the box on the floor and pulled out the small package and wriggled it. "Overstreet found it. He asked if I knew anything about it. Like I would. He's going to check with the pathologist. Maybe it'll be in the autopsy report."

"Geez. When I saw your message I had to come down. I'm supposed to be checking something in the clerk's office."

"Before Overstreet left we sort of had a nice talk, and—"

"Stop right there. Detective Overstreet. Nice talk. What does that even mean?"

"It means he wasn't being an ass for a change. He wouldn't talk about the case but we had a semi normal conversation."

"I overheard Graham talking with Tony. Overstreet will be giving Graham an update on Bradley and his alibi. They just got his credit card receipts for that night."

"You'll have to let me know what you find out. Oh, one other thing. Maybe you can find out why the chief of police thinks I had anything to do with Jane's murder."

"I haven't heard anything. Maybe I'll just ask Randall myself." Claude pulled out an imaginary pen and paper, poised to write. "Alibi, check. Autopsy report, check. Chief, check. Anything else you want me to find out?"

"No, that's it for now."

"What would you do without me?"

"I'd be totally clueless."

"That's for sure. And there's enough of that already around here." Claude nodded in the direction of Susan's office.

"Susan's not clueless. She just likes to play the part."

"Before I go, I overheard Tony telling Cassie how he aced the interview."

"Amanda said she thought she did really well, so who knows?"

"If we weren't such good friends I'd be rooting for Tony to get the job."

"*What*? Why would you do that?"

"Because he thinks very highly of himself. He's not the easiest person to work with."

"I was married to him so I know exactly what you mean."

"What's going to happen if he gets selected?" Claude looked at her friend, concern in her chestnut brown eyes.

"I'll be out of here faster than... than... help me out here."

"Faster than you can say, adios mi amigo?"

"He won't keep me on. And even if he does, I sure as hell wouldn't work for him."

"That would suck. I hope he doesn't get it."

"You are such a good friend." Lauren added, "It would totally suck."

Claude stood by the door. "You know what time it is, right?"

"Time to get back to living the dream," they sang in unison.

Lauren went back to her search of medical spellings she needed for the transcript she was working on.

While online she checked her email, which segued into internet browsing of the non-work-related kind. She ended at a site that sold handbags. When she clicked on a Fendi and saw how much it cost she scolded herself for wasting time.

"What are you doing, checking out a pair of shoes you just have to have? No, wait, don't tell me. You were looking for your next husband."

Startled, Lauren looked up from the screen. Tony, dressed in a charcoal gray suit, leaned against the doorjamb, arms folded across his chest, and a smirk plastered across his good-looking face.

"How long have you been standing there?"

"Long enough to see you drooling over something online. Mind if I come in? I don't want to interrupt you if you're working on something *important*."

"Just checking spellings." She closed her browser.

"And some online shopping? If I remember right, we had fairly big credit card bills because of your online habit."

"Is this why you came down here, to rehash old complaints?"

Tony sat down and stretched his long legs out. "Graham just got off the phone with Overstreet. Seems he had a visit with Bradley."

"Yeah?"

"Brought his lawyer with him. Overstreet said he was some hotshot Denver guy."

"I saw them leaving a while ago. Did Overstreet confirm whether Jane was pregnant?"

"*What?*"

Lauren wanted the question to catch Tony off guard. It did. "I said, did Overstreet tell you—"

"I heard you. What the hell kind of question is that? What makes you think Jane was pregnant?"

"Because Overstreet found a pregnancy test in her office."

Tony shook his head. "Overstreet tells *me* not to tell anyone about the investigation and he's shared it with *you*?"

"He didn't share anything with me. I was here when he went through that box." She motioned to the box on the floor. "I saw him pull it out."

"What else has he shared with you?"

"Nothing."

"She wasn't pregnant."

"What makes you so sure?"

"Because when we were dating she was more concerned with her career. Besides, she was getting a little old to be pregnant."

"Women can get pregnant in their forties. All I know is if someone has a pregnancy test in their desk drawer, they're thinking they might be pregnant."

Tony tapped his foot. "Did you want to hear what Graham and Sam were talking about or not?"

"Of course I do."

"Seems Bradley is worried about his medical license." Tony added, "And he should be."

Lauren straightened in her chair. "Why?"

"He told Sam he didn't want to hinder the investigation in any way but he wanted assurances that the information he provided would stay confidential and didn't get back to the Colorado Board of Medicine. Sam wouldn't make any promises. It depended on what the information was."

"What was the information?"

Tony shook his head. "You do that every time. I'm getting there. You have no patience whatsoever."

"Sar-eee." Lauren slumped in her chair and waited.

Tony inspected his manicured fingernails. Finally, he spoke. "Sam had questions about the Vicodin and Oxycontin found at Jane's house. She had several samples in her bathroom cabinet. According to Bradley Schwartz, the doctor…" Tony drew out the last word "… prescribed them, like he told Sam before, for a ski accident that left Jane with a lot of back pain. The thing is Jane was never a patient of his. He said the Colorado medical board—any medical board—will suspend or take away your license for doing that." Tony snorted. "He was dispensing scripts like some junior high hall monitor handing out tardy slips. What the hell was he thinking?"

"Wow."

"At first he wasn't concerned. He just was trying to help her get through the initial pain. Then when she continued asking for more he began to wonder if she was becoming dependent on them."

"That must have put him in an awkward position."

"That's what the separation was about. He had a feeling maybe Jane was just using him to get painkillers. But according to Schwartz, they had a long talk and it all got worked out. She agreed to seek alternatives to the narcotics and they were going to live happily ever after."

"You sound like you don't believe his story."

"It's my job to question alibis. It's not exactly an alibi but right now there's no one to dispute his story of their breakup or whether they were back together."

"Jane didn't mention that the wedding was off to me. I don't think she mentioned it to Susan either."

"How do you know that?"

"Because if she did, Susan would have shared that with me and everyone else. It would have been all over the courthouse in like ten seconds."

"Not a big fan of Susan?"

"No, not really. I'm sure she's given out my cell number to a news reporter. I asked her what she was thinking. She says, 'Oh, I didn't think you would mind.' It has to be an act. I don't believe she's that stupid."

Tony gave a noncommittal shrug.

"Did you see Susan the other night on the news?"

"No."

"She was interviewed by someone from the Cheyenne news station. You missed a wonderful performance."

"Susan can be entertaining to watch," said Tony.

"There's a reporter from Denver, a Tanya Chamberlain, she's left me a couple of messages. Says she wants to interview me."

"Now her I've seen on TV. Did you speak with her?"

She shook her head in annoyance. "I never called her back. I'm sure she's moved on to the next big story by now."

"That was smart. You might have said something stupid."

"I think I could handle a few questions."

"I didn't mean stupid. Maybe inappropriate. She might have taken what you said out of context or twisted your words."

"Kind of like when you cross-examine someone?" Lauren leaned forward, elbows on the desk, resting her chin in her hands.

"Maybe. That's what I miss about you, Lauren, those little barbs of yours. But, hey, when I'm sitting on the bench maybe I'll let you continue to dazzle me with your witty comments."

"You know as well as I do, if you're in, I'm out." The tone in Lauren's voice grew somber. "If you offered me the job, which you wouldn't, you know what my answer would be."

"I'm sorry if this ruins your life plans of being Crawford's official court reporter until you marry some accountant and have a bunch of kids, or maybe until you turn old and gray, but this is something I want. If I get this, who knows, in a few years I might even join the Supremes."

"*Ha*! You a supreme court judge? Good luck with that." Lauren dropped a few pens into the drawer and slammed it shut.

"What's up with you?"

She looked at him and blurted out, "Why did you cheat on me?"

"*What?*"

"Why? How could you do that to me?" The question had been smoldering inside her ever since the betrayal surfaced, and it chose this moment to ignite. "Why?"

Tony looked at Lauren for a long while before he shook his head. "Drop it, Lauren. It was a stupid mistake, all right?"

"There had to be a reason though."

Tony pushed himself out of the chair. "It's water under the bridge."

"Did you ever really love me?" She braced herself for the answer. It never came.

He ran his hand through his hair. "Are you going to ask me that fucking question every time we see each other? For God's sake, Lauren. Let. It. Go."

Lauren said nothing.

"I came down here to give you the information on Bradley. I told you I'd share, and I have. I don't know why you have to keep bringing up all this other crap."

"You know what? Don't bother coming down here anymore." She pushed herself up from the chair.

"Suit yourself. But remember, you're the one who was begging me for information."

"My mistake." She walked around the desk, folded her arms, and stood at the doorway.

Tony strode past her and down the hall. He swung open the outer office door and slammed it shut behind him. Loose papers on Susan's desk floated to the floor.

"*Asshole.*" Lauren scooped up the loose sheets and glanced at them. There was a letter from Judge Murphy. The top line, in all caps, read, "Improvement Plan." Beneath that were six bullet points, each one spelling out a change Judge Murphy expected from Susan by October 31. She scanned the letter for a date. September 20, two weeks before Judge Murphy was killed. Lauren shook her head. Susan dodged a bullet. She tossed the papers onto Susan's desk and went into the break room.

She opened the refrigerator and stared blankly at its contents, no idea what she was looking for. Suddenly tears blurred her vision. She slammed the refrigerator door shut and charged into her office. She shoved her arms into her coat sleeves, grabbed her keys from her purse, and locked her door.

Lauren leaned into her car and rummaged in the glove box until she felt for the open but untouched cigarettes, along with the lighter. With both in hand, she paced in front of the Volvo, the sharp wind cutting through her. She made her way to the east side of the courthouse, the wind less fierce there. She fished a cigarette out of the pack. Even with her hand cupped around the lighter, it took several attempts for the flame to stay alive. She inhaled deeply. It made her lightheaded. Lauren coughed and looked at the nicotine addiction in her hand. She wiped away an angry tear with the back of her hand. She inhaled again, then threw the cigarette down, and ground it into the small patch of dirt where she stood.

* * *

Gunner looked away from the security monitors as Lauren approached. She hurried past him, her head bowed.

"Well, don't say hello then." He returned his attention to the bank of screens.

Without saying a word, Lauren continued to the staircase and took the stairs two at a time. By the time she reached her office she was breathing hard. She gulped air, then berated herself for slipping up and smoking. Then she berated herself for letting Tony get to her and make her want, no, *need* a cigarette. And, finally, she berated herself for using Tony as an excuse. The cigarettes had been in the glove compartment of her car for eleven months, two weeks, and three days. The thought made her eyes well up with tears again. *What the hell is wrong with me?*

The Marlboros were still in her coat pocket. She yanked them out and hurled them at the trash can, then sank into her chair and pushed the heels of her hands into her eyes.

Lauren heard a faint knock on the door frame and looked up.

"Lauren?" Amanda stood in the doorway, concern on her face. "Are you okay?"

"Um, no...yeah. No, I'm fine."

"You don't look fine."

"I'm fine, really. It's just..." She took a deep breath and blew it out. "Tony was here earlier. It never seems to end well when we talk."

"I see."

"I'm just a little concerned about what's going to happen if he gets the job. There's no way we can work together. I don't know if I'll be able to afford to stay in my house or even in town without this job."

"Oh."

"Crawford was beginning to feel like home, and now…" She shrugged. "But don't mind me. I'm okay."

"I understand. You don't want to lose your cute little place because of your stupid ex."

"You do understand."

"But don't rule me out. I could be the new judge."

"I know. But what's worse is I had a cigarette." Lauren pointed to the trash can.

"I didn't know you smoked?"

"I haven't been. I went almost an entire year without a cigarette. A whole freakin' year."

"We all make mistakes."

"Well, I feel stupid all the same." Tears welled up in her eyes again, threatening to spill out. She swallowed hard. "Can I help you with something?"

"I was down in circuit court. I came up to ask Susan if she had the arraignment list prepared for Friday."

"She isn't in today." The desire to badmouth Susan was hard to resist but Lauren managed to keep quiet.

"Do you know what the docket looks like?"

"I don't. Susan might be in tomorrow and she'll have a list then. I can have her email it to you if you'd like."

"Would you? I need to have an idea how long I'll be sitting in court."

"If she comes in, I'll ask her to send it to you."

"Thanks. I'll see you Friday. And don't let your ex get to you. No man is worth smoking a nasty cigarette for."

"Can't argue with that. Maybe that should be my new mantra." Lauren let out a weak laugh.

* * *

The office clock read four-thirty. Lauren turned off her computer and locked up her office, double checking the lock. She reached the first-floor landing and turned to go out the rear entrance.

Gunner called out. "What, no goodbye?"

She approached him. "Good night. I'm sorry if I was acting weird earlier. I wasn't trying to be rude."

"Don't worry about it. And you weird? I see all kinds of weird pass through here. You're anything but. Have yourself a good evening."

"Thanks. You too."

Lauren hurried out to her car. She tossed her bag on the passenger seat and slid in behind the wheel. She started the engine and replayed the events of her day in her mind. It had been one big roller coaster ride, only instead of her stomach dropping at every sharp descent, it was her emotions. Her soon-to-be favorite song began playing on the radio and she cranked up the volume, wanting to drown out all the thoughts that ricocheted in her mind like a pinball machine.

* * *

After letting Maverik and Percy outside to run off their pent-up energy, Lauren went upstairs and took a shower. Standing under a steady stream of very hot water was her go-to way to unwind. Her problems would come to the surface while she shampooed her hair then they would get washed down the drain. Only tonight the hot shower had failed to do its trick.

Her hand wrapped around a bottle of beer in the fridge. Her stomach rumbled but not for food. She sank into the overstuffed chair, bottle hanging from her hand. Maverik rested his head on Lauren's lap. She absently stroked his fur. Percy jumped up on the arm of the chair. The dogs were not fighting for attention tonight. Lauren chalked it up to the vibes she gave off.

Tony's smug expression pushed its way into her mind. She tried to eradicate all images of him, but they were like dandelions, they kept popping up. She expected another sleepless night and was not disappointed.

Chapter Thirty-Three

The sound of the phone ringing made Lauren scramble to unlock her office door. By the time she picked up the receiver a dial tone hummed in her ear. She stowed her bag in her desk, picked up her laptop and went into the courtroom to set up her equipment.

With the realtime set up and ready, Lauren went to the break room to make coffee. On her way to her office she caught a glimpse of Judge Childers in the "office." Ever since the committee had met there, Lauren no longer thought of it as Judge Murphy's office. Instead, it was just a large space waiting for someone to give it new life, fill the empty walls with someone else's personality. Anyone but Tony's, Lauren desperately hoped.

"Good morning, Your Honor."

The man with the silver white hair and matching mustache smiled at Lauren. He hung up his coat. "Good morning,

Lauren. Thank you for covering today's hearing. I know Vincent appreciates your help very much."

"I'm happy to help out. Are we in for a long day, do you think?"

"I spoke with Judge Brubaker yesterday. He told me I should put these two attorneys on a short leash or risk not getting done today. You've probably worked with both Mr. Brenner and Mr. Rinaldy before, I'm sure."

"Yes. Judge Brubaker is right."

"We can't have that."

"And I guarantee it will be apparent in the first five minutes of the hearing that there is no love lost between them."

"Should make for an interesting day. I think I'll put time limits on them, make sure the case gets completed today. I don't want to come back if it's not necessary."

"I'll keep an eye out and let you know when the parties are here and ready to go."

"Thank you."

Lauren walked toward her office and heard her phone ringing. She sprinted inside and snatched up the receiver on the third ring. "District Court chambers. This is Lauren, Judge Murphy's—good morning, Lauren speaking."

"This is Detective Overstreet. Can you come down to the station this morning?"

"I'm on my way into court."

"What about at lunch time? It's important."

Lauren's stomach tightened. "If it won't take long."

"Good. I'll be here so just come down when you can."

Before the proceedings began, Lauren ducked into the restroom, wondering what the detective could possibly harass her about this time.

* * *

Judge Childers tapped the gavel. "Court will take a fifteen-minute recess." He was in the hallway removing his robe when Lauren came out of the courtroom. He laughed as she approached. "Do those two always behave this badly?"

"Yes, they do. I did warn you they don't like each other."

"Yes, you did."

"I like to think of it as cheap entertainment."

"Not very professional, but I almost laughed out loud when Mr. Rinaldy said, 'I would like the record to reflect that Mr. Brenner's fly is open.'"

Lauren giggled.

Judge Childers gave a small chuckle. "We have one or two 'Brenners' in our district too. It's a challenge to keep a straight face." He shook his head, and walked into his temporary office.

With a fifteen-minute recess there was enough time to check for phone messages and email. Susan's unmistakable scent assaulted Lauren when she opened her office door. There was no mail on her desk and no note but Susan had been there. Lauren had not seen her earlier and assumed she'd taken yet another day off. It was possible, she told herself, that she came in, worked for twenty minutes—Susan's new work schedule—and left for the day.

With court back in session, Lauren once again listened to the questions and answers being volleyed back and forth like a tennis match. She tried to concentrate on the testimony, and made a conscious effort not to look at Mr. Brenner's pants. As far as she was aware there were no more zipper incidents. At twelve-thirty Mr. Rinaldy rested his case.

"We will take a break for lunch and resume at one-fifteen. Court is in recess." Judge Childers tapped his gavel.

Susan sat working at her desk. She said hello to Lauren without looking up.

"Did you need something, Susan?"

"No. Why do you ask?"

"Because you were in my office earlier."

"No, I wasn't."

"Oh-kay." Lauren went into her office and gathered her purse.

"How could you, Lauren?"

She swung around to see Susan, hands on her hips, in the doorway.

"How could I what?"

"Think of me as a suspect."

"A suspect?" She suppressed a smile. "Didn't you just say you weren't in my office?"

"Uh, I forgot. I was in there looking for something."

"Looking for what?"

"I—I don't remember." But how could you think I would be capable of killing Jane? That's very hurtful. She was wonderful to work for."

"Susan, I'm sorry. I was putting down everyone I knew that had contact with her, you know, just like they do on TV. I don't really think of you as a suspect. But wait, she was wonderful to work for? Isn't that a little over the top?"

"No, it's not."

"I've heard her yell at you, all the way from my office."

Susan's face reddened. "She was still wonderful to work for."

"If you say so. Oh, and if you remember what you were looking for in my office, let me know, maybe I can help you find it."

It annoyed Lauren that Susan had been in her office. If she needed something all she needed to do was ask or leave her a note. This was not the first time that Lauren smelled Susan in her office. It was, however, the first time she confronted her about it.

Heather sat behind the glass partition. She escorted Lauren into one of the interview rooms. She had barely sat down when Detective Overstreet entered, clothes rumpled, paisley tie loosened at the neck. Besides the usual blue folder, he carried with him a small bulky envelope.

"I'm going to cut to the chase." He opened the manila package, pulled out a plastic bag with writing on it. He smoothed it out. "Recognize what this is?"

Lauren studied the contents of the sandwich-size container. She did recognize it. It was her Mesmerizing Mango lip gloss. She ordered it off the internet. Guaranteed to moisturize your lips for up to eight hours. Something she desperately needed in the dry winters.

"It looks like my lip balm."

"That would explain your fingerprints on it."

Her stomach churned.

"Can you explain what it was doing under Miss Murphy's body?"

Lauren didn't speak. She wanted to. She wanted to explain how her lip gloss got there.

He sat, all his attention on her face, waiting for her to respond to his question.

"I have no idea how it got there. Maybe it fell out of my pocket when I was checking her pulse." Lauren knew that wasn't the answer. She always kept that lip balm in her desk, in the courtroom, applying it to her dry lips during a pause in the proceedings.

The silence in the room was painful. She watched him as he flipped through some notes in the folder. She waited for him to say, "You're under arrest." When he didn't, she sat a little straighter in the chair.

"If there's nothing else, I have to get back upstairs. Court's going to start up in a few minutes."

He continued to stare at her, his expression unreadable.

"And… and if you have any other questions for me, I—I want my lawyer present." She stood and held onto the edge of the metal desk to steady herself.

To her surprise he did not stop her. "Thank you for coming down."

* * *

Before the afternoon proceedings began Lauren searched her desk. The lip balm was missing, as she feared it would be.

Mr. Brenner presented his case. Unable to concentrate on what anyone said, her fingers automatically wrote the spoken words but her mind was not processing their content. Instead she gazed out the large windows at the cloudless azure sky, her mind focused on the missing Mesmerizing Mango lip gloss.

At five-thirty Judge Childers uttered the words, "Court's in recess" and Lauren let out an audible sigh of relief.

Judge Childers and Lauren walked down the hall side by side. "It's been a long day. Thank you for hanging in there, Lauren. I'm going to tell Vincent he owes you."

"He does, doesn't he?"

Five minutes later Judge Childers stuck his head in Lauren's office. He wore a black wool overcoat. "Have a good evening."

"I will. Drive safe over the hill."

Lauren shut down her computer. She checked her phone. Claude left a text message. "Call me tonight. Have info."

Chapter Thirty-Four

At exactly nine o'clock, in fleece pajama pants and a sweatshirt, legs tucked underneath her on the sofa, Lauren dialed her friend's number.

Claude picked up on the third ring.

"What's the info?"

"What, no hello?"

"I'm sorry. I've been dying to know what you found out, but before you do I have to tell you what happened today." Lauren told Claude about her latest round of questioning by the detective.

"Geez, Lauren."

"I have *no* idea how that lip balm ended up there. Someone had to have put it there on purpose. I didn't even know it was missing. I really thought he was going to arrest me. I almost threw up."

"That sounds bad."

"When he was in the office earlier getting the pregnancy test, it was the first time I felt like I could relax, that I wasn't on his radar."

"Shit."

"It's been bugging me all day."

"This whole thing is getting weird. I'm sorry I didn't get back with you earlier."

"What did you find out?"

"I didn't want to leave a text. I don't want anyone finding out I'm sharing this with you." She whispered into the phone, "She was six weeks pregnant."

Silence.

"Did you hear me?"

"Yeah. I'm just…I'm…"

"That's not all."

Lauren wondered what else there could be.

"Bradley wasn't the father. He had a vasectomy after his last son was born."

"*Holy shit*!"

"Holy shit is right."

More silence.

"Are you still there?"

"Yeah. I'm just shocked. How sad for her. And the baby."

"It's terrible. Remember, this is extremely sensitive information so—"

"I won't say a word. I wonder who she was sleeping with besides Bradley?"

"Good question. Was she acting weird lately?"

An image of a plump soft baby popped into Lauren's mind.

"Lauren?"

"Oh, I was just thinking, if Bradley knew she was pregnant then he would have known she was cheating on him."

"Yeah, but being six weeks pregnant, he probably didn't know."

"Maybe not about the pregnancy but what if he knew she slept with someone?" She couldn't help thinking that somehow Judge Murphy's life had become a soap opera.

Claude's voice interrupted her thinking. "You know whose baby it could be?"

"No."

"The governor's. Governor Sterling's love child. Maybe the rumors were true." Claude let out a snort.

"You're terrible. But thanks for sharing. I owe you."

"Yes, you do."

Lauren went upstairs, sat in bed and sifted through the information her friend had shared. It made her feel sad for Judge Murphy, an emotion she hadn't felt toward her lately. The pregnancy was another piece of a confusing puzzle.

* * *

The judge's chambers were unlocked when Lauren arrived. Susan was not at her desk. Lauren went into the judge's office. "Good morning, Your Honor."

"Good morning, Lauren." Judge Brubaker swiveled in the chair to face her. "Have you seen Susan?"

"No, not yet."

"I was looking for the files for today's docket."

"If you want I can check the list and get them for you."

"Yes, thank you. I want to go over them, see what creative plea agreements are out there this morning."

"I'll be right back." She went to the clerk's office with the day's criminal list in hand and waited while Barbara

Chase, the clerk of court, gathered up the files. Lauren drummed her fingers on the counter and blew out air. *Here I am, once again doing Susan's job.*

Barbara returned and laid the red file folders on the counter. "That's all of them. Where is Susan this morning? She's usually not this late picking up files."

Lauren shrugged. "I don't know."

"I understand the three finalists are going to be announced today."

"That's what I heard too. Won't be long before court is back in session full time."

Barbara nodded. "I'm sure it'll be nice to have a routine again."

"It will. Thanks, Barbara." Lauren balanced the large stack of files against her chest, and made her way to the judge's chambers.

Susan stood in the doorway. "Oh, here, let me get those," cooed Susan. She held open the door for Lauren, then took the stack of files from her arms. Susan walked to the judge's office and placed the red files in front of Judge Brubaker. "Here you go, Judge."

"Thank you, Susan."

All Lauren managed was an eye roll, then went into the courtroom to set up her equipment.

The morning was filled with the usual assortment of proceedings. Arraignments, change of pleas, sentencings, and probation revocations.

It took until one o'clock to get through the entire criminal docket, and once the words, "court is in recess" were said, Lauren sprinted to the restroom.

She took her microwaved meal into her office, and checked

her phone for messages. She read the text from Claude, Lauren's stomach tightened at three words on the screen. "Tony is in."

"Shit," she muttered, then tapped on her phone. "Who else?"

So, there it was, Tony Jenkins one step closer to being the new judge, herself one step closer to being unemployed. Lauren told herself not to overreact. He did not have it yet, but the uncertainty suddenly surrounded her like a cage. She lost what little appetite she had. Her phone pinged again. "Amanda and Sonja Espinoza."

She stared at her phone and glanced up when she heard someone walk in her office.

Lauren smiled at Claude. "Texting and walking, were you?"

"Multitasking at its finest. Sorry to give you the bad news but I wanted you to hear it from me instead of Tony. He's been strutting around like one damned annoying peacock all morning." Claude held a bakery bag, shaking it slightly. "A little something to cheer you up."

"Thanks." Lauren took the token of sympathy and set it on her desk. "Can you stick around for lunch?"

"No. I just wanted to bring you dessert."

"You know he has a good shot, don't you?"

Claude nodded.

"As much as I detest him for—well, all this crap I've had to relive, deep down I know he would make a good judge."

"I can't believe—"

"If you ever tell a soul I said that, I'll have to kill you." Lauren sat behind her desk. "But it's true, I know he'd do a good job."

"Ooh, ooh, I know what you should do." Claude raised her hand in the air school girl style.

Lauren eyed her friend with suspicion. "And what's that?"

"Sleep with the governor."

"Huh?"

"You know, like Jane did… was rumored to have done. And in exchange for sleeping with him he has to agree to nix Tony." Claude giggled.

"Yeah, right."

"And if you do…" Claude paused. "… just don't forget to use protection."

Lauren shook her head, but not before a hint of a smile crossed her lips.

"I better get going. I just wanted to make sure you were okay."

"What? Did you think I would hurl myself out a window?

"No, but—"

"They don't even open. Quit your worrying."

"I don't like seeing you stressed out like this. And don't tell me you're okay. I can tell this whole thing has got you upset."

"It has, but I'll be okay. And now…" Lauren clutched the little white sack… "I have a distraction. I think I'll skip my usual frozen, tasteless crap lunch and go straight to dessert."

"You have my permission." Claude waved goodbye.

Lauren opened the small bag, and inhaled the scent of cinnamon and vanilla frosting. She leaned her head back and stared at the ceiling. *What if that asshole makes it?*

Chapter Thirty-Five

Reporting various criminal cases filled up the entire afternoon, and the end of the day couldn't come soon enough for Lauren. The same thought kept replaying over and over. *What if Tony is selected? What if Tony is selected? What if?* More than once during the proceedings Lauren told herself, *pay attention to what people are saying.* If she didn't listen to her inner voice she would pay the price later when editing the transcript.

Lauren gathered her writer and computer from the courtroom and lugged them to her office.

Judge Brubaker stuck his head in. "Lauren, I left the files on Susan's desk. She can take care of them on Monday."

"Okay."

"Have you heard the latest?"

She looked up from her computer screen. "You mean who the final three are?"

"Yes."

"I heard." Lauren tried to sound unfazed.

"Things have a way of working out. I wouldn't worry too much."

"I'm sure you're right." She offered up a feeble smile to convince him, and herself, that she was not concerned about Tony. Apparently even Judge Brubaker had learned about Tony and Jane.

"And I have it from a reliable source they will be adding a new judge to the district. It's just a matter of working out the details. There's plenty of room on the third floor for another courtroom. There will have to be a fair amount of remodeling involved but I understand the design phase is already in the works."

"That's good. Makes me feel better knowing it wasn't my imagination that I was overworked."

"Yes. I think I retired at the perfect time." He winked, and turned to leave. "Have a good weekend."

"I will." Lauren's voice held no enthusiasm.

The comforter and blanket were bunched up, evidence of another night of tossing and turning. Lauren lay in bed in a state of semi-wakefulness. The weekend loomed ahead. She forced herself to get out of bed. She shuffled over to the window and peered out. Beyond the bare aspen branches, steel gray clouds hung low in the sky. After the recent snowstorm she feared Mother Nature had forgotten the calendar still said October, and was going straight from summer to winter, Crawford's Indian summer but a fond memory. A sprinkling of frost on the ground hinted which way Mother Nature was leaning toward.

Dressed in what was becoming her signature I-don't-care-who-sees-me Saturday attire—yoga pants, a long-sleeve T-shirt, and UW hoodie—Lauren snatched up her phone off the kitchen table, reached for her keys from the side pocket of her purse, locked up, and drove downtown.

Her first stop, the local coffee house. From there, the library. She needed to check out some books on dog training.

The double-shot macchiato latte tasted rich and smooth. Lauren sat and embraced the aroma escaping the large to-go cup. The sidewalk in front of High Altitude Roast buzzed with people passing by or stopping in.

Amanda Capshaw entered the shop. She placed her order and turned from the counter. Lauren waved, and she walked over to the table.

"Amanda, congratulations on being a finalist."

"Why, thank you."

"You must be excited."

"Oh, I am."

"Are you meeting anyone," asked Lauren, looking around.

"No."

"Why don't you join me? I just sat down myself."

"Sure. Thanks." Amanda set her purse on the table and waited for her drink order.

A young barista called out, "One large double shot pumpkin spice latte, skim, extra whip."

Amanda retrieved her drink and joined Lauren.

Skim and extra whip. Does that make it an oxymoron beverage?

"I don't think I've ever seen you here on a Saturday."

Using a long plastic spoon, Amanda popped a dollop of whipped cream into her mouth.

"I'm usually at home working on transcripts on Saturdays. I'm finally getting to the point where I'm getting caught up with my appeals and can relax a little more."

"That must be nice. How are you doing otherwise?"

"I'm good."

"Any exciting plans for today?"

"My exciting plans include going to the library after this." Lauren gestured toward her cup. "Did the committee tell you when to expect a call from the governor?"

"By next Friday." Amanda sipped her latte. "Mmm. This is decadent and I really shouldn't but this is my little splurge for making it to the final three."

"You deserve it."

"I was going to ask you, have you heard anything from Tony? About how the investigation is going," said Amanda.

"No. And I won't be, which is fine by me. Life is stressful enough these days without him adding to it."

"Oh, that's right, you mentioned you two sort of had it out the other day."

"If I want information I can always ask Claude." Lauren watched the steam rise from her coffee.

Amanda nodded. "I remember Claude." Amanda wiped whipped cream from the corner of her mouth. "What about Overstreet? Has he questioned you again?"

Lauren explained where they found her lip balm.

"You should have called me and let me know."

"I don't want to be using my retainer on the small stuff." Lauren tried to smile, but the thought of being thousands of dollars in debt stopped her.

"Did Overstreet ever get in touch with you regarding that list of names?"

"List of names?"

"Remember, I found that sheet of paper in Judge Murphy's office? There were three names on it? You took the list. I think he was going to contact you to see if you had any information."

"I haven't heard from him. Did you give me the names?"

"Yeah."

"I'm sorry, I forgot all about it. I've been so focused on this whole selection process that I've been a little out there." She said the last two words with air quotes.

"I understand."

"What were the names again?"

"The one I can remember for sure is Cochran, Duane Cochran. I don't remember the others but they both were divorce cases."

"How do you know that?"

"I looked them up on the court system."

"Of course you would."

Lauren detected a note of sarcasm in Amanda's comment.

"Duane Cochran? Doesn't ring any bells."

They watched a young couple, holding hands, pass by their table. The place began to hum with customers.

"Did you hear the police picked up Hector Ortiz the other day," asked Lauren.

"No."

"Did you tell him the police were looking for him, when you saw him at Dominick's?"

"No. Where did they find him?"

"It was during a traffic stop. They brought him in for questioning. But I'm pretty sure he's been released."

"*Released*?"

Lauren had Amanda's full attention.

"The police must not have had enough evidence to hold him," Amanda said.

"That's what I assumed. I've been trying to come up with ideas or—I don't want to say suspects, but people that had something against Judge Murphy. Enough to… So far I've come up empty..." Lauren stopped and frowned.

Amanda turned in the direction Lauren was looking.

Tony came over to their table. He smiled at the two women, insincerity stretched across his lips. "Lauren. Amanda."

"Good morning, Tony." Amanda returned the insincere smile with one of her own.

"Congratulations, Amanda. I hope there won't be any hard feelings when I take the bench." Again, Tony flashed the insincere smile.

Lauren coughed. Coffee almost came out her nose.

"Just remember those words, Tony." Amanda turned to Lauren. "So, you were saying?"

"Nice seeing you both." Tony took Amanda's hint and went to stand in line.

"What did you ever see in that jerk anyway?"

"Good question."

"I'm sorry, I shouldn't have said that."

"No, no. You're right, he is a jerk."

The women took in the constant stream of customers. "You said you've been making headway on your transcript appeals now that you're not in court all day?"

"It's nice not to be rushed, to actually have weekends to myself. See," Lauren pointed to herself, "This is me on a Saturday. Not working," and gave a little laugh. "I even have time to paint my bedroom. That's my next project."

"I'd rather pay someone else to paint."

"I enjoy it. I just haven't had the time. Until now." She looked up at Amanda. "Pretty soon you'll be on the bench and it will be work work work."

"When I am, my plan is to work five days, and possibly four-and-a-half, and definitely not work weekends. That goes for my staff too."

"Wow."

"I think with proper time management that job can be done in forty hours. You won't be hearing from me demanding transcripts ASAP. I pride myself in taking good notes. I won't be needing rough draft transcripts, especially in divorce matters."

"I like the way you think." Lauren stuffed her napkin into the empty coffee container.

"And I don't plan on covering for other judges. I've done enough traveling on I-80 to last a lifetime. I think my car could drive itself to the state pen. And that stretch in the winter is treacherous, but I'm sure I don't have to tell you what it's like. You used to travel too, didn't you, when you freelanced?"

"I don't miss it one bit."

Amanda patted her coat pocket in search of her keys. Getting up she asked, "How is Percy? Is he still with you?"

"Yeah, he is."

"I've been meaning to stop by and see him but I just haven't had any spare time."

"He's sort of growing on me."

"It was nice chatting with you." Amanda smiled. "I think we'll work together nicely. Don't you?"

"Oh, yes, I do."

Chapter Thirty-Six

Amanda walked out of the coffee shop wrapped in a coat of self-confidence. Lauren saw it in her stride, heard it in her voice, talking about when, not if, she became the next judge. Lauren felt a twinge of guilt for telling her she would be the new judge, a complete case of sucking up, but rationalized that no harm could be done trying to get on her good side and secure her continued employment.

The comment about working only forty hours or less a week had made Lauren want to laugh out loud. She was proud of herself for keeping silent. The likelihood of working forty hours was about the same as winning the state lottery. Sure, it would be awesome, but it was close to pure fantasy.

Lauren zipped her hoodie, ignoring Tony who sat a few tables away. She walked the short distance to the Albany County Library. She'd pick up her books on dog training and maybe also a light read, a cozy mystery or something with comic relief, and go home.

People milled about on the first floor of the library, three teenage boys sitting at computers with headsets, an elderly man with his head cocked sideways to read the spines of the science fiction novels. Moms with their little ones were in the children's section. Lauren went to the reference section on the second floor.

With an armful of instructional books, Lauren took the stairs to the first floor and made her way toward the fiction area. She stopped when she saw Detective Overstreet walking in her direction. She relaxed her shoulders when she caught a smile on his face. She wished she wore something besides yoga pants and trainers, or at least put on some makeup. Everyone told her the sprinkling of freckles on her face was cute but Lauren was not convinced and often hid them under foundation.

"Hello, Lauren."

"Hi." She looked around the library. "I'm surprised to see you here. What are you doing here in the children's section?"

He cocked his head. "Waiting for Jonah."

"Oh." Lauren turned around to see several children engrossed in building Lego creations.

"He's the good-looking fella over there, the one in the red and blue striped shirt."

"I was going to say, he takes after you." Lauren regretted the words as soon as they passed her lips. Her cheeks burned.

He pretended not to notice. "I saw you coming down the stairs, thought I'd say hello.

Lauren shifted her weight. "Do you come here often?" She covered her mouth. "I'm sorry, that sounded like some pickup line, something a guy would say."

He repressed a smile, then answered. "Jonah found out the library was putting on Lego Lollapalooza today, and since he's crazy about Legos, here we are."

"That sounds like fun. Is your wife here?"

"We're divorced."

Lauren remembered her Aunt Kate's failed attempt to play matchmaker the other evening. "Oh, I didn't remember—know. I shouldn't have asked. It's none of my business whether you're married or not. It's not like I care whether you have a wife. I don't mean I don't care—I care but not—" Lauren stopped and cleared her throat. "I'm sorry. Too much caffeine this morning." She pressed the books tight against her body.

"Jonah's my step-son. Or I should say, ex-step-son. It's complicated."

"How old is he?"

"Six."

"A fun age I'll bet."

"It is, it is. The divorce had been hard on him, so I still keep in touch and see him when I can. I'm sure that will change once Ashley gets serious with someone else."

"Relationships. Don't get me started." Lauren gave a fake shudder.

"And speaking of the little guy, here he comes now."

A boy with unruly blond hair came running to Detective Overstreet. He held some sort of Lego contraption in his hands. "Hey, Sam, look what I made." Jonah lifted the colorful Legos and spun around with it. "And I almost came in third place," he added.

"Way to go, buddy! That is one awesome looking race car."

"Uh, it's supposed to be a spaceship." He turned to Lauren, and flew the spaceship in the air for Lauren to admire.

"Very cool spaceship. Do you get to keep it?"

"Naw." His voice dropped. "We have to leave the Legos here."

Detective Overstreet patted the boy's shoulder. "You put the spaceship back and then we'll go get something to eat."

"Can we have pizza? *Please*?"

"I think we can do that."

Jonah ran over to the other children, who were flying and crashing their newly made creations in pretend battle.

"Any new leads in the investigation? Is Hector Ortiz still around?" Lauren asked.

"Yes and no. Hector is still around as far as I know. And no, there's nothing I want or can share."

Cop-mode overtook his friendly expression and Lauren regretted bringing up the subject.

"I shouldn't have asked. You should be enjoying time with Jonah and not thinking about work. I'm sorry."

"No, that's okay. It comes with the territory." His voice grew serious. "That was one of the many things my ex and I fought about, me not being able to leave work at the office. She told me I was just like the meth addicts I arrested, only with me I'm hooked on adrenaline."

"Ouch. That sounds a little harsh."

"Yeah, but it's not far from the truth."

"But your job is different than an ordinary nine-to-five job. Your day doesn't end until the perps are behind bars, right?"

"Perps? I see you know the lingo. What TV show did you get that from?"

"I've watched one or two episodes of *NCIS*." She blushed. "But I also pay attention to what people are saying on the witness stand." She let out a small laugh. "Though sometimes it's pretty boring stuff. Put an economist on the stand, and it's a challenge to stay awake."

He smiled, revealing his dimples.

Jonah returned.

"Well, I better let you guys go. It was nice to meet you, Jonah."

Jonah smiled and leaned into Sam's side. They walked away but not before Lauren heard Jonah ask, "Who was that lady, Sam?"

Lauren wondered what the detective's answer would be.

Before going home Lauren stopped at Dominick's to pick up something sweet for later in the afternoon. It was also an excuse to find out if Hector was working at the bakery again. She hoped there would be a cheese danish left with her name on it. It was a few minutes past noon and Saturdays were Dominick's busiest day of the week, and he was often sold out of all his pastries by twelve o'clock.

The only empty parking spot Lauren could find was around the corner from the bakery on a side street.

The tinkle of the bell above the door was drowned out by the sounds of the multiple conversations going on at once. Lauren walked to the counter, bent her head, and peered into the glass pastry case.

"What can I get you, miss?"

She straightened and smiled.

"Oh, it's my favorite customa."

"Hi, Dominick. How are you today?"

"No complaints here."

"I see business is good, as usual. And I also see you've run out of almost everything. I'll take your last cheese danish."

Dominick grabbed a little square of white paper and reached into the pastry case.

Lauren searched the opening to the kitchen for Hector. Her line of sight was limited, but the sound of metal pans clanging and water running told her somebody was in the back room.

While she waited for her change, Hector came out of the back area and grabbed one of the large empty trays from the pastry case. He spotted her. Their eyes met. His face showed no emotion. Lauren looked away.

Dominick asked her about the progress on selecting a new judge, and they chatted a few minutes until a customer approached.

Lauren stepped out onto the sidewalk and held onto the small white bag. She turned north and was hit with a sharp wind as it barreled down the street. She walked briskly to the end of the street, turned west, bowed her head into the gale force and jogged to her car. As she opened the door a hand grabbed her shoulder. She whirled around and caught sight of a dark figure wearing a black hoodie. Her breath caught.

Even with the hood up around his face, Lauren felt Hector Ortiz's penetrating eyes on her.

"I did not mean to scare you."

Lauren exhaled.

"I wanted to thank you. Dominick said after talking to you, he decided to give me another chance at the bakery." His expression was hard, his eyes unfriendly.

Maybe that was just his normal look. Don't analyze it, just accept the apology and go.

"It's a good job. I like working for Dominick."

"As long as you had nothing to do with Judge Murphy's death, there's no reason for you not to stay in town and work for Dominick."

"I did not hurt that judge. I just wanted to be left alone. I did my time. I knew them cops would start asking me questions. They are trying to pin this on me."

The frustration in his voice was palpable.

"I'm just an easy target. Miss Capshaw was right."

"Well, you'd been out like, what, two weeks, and she ends up dead? I mean it might look a little suspicious to some people. Did Amanda, Miss Capshaw warn you that the police were looking for you?"

"Yeah. I told her I didn't do nothing to the judge. I told her I don't have to answer to nobody no more. No fuckin' probation officer, nobody. I killed my number. Everyone can just fuck off and leave me the hell alone." He clenched his fists. "But when she said the cops were going to bring me in for questioning, I got scared and tried to leave town. Them cops will try to say I killed her."

"It's true then, you did all your time?"

"Yes. I come back here to start over. Dominick is nice enough to let me work for him but the cops are going to ruin it for me." His eyes darkened. Anger vibrated off his body.

Lauren crossed her arms over her chest, pulling her hoodie tight. "If they let you go, they must not think you did it. I'm sure they won't bother you again." She was not sure of anything but was trying to say something, anything to reduce his agitation. "And—and would you believe they questioned me too? I'm a suspect. Their first one as a matter of fact."

"You?"

"Didn't Dominick tell you?" As she spoke the words, it occurred to her that she and Hector had something in common, being a suspect in a murder. What a thought.

She waited for a reaction. Her words had the desired effect. The muscles in Hector's jaw relaxed.

"Cops, pendejo."

Though Lauren did not understand the word pendejo, she assumed it was not a word of praise.

Hector thrust his hands into the pockets of his hoodie. "I better get back to work. Like I said, I just wanted to say thank you."

"You're welcome." Lauren didn't wait for him to walk away. She got in her car, locked the doors, and cranked the engine to life. She did not drive away. She needed to wait for her hands to stop trembling.

Chapter Thirty-Seven

The sound of a car door slamming awakened Percy from his nap on Lauren's lap. He yipped and jumped off. Lauren set the book she had been reading on the arm of the couch, stood, and peered out her living room window. A maroon Crown Vic sat parked at the curb.

Detective Overstreet came up the walkway wearing the same clothes he had on at the library, a gray sherpa-lined hoodie, unzipped, exposing a dark blue polo shirt underneath. He wore faded blue jeans and cowboy boots.

His hand was in mid-knock when Lauren opened the door. Maverik rushed out. "Maverik, no."

The dog ran around the detective and then back inside.

She looked to see if he carried any paperwork or handcuffs.

"Hello again. If you don't mind I'd like to ask you a few questions. Is now a good time? Am I interrupting anything?"

"Yes. I mean no... I don't mind. Where's Jonah?"

"Ashley had a change of plans and she picked him up early."

Since the detective didn't suggest going to the police station, Lauren's muscles relaxed and she ushered him inside.

Percy jumped on the sofa and sat on the arm. Maverik followed behind the detective, sniffing his pant legs.

"Nice looking dog. Border Collie?"

"The vet says he's part Border Collie, part anybody's guess. I found him at the Maverik's on West Eleventh."

"Hmm. Clever."

Unable to see the detective's face, Lauren could not tell from the tone of his voice if the comment was meant to be sarcastic. "The cashier said he had been hanging around for days. I even posted a picture of him on Facebook."

"How long have you had him?"

"Two months. We're still getting used to each other. Or more me getting used to him. I've never had a dog."

"Never?"

"Unh-unh. My sister was allergic to dogs, to cats, to horses—pretty much everything when we were growing up."

"That's too bad."

"Do you have a dog?"

"Used to." He rubbed Maverik behind the ears.

"Would you like some coffee?"

"If it's no trouble."

"No. We can talk in the kitchen."

As he followed her into the kitchen he read the title of the book Lauren laid on the couch. The corners of his mouth turned up a fraction. "*Turn Your Dog from a Scooby to a Lassie*"?

"I keep telling myself Maverik's a work in progress but I could use a little help. Ever since Percy came to stay with us, Maverik's behavior has been sliding."

"Haven't found a home for the little guy?"

"Every time I ask someone if they want him, as soon as they find out what kind of dog he is, the answer's always the same. 'Oh, he's too small. If I let him out in my backyard he could get carried away by a hawk.'" Lauren mimicked the words.

"Don't forget coyotes and foxes."

"No, can't forget those. I hate to admit it but he's growing on me. If I keep him, then I'm going to have to start worrying about hawks and coyotes."

"I don't think you have to worry about that in your neighborhood. Maybe if you lived further out of town."

He sat at the small table.

Lauren reached over and grabbed a neat stack of junk mail from the kitchen table and set it on the white Formica countertop. She started the coffeemaker. Over her shoulder, she asked, "What did you want to ask me?" *How odd, I'm making coffee for a man I don't even know, but he knows a heck of a lot about me.* She grabbed the pumpkin spice creamer from the refrigerator and gestured with it to Overstreet.

"Sure, I'll give it a try."

She poured them each a cup of coffee, then sat opposite the detective.

He added the creamer and sipped the flavored coffee. "I think I'll stick to plain old cream." He sat at the kitchen table, legs stretched out under it.

"I looked at what was on that flash drive that was in Jane's box of stuff."

"And?"

"It was the electronic version of the letters she wrote regarding your performance."

Lauren set her cup down.

"Didn't you say that you had no idea that flash drive was in that box?"

"Yes. I didn't know. It must have been in that same drawer with the pregnancy test." Lauren thought about the flash drive. "Did you check to see when those documents were last modified?"

Detective Overstreet thumbed through the little pages of his notepad. "I didn't write that down. I don't know that I even thought to check."

"Maybe you should."

"What are you thinking?"

Excitement made Lauren's hazel eyes sparkle. "What if it were last modified when Judge Murphy was out of town or on the bench? I mean literally on the bench, you know, a time when she couldn't possibly have written it? Every time you open a document it shows the date and the time it was last modified."

"Right."

"What if someone—what if the killer typed up the letter and planted the flash drive to make it look as if Judge Murphy didn't like my work? Or to make it look like I had a reason to be mad at her?" Lauren's excitement grew. "Do you think I could look at those letters again?"

"Sure. Why?"

"I want to see the signatures."

He tapped his pen on the notepad. "Do you think you would recognize her signature?"

"Yes, I do." Lauren leaned forward in her seat. "If the dates correspond to a time when she was on the bench then that means—"

"Someone else created those documents."

"It could have been anyone. I take that back. Not just anyone. It would have to be the killer. He or she planted the letters in her house and planted the flash drive in her drawer."

"The question is, who would want to point the finger at you?"

"No one. Everybody likes me." Then she let out a hollow laugh. "I better rephrase that. I didn't think I had any enemies—any enemies like that but someone out there must not like me." Goosebumps rose on her arms. "At least they didn't plant the murder weapon in my house." The attempt at humor was lost on the detective.

"Who has access to the offices?"

Lauren focused on one of the tiles on the floor while she thought. "Lots of people would have access." She turned her gaze to him. "But two people come to mind that wouldn't. Hector Ortiz and Danielle Armstrong."

"Not unless they knew someone that worked there."

"Maybe one of them knew one of the janitors. They have keys. But anyone that was able to get past security could get in."

He wrinkled his brow.

"What I mean is they could pretend to have legitimate business in the courthouse, and once they got past security, all they'd have to do is look in the courtroom. If court was in session they could just come in and drop the flash drive in Judge Murphy's desk."

"They'd still have to get past Miss Mumford."

A snort escaped from Lauren. "Yeah, if she was ever at her desk. With no judge, she barely makes the effort to show up for work anymore. Anyone would have easy access. The judge's office is open during business hours."

Lauren cradled her mug. "Were there other files on the flash drive?"

"No."

"Nothing? No other files at all?"

He shook his head.

"Don't you think that's a little odd?"

The detective gave the question some thought. "A little. It does add to the idea that Jane didn't create that file."

"I agree. I think there would be other documents, other files on it if it were truly her flash drive." Lauren made a steeple with her slender fingers. "How many of those do you go through?" She jerked her chin in the direction of his notepad.

He grinned. "These? Quite a few. I haven't been able to bring myself to go completely digital. I need to. I just don't trust the technology. I worry that if I put everything on my phone or a tablet, what am I going to do when it crashes."

"That's what backing up is for but I know what you mean. I worry about losing files all the time, or have my computer crash or something happen with the internet, you know, they somehow just disappear from…" Lauren made air quotes… "the cloud. I have a triple back-up system, cloud, flash drive, external hard drive, but I still worry."

The detective turned to a clean sheet on his notepad. "I want you to think back, think back to that day, before her murder. That afternoon at the courthouse, describe everything that happened, everything you remember involving Miss Murphy and her movements. Anyone that came to see her. Any detail, no matter how small, that you can remember."

The hum of the old GE refrigerator sounded loud in the small kitchen.

Lauren concentrated on the events of that ordinary day. "Let's see. We had motions in a custody matter which took up the whole morning. Judge Murphy had an appointment and left at noon. Before she left she stopped by my office and asked if I had the transcript she asked for on Sunday."

Lauren was quiet for a moment, then continued. "She did tell me she might be running a few minutes late for the one-thirty hearing, that she had an appointment."

"Did she say who the appointment was with, what it was for?"

"No, she didn't but I assumed it was a doctor's appointment." *Maybe it was an obstetrician.*

"Why do you say that?"

"She said something, about hating to sit in a waiting room when she had more important things to do. The doctor appointment is my assumption. And turns out she wasn't late getting back. The hearing lasted all afternoon. We got done, I want to say four o'clock.

Lauren rubbed the lone pearl on her necklace. "What else? She was in her office after that. The only odd thing about that was her door was closed. She usually left it open."

The detective wrote, then flipped to a fresh page. "Did she seem any different after lunch? Was she upset, distracted?"

"I can't answer that. We don't always have a chance to talk between hearings. She goes straight to her office."

Lauren sat in thought. "She was quieter than normal. After she got off the bench she often made a comment or two about the attorneys or what she thought of their presentation but she didn't say anything that afternoon." Lauren added, "Maybe I'm reading more into it because you're asking me. I mean she didn't always comment on a case after she got off the bench, but Mr. Brenner was one of the attorneys in that afternoon case, and he's sort of known for saying, um—you've got to know him to understand what I mean. But she didn't say anything about him."

Detective Overstreet nodded. "I've had dealings with Mr. Brenner. I think I understand. What time did you leave the courthouse?"

"Around five-thirty. I needed to finish up the transcript I told you about. I had to print it out and give it to her before I left. I didn't want to work on it that evening. She prefers… preferred a hard copy to an electronic one."

Lauren drummed her fingertips on the coffee cup. "You already know about the texts."

He nodded.

"Other than that, I can't think of anything. When I left she was still in her office. Susan was gone, so she was there by herself."

The sound of the detective's pen tapping on his notebook added to the hum of the refrigerator.

Lauren cocked her head and looked at the detective.

"What is it?" he asked.

"I just realized Jane had to have been killed Monday night, not Tuesday morning."

"What makes you say that?"

"Her clothes. Her suit, her gray suit. That's what she

was wearing Monday at work." Her voice grew quiet. "That's what she was wearing when I found her."

"You're right." The detective watched Lauren's expression.

"Can I ask you something, Detective?"

"You can always ask. I may or may not answer."

"I was curious about the glass, the broken glass that was—that I stepped on and that was on Judge Murphy."

"What about it?"

"Did they find glass underneath her?"

"No."

"That means it was broken after she was already lying on the floor?"

"Yes. Yes, it was, Miss Marple."

"Ha-ha. I wish that's all this was, some mystery in some book." Lauren stood at the sink and attempted to look out the window. Her sleep deprived reflection stared back at her. She refilled their mugs and sat down.

"Just a couple of more questions, if you don't mind?"

"No, go ahead."

"What can you tell me about Susan Mumford." He sat, his pen poised to write.

"We've worked in the same office for two years now so I know her, but we don't socialize outside of work. I can't say I know her well. She worked for Judge Brubaker close to twenty-five years, I'm not sure on the exact number. I assume you've interviewed her and know her background."

"Yes, but I'd like to get your take on how she interacted with Miss Murphy."

Hmm, my take. "She was a slacker and I think Judge Murphy thought the same."

Detective Overstreet began writing.

"The last year Judge Brubaker was on the bench she quit scheduling hearings on Fridays altogether. He didn't mind but it's a busy district and things should have been scheduled on Fridays. Plus, she would leave early all the time for one reason or another. And she called in sick a lot. I mean a lot."

"Brubaker didn't mind?"

"No. And she had an assortment of prescription bottles on the corner of her desk. I think most of them were just for effect."

"Care to elaborate?"

"It was her way of saying, 'Poor me, look how ill I am, I have to take all this medicine.'"

"And I assume that changed once Miss Murphy came on board?"

"The pill bottles were still there but Susan only called in sick two or three times at the most since Judge Murphy started. And I heard her ask Susan one day why nothing was ever set on Friday afternoons, no pretrial conferences, motions, nothing. Susan said Judge Brubaker liked it that way. Judge Murphy told her, 'I'm not Judge Brubaker, and we're not running a dental office. Start scheduling things on Friday.' Susan did, of course, but she wasn't happy about it. She complained to anyone that would listen."

Lauren checked the time on the microwave. Five o'clock.

The detective watched Lauren fill the dogs' bowls with kibble and place them on opposite sides of the kitchen. He raised an eyebrow.

"Maverik eats too fast. When he's done he tries to steal Percy's food. You wouldn't know it to look at him but

Percy is no pushover when it comes to what's his. I've had to break up more than one food fight. I have to baby-sit them when it's meal time."

He gave her a slight grin. "What do you know about her personal life?"

"She's divorced."

"For how long?"

"I'm not sure. Maybe three years ago." Lauren slapped the kitchen table. "Jane was her lawyer."

"She was? Did Miss Mumford ever talk to you about that relationship?"

"When Judge Murphy would show up for a hearing in front of Judge Brubaker, you know, when he was still on the bench, Susan would say things that left me with the impression she wasn't too happy with Jane's representation of her."

"Such as?"

"Oh, like, 'If I had gotten my share of my lazy husband's retirement like I was supposed to, I wouldn't have to be eating leftovers for lunch every day.' She didn't end up with any of his retirement."

"Is that unusual?"

"If a couple has been married as long as they were, you know, close to thirty years, the spouse is often entitled to half of the ex's retirement."

"I didn't know that."

"It's not in a statute anywhere but it's one of those marital assets that usually gets divided in half."

"Was it a good-sized retirement?"

"I have no idea. He worked for the railroad, in management, so I assume so. She commented that Jane was just another overpriced lawyer."

The detective digested the information. “What else can you tell me?”

“She likes to gamble.”

“And you know this how?”

“She’s told me about going up to Black Hawk on the weekends. Plays the slot machines, has a few drinks and unwinds.”

“What do you know about her drinking habits?”

“Nothing.” Lauren let out a small laugh. “Though she has called me at home two or three times in the past couple of years, and she sounded like she’d been drinking. Super friendly and slurring her words. I could hear the sound of ice tinkling in a glass in the background.”

“Why would she call you at home?”

“I don’t think she had a reason. Drunk dialing maybe?”

Looking up from his notepad Detective Overstreet asked, “Do you think Susan had a grudge against the judge? Any thoughts about that?”

“I don’t think so. Judge Murphy did mention to both of us one time, we were state employees and she expected us to act professionally and be available Monday through Friday. The ‘act professionally’ I believe that was meant for Susan. Come to think of it, the judge gave Susan one of those needs improvement plans. Maybe she did have a grudge.”

“Did you actually see a written plan?”

“I did. Just the other day as a matter of fact. It was on Susan’s desk.”

A low growl came from under the table. Maverik stood near Percy’s dish with Percy giving Maverik a sideways look and showing his pearly whites.

"No, Maverik." Lauren wagged a finger at him.

At the sound of his name he came over to Lauren and sat by her feet. Percy trotted over and pawed at her pants. She picked him up, set him on her lap, and stroked the soft white fur of his chest.

"Any other reasons you can think of that Susan might want to harm Judge Murphy?"

"No." She cocked her head in thought. "But that lip gloss you found under Judge Murphy? I always kept it in my desk drawer in the courtroom. Not too many people have access when there's no trial going on."

"But Susan does, is what you're saying?"

"Yeah."

Maverik gravitated to Detective Overstreet's left thigh and leaned into it. He scratched Maverik behind his ears.

Lauren gestured to the coffee pot.

He shook his head. "One more question. Were there any big cases coming up?"

"Big cases? We do—or we did have a drug case coming up. Ordinarily that's not a big deal, but because of who the defendant is, it is a big deal."

"Oh, is that the one with the assistant attorney general?"

"Pretty big news, Wyoming Assistant Attorney General Leland Langford up on drug trafficking charges. Doesn't get much bigger than that, not in Wyoming."

The detective flipped his notebook shut. "I've taken up enough of your time. Well, if you think of anything else, call me. You still have my card?"

"Yeah, I do. And I will." She watched him as he got up and put his cup in the sink. Lauren imagined the stress he must be under. Jane Murphy's death, after all, was a huge deal. People, especially a judge, don't often turn up dead in Crawford or even in Wyoming for that matter. He had been doing his job when he focused in on her as the likely suspect, but in the process, had wasted valuable time. After talking with the detective she asked herself, *Could Susan have been angry enough to kill Judge Murphy*?

Chapter Thirty-Eight

"Morning." Lauren was surprised to see Susan at her desk so early. She hadn't come to work at all yesterday, and thought if she saw her at all it would be well past ten o'clock.

"There's your mail." Susan nodded to the edge of her desk.

Without exchanging any more words, she scooped up the neat pile of envelopes, unlocked her office, and flipped on the lights. She turned on her computer and waited for it to fully awaken. It took some time because, after all, it was a dated state-issued desktop.

While waiting, she flipped through her mail. On the bottom of the small stack was a letter from the Wyoming Supreme Court. Turning it over Lauren saw the envelope flap was barely attached to the envelope. Lauren looked out her door and shook her head.

She removed the heavy-weight cream-colored paper, and smoothed it out. *Dear Ms. Besoner: This letter is to inform you that as of November 30th, your position as the official court reporter of the Second Judicial District will terminate.*

There was more to the letter, explaining that the Second Judicial District was now without a sitting judge and, therefore, there was no need for her position.

The urge to tear up the letter into itsy-bitsy pieces and stomp on them was powerful but instead Lauren carefully refolded the letter and tucked it back in its envelope. The office walls began to close in. Lauren pulled up the blinds, needing the outside light to filter in. She rested her palms on the cold glass. Stratus clouds raced southward. She felt like one of those clouds, the wind in complete control, pushing her, pushing her until she had no strength left to push back.

"And what, may I ask, is so interesting out there?"

Cowgirl up. Lauren straightened her shoulders and turned to face Susan. Her mouth opened at the sight of her. Susan had been seated when she retrieved her mail and had missed the full-on effect of her outfit, a black camisole underneath a brown gauzy blouse which cascaded over leopard-print leggings. Her long black talon acrylic nails shone bright under the fluorescent lights. Susan was balancing her pear-shaped frame on leopard-print stiletto heels. If she didn't know better she would have bet her lunch money that Susan just walked off the stage of Crawford's community theater production of *Cats.* The only things missing were whiskers and a tail to complete the ensemble. Maybe they were in her desk. She swallowed the laughter that bubbled up inside.

"Is there a Halloween party in the clerk's office today?"

"No. I think Friday is when they're having their party." Susan stepped further into Lauren's office. "I wanted to ask you, were you here yesterday?"

"Yes, I was." Lauren sat down.

Susan shifted from one leg to the other. "I'll be leaving soon, and I don't think I'll be back. I don't feel well."

"Oh-kay."

"Would you mind answering the phone today?" Susan asked, exasperation in her voice. "There must have been at least twenty voicemails left for me yesterday. Didn't you answer my phone at all?"

Her jaw muscles tightened. "Excuse me?"

"I'm saying, I had a lot of messages. Maybe you could answer my phone this afternoon while I'm gone."

"You're kidding, right?"

"No. What do you mean?"

Lauren stood, grasped the edge of her desk and leaned forward. "I mean I'm tired of answering *your* phone. I'm tired of doing *your* job. That's what I mean."

"I wasn't feeling well yesterday."

"*Of course* you weren't."

Susan put her hand to her throat. "What are you saying, that—that I'm lying about not feeling well?"

"I'm saying you're *never* here!"

"You don't have to raise your voice. I can't help it if I've been feeling ill."

"I'm sorry you're ill," Lauren put the word ill in air quotes, "but I just don't care anymore. If you're not here to do your job, the calls are just going to have to go to voicemail. So the answer is, yes, I do mind."

"Is this about me not being here yesterday or is something else upsetting you this morning?"

Lauren gripped the edge of the desk harder, her knuckles whitening. "What would be upsetting me this morning?"

"I don't know but you're not acting like yourself. I thought maybe you were having a bad morning or something."

The fake innocence in Susan's voice was not lost on Lauren. She was about to accuse Susan of opening her mail when the phone on Susan's desk rang.

Susan turned her head in the direction of the ringing.

Two more rings and the call would go to voicemail.

Lauren snatched up the receiver, punched a few buttons, and shot Susan a look that said, *See how easy it is to answer a phone?* "District Court Chambers, Lauren speaking."

"Hi. This is Nancy from Tres Chic. Is Susan there?"

"No, she's not at her desk right now, but I'd be happy to take a message."

Susan walked closer to Lauren's desk and held her hand out for the phone.

Lauren ignored the gesture and cradled the receiver between her ear and neck.

"I'm calling to confirm her hair appointment at two today."

"Well, I'm afraid the poor thing went home sick. I don't think she'll be able to make it."

"Oh."

"She must have forgot to call you and cancel."

"Just tell her to phone me when she's feeling better and we can reschedule."

"I'll be sure to tell her."

"Thank you."

"No, *thank you*. Bye." Lauren placed the receiver into its cradle and looked at Susan, whose cheeks were red. "In case you didn't figure it out, that was Nancy from Tres Chic. You need to call and reschedule your appointment when you're feeling better."

"Was that today?" Susan blinked several times. "I totally forgot I had an appointment, but you should have let me speak with her."

"Un-fucking-believable." Lauren swore under her breath. "Oh, and that was the last call I'm answering for you today." She sat down and concentrated on the blank computer screen and tapped away on the keyboard. Conversation over.

"Hmmph." Susan twirled around and teetered down the hall out of sight.

The cream-colored envelope from the Supreme Court stared up at Lauren. She leaned back in her chair and closed her eyes thinking, *I will be unemployed in less than four weeks unless, A, they hire a new judge, and, B, the new judge is not Tony.* This totally sucks. Out loud she said, "Well, Lauren, are you just going to sit here and take it or do something about it?" She pounded her fist on the desk and got up out of her chair. It rolled backwards. The phone rang and interrupted her tirade.

Amanda was checking on the criminal calendar, wondering if there would be court on Friday. Lauren informed her that, yes, Judge Brubaker would be holding court Friday, and either she or Susan would call her back when the criminal docket list was firmed up.

The phone call and the reminder of working Friday calmed Lauren. She printed off more of the fourth day of the Howard trial, intent on proofreading it.

* * *

"Hey, sweetie." Aunt Kate stood in the doorway. "I was over at the co-op and I thought I'd swing by and take you to lunch if you haven't already eaten."

"Sure. No, I haven't eaten." Lauren had not thought of food since she read the letter from the Supreme Court. A glance at the clock told her it was after one. "Just give me a minute."

"If you're busy we can do it another time."

"No, no. And I didn't bring lunch. This is perfect."

"Where's Susan?"

"Don't get me started on Susan." She stacked her proofreading in a neat pile.

The two mulled over the choices for lunch while Lauren put on her coat and locked her office.

* * *

Aunt Kate and Lauren sat across from one another at a small table in the bakery. They both chose the day's lunch special. Lauren brought Kate up to speed on what had been happening the last few days. She mentioned Chief Newell's name, and the comments Dominick had shared with her.

"That might have to do with the fact that he and your father never got along."

"I didn't even know they knew each other."

"Yes. Raymond grew up in Casper too. He was in the same grade as your dad. The animosity started during the time your father was on the Casper City Council and Raymond was the chief of police in Casper."

"Why didn't they get along?"

"I don't know the details but your father was involved in an internal investigation of the Casper Police Department. There had been complaints against the chief from the officers underneath him. Afterwards, the city council recommended he be let go and the mayor asked for Chief Newell's resignation. He ended up resigning."

"I had no idea."

"Well, you wouldn't. It was politics, and you were young at the time." Kate thought for a moment. "Ten or eleven when that all came up."

"He must still hold a grudge." Lauren pushed away her half-eaten sandwich. "And on top of everything else, I got a letter today." Lauren shared the details of the letter from the Supreme Court with her aunt.

"Oh Lauren. Can they do that?"

"If there's no judge there's no reason for me to be there. I knew the letter was coming. Just a little unnerving to see it in black and white. I'm not too worried."

"Are you sure?" Her aunt looked at her doubtfully.

"A new judge should be on the bench by then. Maybe. I didn't bring it up to make you worry." She rubbed her eyes. "It just feels like I have no control of my life right now."

Kate reached out and lightly touched Lauren's arm. "But you do have control."

"I do?" She uncovered her eyes.

"Yes, you do. You have control, control over how you react to what's been happening around you."

"Oh, *that's* helpful."

"Don't roll your eyes. I'm serious. You're young. You have your health. You have a good skill set."

"I guess."

"If Tony does get the job, you can stay in Crawford and go back to being a freelance court reporter. If you have to travel, Tess can help with Maverik."

"I know."

"Or you can relocate. I hope you stay here, but what I'm trying to say is, it is *not* the end of the world." Kate took a bite of her chicken and brie sandwich. "I'm a perfect example of what I'm talking about. When things didn't work out with me and John, I moved here to Crawford and started over. I eventually met Jack, and the rest, as they say, is history."

Lauren studied her aunt's face. It held a softness despite the many fine lines crisscrossing her cheeks. The woman gave off a calming effect.

"What are you telling me? You've had enough of my whining?"

"Yep." Her aunt laughed, the corners of her eyes crinkling. "No. I'm saying there's more than one way to look at your situation. Yes, things have changed and things will continue to change, but you will get through this. It's your attitude which you have total control over. It's time, Lauren, to take the wheel and steer. Stop letting fear do all the driving."

"Isn't there a song like that, something about not letting fear take the wheel and steer?"

"Maybe I should start writing songs again," her aunt quipped.

"Again?"

"Didn't I tell you I played guitar and was lead singer in a band when I was in high school?"

"No, you didn't." Lauren laughed. "You're full of surprises."

For the next few minutes Lauren sat in a virtual passenger seat while her Aunt Kate drove down memory lane.

"I better stop with the stories or you won't want to hang out with your old auntie."

Lauren shook her head. "Nope, not gonna happen. But I get your message, no more whining."

"I didn't say you couldn't whine. I'm always here for you. You know that."

"I know. You've been there for me my whole life. You've been like a mother to me." Lauren blinked back tears.

"Don't go getting all sentimental on me now."

But it was true. She had the love of a mother all these years and never once told her aunt what she felt inside. Maybe it was because she just now realized it for the first time. Lauren cleared her throat. "I don't think I ever thanked you."

Kate now blinked back tears. "No need to thank me, sweetie. I think of you as the daughter that I never had." Kate wrapped her soft hand over Lauren's.

They were finishing up their last sips of coffee when Lauren's cell phone rang. She looked at the screen. A Rawlins number. "Hello, this is Lauren."

"Lauren, it's Emmett Murphy."

"Hi, Emmett."

"I'll be in Crawford in about an hour. I'd like to pick up Jane's things. Will that work for you?"

"Sure. Everything's at my house." Lauren recited her address and ended the call. "That was Mr. Murphy. He's going to pick up Jane's personal effects from her office. They're sitting at my house."

"Poor man." Kate sighed.

When Lauren returned to the office she was surprised to find the door unlocked and more surprised to find Susan working at her desk.

"Feeling better?" The question was laced with sarcasm.

"As a matter of fact I am. And since *someone* canceled my hair appointment I decided to work on Friday's docket."

Lauren went to her office and backed up her files to the cloud and a flash drive. She passed Susan's desk.

"Leaving *already*?" It was Susan's turn to sound sarcastic.

"Emmett Murphy is stopping by my house to pick up Judge Murphy's things."

"Oh." Susan turned to her computer screen but continued talking. "Lauren, I'm a little surprised at you."

Irritation crept into Lauren's voice as she asked, "Why?"

"Even with Judge Murphy gone, we should not be discussing the Blackburn case."

"Oh-kay, but I don't know what you're talking about. I haven't spoken to anyone regarding the Blackburn case."

"When I returned from lunch Amanda was coming out of your office. She was looking for you. She said something about the Blackburn case. She wants to be up to speed on all of Judge Murphy's open cases when *she* takes the bench." Susan let out a snort.

"Why would she be asking me?"

"I assume because you've been discussing the case with her."

"You *assume* wrong. I haven't." Lauren's jaw tightened.

"Anyway, I told her it was confidential and you shouldn't be talking about it."

"I told you I *wasn't* talking about it." Lauren shouldered her purse. "I gotta get going." She walked out of the office and shut the door harder than intended.

* * *

"Who are you talking to?"

"I'm sorry, what?" Lauren stopped on the landing of the staircase noticing the detective for the first time.

"You were mumbling something." He arched an eyebrow and gave her a small smile.

Lauren blushed. "Uh, nothing. It's just sometimes Susan doesn't make any sense."

"Does that mean she's in this afternoon?"

"Yeah."

"Good."

"She's in. I don't think she's all there but she's in."

Chapter Thirty-Nine

Judge Murphy's boxes sat in Lauren's garage. She carried them inside, and with the last one in her arms, used her foot to close the door behind her. She rested the box on one of the kitchen chairs.

Percy scampered into the kitchen followed by Maverik. The Papillon circled the box sniffing.

"Oh, you probably smell Jane's running shoes." She lifted the lid and watched as Percy danced on his hind legs, excited. Lauren burst into tears. She grabbed a box of tissues off the counter and sank onto the floor. "I have got to quit..." she sobbed into a tissue "...all this crying." Percy came over, stood on her lap and sniffed. "I've done nothing but feel sorry for myself. And you, I forget how hard it must be for you. Jane loved you. Maybe you were the only one she really loved."

Maverik came over. Before she could put an arm around

him, he stuck his face in the box, snatched one of the shoes, and dashed out of the kitchen.

She blew her nose and yelled, "Hey you. Drop it!" Percy hopped off her lap and into the box and got ahold of the other shoe. He jumped out and the box fell off the chair, spilling its contents. He ran off. Lauren followed them out of the kitchen shouting, "Bring those back." Percy was at the bottom of the stairs. "Come. Percy, come here now.H" He did not.

Lauren righted the box and picked up some of the mess the two dogs left behind. A tin of Altoids managed to get itself wedged under the refrigerator. With the help of a spatula, Lauren retrieved the mints along with some dust bunnies. She brushed them away and popped open the container to see if the mints were still any good. Inside were three white candies and a tiny memory card. Lauren examined the small card she held between her thumb and index finger, then put it in the tin and pocketed it. She gathered up the diplomas, pictures, and other items and placed them in the box.

Growling sounds came from upstairs. Lauren ran up the stairs and stuck her head in the bedroom. Maverik and Percy were playing tug of war with one of Judge Murphy's shoes. "Hey, give me that." She easily took the sneaker out of Percy's mouth. She turned to Maverik. "Drop it." He held on tighter. "Drop it now." She twisted the shoe and pried it out of his mouth. "I suppose that's one more thing we have to work on. Yeah, you heard me."

Maverik opened his mouth and panted. His upper teeth showed.

"Smiling at me is not going to work."

She searched for the other shoe for five minutes before giving up. "Maybe it would be better not to have such a personal item in the box anyway. It made me cry." Tears, once again, tugged at Lauren's eyes, but then she remembered the memory card in her pocket. In her office, she fired up the computer and inserted the card into the small slot. A dialogue box popped up with several choices, including the choice to open files. Lauren stared at the screen trying to decide what to do. *This is not mine. I should just let Mr. Murphy have it. He can open the file. But what if it has some embarrassing photos, selfies or something worse?* Lauren convinced herself that she was protecting Emmett Murphy from further grief when she clicked "open file."

Four document files on the card, no images. Lauren let out a small sigh of relief. The first file was a letter written by Judge Murphy, addressed to the Wyoming Bar Association.

Lauren read the document. The letter ended with, "See enclosed attachments." She exited out of the first document and opened the other three, the "attachments" to the original letter.

After viewing them, she exited out of the files, right clicked to copy them to her computer, and as an extra precaution, sent a copy to the cloud. Next, she dialed Detective Overstreet's number which she now had memorized. The call went straight to voicemail. "Detective, this is Lauren Besoner. Listen, when you get this message please call me. I found something that I'm sure you'll want to see. I'll be home the rest of the day." She left him her number, though she knew he had it, and hung up. She did not like leaving messages on people's voicemail and it showed. She always began speaking slow and clear but by the time she said goodbye, she all but told her life story, and more than once rambled on for so long that the call ended before she finished. During those times, she had to resist the urge to call back and finish her message.

With the SD card back in the tin and in Lauren's pocket, she turned to leave and spied Judge Murphy's lone sneaker sticking out from behind the door. She ignored it.

Mr. Murphy wasn't due for another thirty minutes. Lauren put on a pot of coffee and then went into the laundry room and grabbed the dogs' brush. She called for Percy to come, which he did. "No, not another treat. Come here. Let me brush you. Maybe you'll look irresistible and Mr. Murphy will break down and take you home with him." Lauren sat cross-legged on her laundry room floor and brushed Percy's long fur.

* * *

The dogs barked. Lauren heard a knock on the front door. She reached for Maverik's collar before opening the door. "Hi, Mr. Murphy. Please, come in."

He entered and removed his cowboy hat. "Hello, Lauren." He noticed Percy. "Hey there little fella." Percy hopped on his hind legs in excitement.

"And who is this big guy?"

"That's Maverik."

"Nice looking dog."

"Thanks. I just made some coffee. Do you have time for a cup?"

"Yes. Thank you."

"Have a seat."

Mr. Murphy stood by her couch.

"Excuse my sofa. Someone was being naughty." *Uh-oh, what if he thinks Percy did it? Should I lie to him?* "Milk, sugar?"

"A little sugar, please."

Before grabbing two clean cups from her dishwasher Lauren checked her phone to see if Detective Overstreet returned her call. No missed calls, no texts.

She brought out the two mugs of hot coffee and handed one to Mr. Murphy.

"Thank you." He sat on the intact cushion. He placed his well-worn cowboy hat on the end table next to him. Lauren sat opposite him in her overstuffed chair. Percy jumped up on the arm of the chair. An awkward silence passed between the two as they each sipped their coffee.

Emmett broke the quiet. "Are you going to keep Percy?"

Lauren stroked the fur that dangled from Percy's ears. "Maybe. I have asked a few people around town but I haven't had any luck. Have you and Mrs. Murphy changed your mind by any chance?"

He shook his head. "Margaret isn't going to change her mind."

"Has Detective Overstreet been in touch with you?"

"He has. He said he's following up on some very promising leads. I asked him what the leads were but he wouldn't say."

Not wanting to get his hopes up, Lauren said nothing about the files she had found.

"How is your wife doing?"

He let out a deep breath before answering. "These past few weeks have been very difficult. If that detective doesn't come up with something soon…"

"I'm sure he will. He probably wants to be very thorough before he takes his case to the county attorney."

Emmett set the barely touched coffee down on the steamer trunk and stood. "I better be going." He loaded the boxes in his truck, then returned and shook her hand. "Thank you, Lauren."

She stood by the open door and watched him walk to his truck. She retrieved his coffee mug, took it to the kitchen sink and began loading the dishwasher. The dogs barked and interrupted her cleaning of the coffee pot. As she strode to the front door she caught sight of Emmett's hat sitting on the end table.

Chapter Forty

She swung the front door open. "You forgot this, didn't you?" Mr. Murphy's hat hung in her hand.

Amanda stood on the front porch.

Maverik shot past the two women, onto the front lawn and barked.

"It's chilly out here. Aren't you going to invite me in?"

The sight of the black pistol pointed at her made Lauren flinch.

"I wouldn't worry about your dog." Amanda stepped inside and slammed the door shut.

"Amanda—"

"Shut up."

Maverik barked and scratched at the closed door.

"Turn around."

Percy jumped off the couch, ran over to Amanda, bared his teeth, and growled.

"Shut him up or I'll shoot him first."

Lauren's stomach tightened. She bent and picked up Percy. His body quivered.

"We're going to go to your basement. Move."

The sound of Maverik, his barks and scratching, grew faint as they made their way toward the basement.

"Amanda, what's—" The cold metal shoved between her shoulder blades silenced her. She opened the basement door.

"Down."

Percy growled in Lauren's arms. She took a step down. The loud crack and excruciating pain behind her right ear were the last things she remembered.

Lauren awoke to find herself sprawled at the bottom of the staircase, staring up at a bare bulb that hung from the ceiling. Percy licked her cheeks. She tried to sit, and pain coursed through her right shoulder like a hot poker. Nausea lurched in her stomach. Her eyes began to focus, and as they did, she saw a figure crouched several feet from her. The memory of Amanda with the gun came back to her.

Flames grew from piles of newspapers scattered throughout the room. It looked like some satanical ritual was about to start.

Amanda stacked paint cans, with the cornflower blue paint she recently purchased, behind the staircase.

Fear snaked its way through Lauren's mind. "Amanda?"

The tall woman straightened and faced her.

Lauren looked into Amanda's eyes. Crazy looked back.

Percy growled.

"I don't understand." Lauren rolled to her side and tried to sit. A stabbing pain radiated from her ankle up her shin. She slumped back.

"Spare me. You know. And even if you don't you'd be putting it all together soon enough."

Percy continued a low throat rumble. Lauren put her left arm out, patted him, and made ssh-ssh-ing sounds.

"I was hoping that hit on the head hadn't killed you. We can't have you dying by blunt force trauma now, can we?" Amanda's voice carried a sing-song quality to it. She touched the cigarette lighter's small flame to more newspapers, then fished out a pack of cigarettes from her pocket, tapped one out and lit it. She inhaled and promptly coughed.

"I didn't know you smoked."

A harsh laugh escaped from Amanda. "I don't but you do. Such a bad habit, don't you think? Especially when you get careless."

"Why would you kill Judge Murphy?"

"*Why*? Because she was going to ruin my career, that's why." Amanda watched the cigarette smoke swirl around in front of her. "It was bad enough that she dumped me."

"She didn't dump you. She became the new judge. Your partnership had to end."

"Thank you for enlightening me, Little Miss Know It All, but that isn't what I meant." Amanda tucked newspapers around the paint cans.

"I don't understand."

"Do I have to spell it out for you? We were more than law partners. We were lovers." She touched the flame gingerly to three more piles of paper, lighting them as if they were little candles on a birthday cake. She glanced at her handiwork, then spoke. "Don't look so surprised. Our relationship started after Jane broke up with your jerk-of-a-husband, Tony. It coincided with our fifth anniversary as Murphy and Capshaw. We went out to celebrate. She confided in me how glad she was to be rid of him. By the end of the evening, one thing led to another and we ended up at my place. In bed." Amanda's voice sounded far away. "I'd been attracted to Jane ever since I first met her in college."

The cold of the cement floor could no longer compete with the rising flames. Beads of sweat formed on Lauren's face.

"But when Jane applied to replace Judge Brubaker she said we should keep our relationship quiet, that if Governor Sterling knew about… about us, it would ruin her chances. She said it was only temporary, and it would be worth the sacrifice. Once she was on the bench we could take our relationship to the next level. She even mentioned marriage."

Amanda surveyed the hot room. "I agreed. After she got the appointment I waited for her to contact me. I tried getting in touch with her but she kept putting me off."

While Amanda rambled on, Lauren's eyes darted around, desperate to find a way out. She moved her leg and was still met with a sharp pain. "That must have been hard on you."

"Don't insult me. You don't give a shit about me." Ashes fell from the cigarette.

The pounding in Lauren's head made it hard to focus on Amanda's words. She reached up and touched her right temple, felt thick blood on her fingers.

"Then the day that Jane came to our office to supposedly sign papers to dissolve our partnership, she tells me it's over between us and not just our business. Just like that." Amanda shook her head. "I had heard rumors about Bradley Schwartz but I knew she was only using him to get pain killers. Deep down Jane loved me. I knew we would be together again. I knew she would come back to me. I thought she would come back..."

"Judge Murphy could—"

"*Quit calling her judge.* Everybody can just *quit calling that bitch judge*!" Amanda's shrill howl pierced the hollow basement.

Percy's body quaked. Lauren watched as first one, then a second storage box burst into flames.

"You brought this all on yourself." Amanda gestured around the growing inferno. "You had to go digging up names, snooping around Jane's things."

"What did you expect me to do? The police thought I killed her. I couldn't just stand around and do nothing."

"I underestimated you. I didn't think you had it in you to stand up for yourself." Amanda's voice droned on.

Holding Percy, Lauren took comfort in the fact that Maverik had rushed out the door, not listening to her. At least he was out of danger.

"She was going to tell the Bar everything I did. I couldn't let that happen. I'd lose my license, I'd lose everything. I'd disgrace my whole family. I had to stop her."

Lauren remembered the letter she just read, written by Judge Murphy, and the accusations contained in it, the main one, that Amanda had signed her client's name on a waiver of speedy trial.

"When I found out Hector Ortiz was in town I thought, perfect timing. Nobody would think twice about putting him back in prison. Once a gang banger, always a gang banger. But I worried they wouldn't have any physical evidence tying him to the scene. As an added precaution, I sent the police in your direction too. Spread the suspicion around."

"It was you." Lauren struggled to get the words out. "You typed up those notes—those lies about me. You left them at Jane's house that night, after you killed her."

"You are catching on. See, I knew you would."

"And you planted the flash drive in her desk too."

"That I dropped in that box in your office when I was feeling chatty and visiting with you. And don't forget the lip gloss. I thought it added a nice touch."

"And there were no real threatening letters from Hector. That was you also."

"Me again." Amanda's burgundy lips stretched into a thin icy smile, then her face went dark. "I went to her house that night to ask her one last time to not destroy me, not destroy everything I worked so hard for. I came prepared to do what I needed to do. Oh, she had a smug look on her face when she told me that the wheels were almost in motion. She was going to turn over the information once she returned from Casper. Everything." Amanda's eyes shone bright. "Not so smug when she saw the knife."

The heat, the nausea, the ringing in her ears intensified. Lauren tried to focus on Amanda's words.

"I searched her study and found the letter she had written, but I couldn't find the original file. She had to have saved it somewhere. I even searched her office when Susan was gone. Then I saw you that day loading up her stuff into your trunk."

"You broke into my house to search those boxes. But how did you get in?"

"A flowerpot is no place to hide a key. I didn't break in. That damned beast of yours wouldn't stop barking. And that little mutt..." Amanda glared at Percy "...tried to attack my ankle."

Lauren's mind slid another piece of the puzzle into place. "You saw the transcript I prepared for her, there in her living room. That's why you were asking Susan about the Blackburn case."

"Yes. I regret mentioning that to her. I had a suspicion she might say something to you. She can't seem to mind her own business." The cigarette had gone out, and Amanda flicked it onto the floor. It landed near the bottom of the stairs.

Lauren glanced at the newspaper on the floor by her feet. "Crawford Judge Slain in Own Home." Jane Murphy's smiling face contorted, then succumbed to the flames and vanished.

"Don't do this, Amanda. It'll only make things worse. Detective Overstreet is going to find out what happened. I left him a message. He's probably on his way over right now." Lauren tried to sound confident, hoping to convince Amanda she spoke the truth.

"I think you give him too much credit. And everyone knows how hard it is to quit smoking. You get a little careless and, whoosh, flames everywhere." Amanda's gaze went to the wooden-beamed ceiling. She wiped her brow with the back of her hand. "Besides, when he finds the knife in your evidence room, he'll be convinced that it was you all along."

"*What?*"

"I took your keys while you were in court one day, made a duplicate."

Lauren sank against the beam. The crazy bitch thought of everything.

"I think I'll have to hire a new judicial assistant when I'm on the bench. That Susan is just never at her desk. Anyone could walk right in."

Amanda coughed. "It's time I say goodbye Lauren."

"Take Percy with you. There's no reason to leave him here. He hasn't done anything to deserve this. Take him, please."

Amanda trotted up the stairs, and without a backward glance, shut the basement door behind her.

Lauren sat helpless on the floor and stared at the closed door. Hot tears, mixed with sweat, ran down her cheeks. Flames crackled and popped around her. Percy barked and Lauren hugged him. The tiny dog stood on her lap and licked her hot cheeks.

Do something. At least save Percy. With her good foot, she scooted the cigarette butt Amanda left behind toward her. When it was close enough, she reached for it with her good arm and put it in her pocket. Then again with her good hand she pulled herself up along the beam. Percy sat in the crook of her arm. She took a step, sending waves of pain up her leg. She turned her head, vomited, then wiped her mouth on her sleeve and hobbled forward.

The fire blocked the bottom of the staircase, and flames teased at the paint cans.

Lauren pivoted and made her way over to a small window, a little wider and longer than the frightened dog in her arms. It faced the backyard. She set Percy on a cardboard box next to her. "Stay." With her good shoulder, she reached up as high as she could and managed to unlatch the window. She pushed against it. It did not budge. The frame and sill had been painted over many times, sealing the wooden frame tight. Lauren frantically looked around until she spotted a wooden lamp minus its shade next to the box near Percy. She grabbed it and swung hard. The glass shattered. Lauren yelled into the black night, "Help! Somebody help!"

Smoke took flight through the broken window. Flames sprung up around her.

Lauren picked up the shaking Papillon and pushed him through the small opening. "Go. Percy, go."

He faced Lauren. "Yip-yip-yip."

"Damn it, just go!" Lauren's now damp hair clung to her neck. The wall of heat inched toward her. She turned. Flames engulfed several more cardboard boxes that she had meant to unpack and now never would. Their burning contents filled her nostrils with an acrid stench.

She reached into her pants pocket, felt for the tin, pulled it out, and with a flick of her wrist, sailed it out the window. It landed somewhere in the blackness. Next, she fished out the cigarette and flicked it out into the night.

Lauren slid down the wall and collapsed in a ball of pain. She did not want to inhale. Each new breath scorched her throat. She buried her face in her arm. Percy's barks grew faint.

Chapter Forty-One

"Just relax," came the sound a man's deep voice.

Lauren blinked and tried to look around. She put a hand to her face, felt something and automatically grabbed it.

A hand gently touched the mask. "No, no, you need to leave that on. Just relax."

Cody, the firefighter who Lauren had met weeks earlier, now leaned over her, his expression full of concern. She lay on a gurney, not knowing how she got there. Next to him a paramedic held an oxygen mask over her nose and mouth. "You need to keep this on to get your oxygen saturation levels up, okay? Lie still for me and breathe."

The flashing lights of the emergency vehicles lit up the night sky. Lauren closed her eyes against their harshness and inhaled the oxygen. Her lungs felt like they were on fire. She removed the mask and tried to sit up.

"Ah-ah-ah, you need to keep that on," came the paramedic's voice off to her left.

The attempt to put weight on her elbow reminded Lauren she was in no shape to sit up. She dropped back, closed her eyes again and inhaled the cool oxygen.

When she opened her eyes she saw a shorter paramedic approaching. With an EMT on each side of her they rolled the gurney toward the ambulance. Ignoring the pain, Lauren managed to pull off the oxygen mask. "I'm not going anywhere until I find out if my dogs are okay."

The paramedics stopped. "Cody, have you found any dogs—how many dogs do you have," the shorter paramedic inquired.

"Two."

"Cody, she has two dogs," said the shorter EMT. They rolled the gurney closer to the ambulance. "We'll just get you ready for transport."

The movement made her wince.

"Sorry," said the taller paramedic as they continued down the sidewalk.

Once inside the cramped space, Lauren waited to hear from Cody.

Someone approached the rear of the ambulance. Jeff, her neighbor, leaned in. Maverik stood at his side panting. He asked the shorter paramedic if he could speak to Lauren.

"Okay, but make it quick."

"Oh, my God, are you okay?" Jeff's eyes were large with concern. "Is there anything I can do?"

Lauren's words came out in a hoarse whisper. "Can you take care of Maverik?"

"Of course, of course. Don't worry about him."

Another familiar face appeared at the back of the ambulance. Detective Overstreet stood by Jeff. Percy sat cradled in the crook of his arm.

"Percy, thank God." She pushed herself up on her good elbow. Words tumbled out. "It was Amanda, Amanda Capshaw. She killed Judge Murphy. She set my house on fire, she tried to kill me. And…" Lauren coughed hard. Her head throbbed to the point of nausea.

"Slow down, slow down. She's been picked up."

The baritone voice calmed Lauren. Then tears of relief ran down her cheeks. "But—"

"I'll explain everything later." He patted her hand. "Right now you need to get to the hospital."

"What about Percy?"

The sound came of squeaky wheels made the detective turn around. Twila Nash's red curls peeked out from behind Detective Overstreet. Her thin body was hidden inside a calf-length maroon coat. A pair of turquoise colored polyester pants poked out from underneath the parka, and her feet were encased in pink slippers.

"Oh, heck, I guess he can stay at my place." Twila nudged the detective with her elbow. "Give 'em to me," she snapped and held out her arm.

Detective Overstreet waited for Lauren's approval. She nodded.

"And you got me to thank for saving your life, young lady." She moved closer to the ambulance door, "Yep. I was watching TV and I heard that dog of yours barking his fool head off. I opened my back door to yell at him to get off my property. Then I heard glass breaking and you yelling for help, making one helluva racket. And then the smoke, I saw all that smoke pouring out of your basement. I thought to myself, 'My God, what has she gone and done now.' I called nine-one-one right away." Twila nodded matter-of-factly.

Exhaustion overtook Lauren. Before she lay back she managed a weak, "Thank you, Mrs. Nash."

With Percy tucked under her arm, the frail woman turned away and shuffled off in the direction of her house. "Come on... Percy, is it? *Wheel of Fortune* is about to start."

The shorter paramedic got in the back of the ambulance and was about to pull the doors shut behind him when Lauren reached out and touched his arm. "Please, one more thing. I have to tell the detective one more thing."

"Okay." The paramedic motioned for him to get in.

The detective climbed in and crouched next to Lauren. She turned her head toward him. "The mints, check the mints. And the cigarette."

"Mints? What mints?"

"Backyard. Mints and..." She coughed and fell back on the gurney.

"We need to get going."

"I'll come by the hospital later." Detective Overstreet patted the foot of the gurney.

The ambulance turned the corner, sped down the street. Lauren's sore muscles felt every movement it made.

Chapter Forty-Two

Aunt Kate loaded dirty breakfast plates into her dishwasher.

"Lauren, let me help you to the recliner." Jack held out his arm.

Using Jack as her crutch, she made her way to the worn leather chair and gently lowered herself into the soft cushion.

"Can I get you anything before I go?"

"No, I'm good. Thanks." Lauren watched Jack back out of the driveway and head in the direction of town, then turned her attention to the fat snowflakes that drifted lazily to the ground.

"I'll bring you a cup of hot chocolate after I feed the pack," called Aunt Kate before going out the back door.

"Sounds good."

With no more chances for table scraps, Maverik trotted out of the kitchen and lay by the recliner.

A 2007 blue Dodge Ram 2500 made its way up the gravel drive. With effort, Lauren maneuvered out of the chair, to the front door, and let Detective Overstreet in. "More questions?" she asked.

"No, no. The statement I took from you at the hospital has pretty much everything I need. I'm on my way to work but I wanted to see how you were doing."

"Better. Still trying to process everything that's happened but I'm okay." She motioned for him to have a seat.

He unzipped his Carhartt hoodie and sat on the leather sofa. "We're working on getting Amanda to confess. Or I should say Oscar Gordon, the district attorney from Cheyenne is. He's working with her attorney, seeing if they can cut a deal."

"A *deal*? What kind of deal? She shouldn't be getting any deals. She killed Jane, she tried to frame me, and then she tried to kill me."

He raised his hands. "Hey, hey, don't get so excited. The only deal out there is if she pleads guilty to all the charges the state won't seek the death penalty."

Lauren's jaw muscles relaxed.

"Those files on that SD card certainly add to the premeditation theory." He ran his fingers through his wavy hair.

"I got lucky and stumbled across it."

"Without luck, that information might not have ever surfaced and Amanda might have gotten away with murder. And saving that cigarette butt was quick thinking on your part."

Lauren shifted in the recliner. "I was desperate to leave some clue behind, you know, in case..."

The unspoken meaning of the statement hung between them for a beat.

"How did Amanda get picked up so soon?"

"When I got your message, I decided to come over rather than call. And then I heard over the scanner that there was a fire at your address. I decided to put out a BOLO, be-on-the-lookout for her just in case. She was picked up two blocks from your house."

"Did you know it was her? I mean that she killed Jane?"

"I was almost to that point. Remember that list of names you gave me?"

"Yes."

"I spoke with Duane Cochran. He's at the pen. He confirmed he spoke with Judge Murphy and told her he never signed a waiver of speedy trial. That alone would have gotten Miss Capshaw disbarred."

Lauren nodded.

"And I was able to get ahold of the other two names. Amanda represented them both in their divorce cases. Turns out Amanda was working on a contingency fee basis in each case. I spoke with Graham. Even though all he does is criminal law, he filled me in, that that's a definite no-no. Her clients didn't realize at the time she was not allowed to take a percentage of what the judge awarded them in their divorce. Jane somehow found out. Made me want to dig deeper into Miss Capshaw and her whereabouts at the time of the murder."

He leaned forward, resting his elbows on his knees. "And after talking to Susan—"

"*Susan?*"

"Yes. I spoke with her that afternoon. Remember? You were talking to yourself as you were heading down the stairs that day?" He grinned at Lauren.

"Oh, uh, right."

"Susan said something that just didn't fit. She said when she returned from her lunch break Amanda was coming out of your office. She was looking for you."

"So? Susan told me that too."

"Think, Lauren. How would she have gotten into your office? You leave a door unlocked? I don't think so."

"You noticed that little habit, huh?" Lauren looked sheepish.

"I did. It got me to thinking."

Lauren let the information sink in. "Do you know she planted the knife in the evidence room?"

"I'll have to get over there and check that out. The flaw in that part of her plan was you were no longer on my radar. I never got to the point of getting a search warrant for your offices."

"No longer on your radar? Really? You could have fooled me. Every time I saw you I thought I would hurl."

"Maybe I was a little overzealous."

"I know Chief Newell had a hand in that. But you, you tried to get me to confess to something I didn't do." She caught the apologetic look in his eyes.

"After Amanda began spreading false clues around like they were cow manure, she began to relax, that is until you started snooping around."

"I wasn't—"

He held up his hands. "*She* thought you were snooping, let me put it that way." The detective studied Lauren with her leg propped up on the recliner and her arm in a sling. "What do the docs say about your arm and your foot?"

"I have a doctor's appointment tomorrow. X-rays at the hospital didn't show anything broken. Emergency room doctor said he thought it was just a sprained ankle. And my shoulder, probably just pulled muscles. I should be able to go home in a few days." Lauren nodded toward the kitchen. "Though I am getting used to all the pampering from my aunt and Jack. It's been kind of nice."

"No broken bones, that is good news." The detective stood. "I need to get going. I thought you'd appreciate an update on where things were."

"I do. Thanks for stopping by."

Chapter Forty-Three

Six days after the fire Lauren stood in front of her house, Aunt Kate at her side. She opened the door and Maverik bumped past the two women and began his inspection of the house. Aunt Kate carried Lauren's suitcases upstairs.

"I can't smell anything up here," Kate called out. She came downstairs and stood next to Lauren. Like two bloodhounds they continued to sniff the air.

"I smell a slight chemical odor."

Kate nodded. "I don't smell any smoke." She turned to Lauren. "You call me if you need anything, anything at all. You understand?"

"Yes. And thank you for everything. You and Jack are the best." With her arm no longer in a sling, Lauren reached out and gave Kate a hug.

Alone, Lauren called out to Maverik. He bounded into the living room. "I think it's time."

He cocked his head to the left and swished his tail.

"You behave. I'll be back soon." Lauren gathered up a few empty cardboard boxes, loaded them in the Volvo and drove to the courthouse.

* * *

Gunner sat in his usual spot. He spoke as Lauren approached. "Hey, what's with the boxes?"

"I'm moving on." Lauren went through security and punched the up arrow on the elevator.

"The rumors are true then?"

"About me leaving? They're true."

"I'm going to miss that smiling face of yours."

His words made her smile. She stepped in the elevator. "I'm going to miss yours too, Gunner."

"Call me when you're done packing. I'll help with those boxes."

"Thanks, I'll do that." The doors closed.

The second floor was quiet. Lauren let herself in to the judge's chambers, took out her cell phone, and texted Claude. "In my office. Come down if you can." She set the boxes on the desk, went over to the window, and gazed out to the courtyard below. People walked in and out of the courthouse. Just an ordinary day.

"Hey you."

Lauren exhaled and turned. "Just in time to help me pack up."

Claude swiped at the corner of her eye with a finger.

"Don't go getting all teary-eyed. You'll make me start to cry. Besides, we both knew this day was coming."

"I know. But did Tony at least offer you the job?"

"He did, but only because he knew what my answer would be." Lauren did her best imitation of Tony. "'You don't ask a witness a question that you don't already know the answer to.'" She sighed. "He knew. But we did talk for a long time. I even told him I think he'll make a good judge."

"You *didn't.*"

"It was my way of saying, I'm over you. And I truly am."

"Good for you."

"I've had a lot of time to think about everything. I've decided to let go of all the negativity. I know it's cliché, but I have so much to be thankful for." Lauren shook her head. "No more wasting my time with negative emotions. It feels pretty sweet."

Claude sat on the edge of Lauren's desk. "But it sucks that you're out of a job. What are you going to do?"

"I'm going to update my résumé. Judge Brubaker called me yesterday. He told me the district got funding for another judge. My plan is to apply as the new court reporter." She put her cactus plant gently into one of the boxes. "In the meantime, I still have a few more weeks of rehab for my shoulder. With a little luck my physical therapy will end at the same time the new judge starts interviewing for a court reporter." Then added, "And if the planets don't align, I'll go back to freelancing."

"How is your shoulder doing?"

"It's getting better. I'm looking forward to sleeping in my own bed tonight. With Amanda in jail, I can finally relax."

Claude took the various reference materials and dictionaries that Lauren handed to her and added them to the boxes. "I'm going to miss coming down here, you know, BS'ing with you."

"It's temporary. And my new mantra? Change is good." She placed her coffee mug on top of the now full box. "And you know what the best part of this whole thing is?"

"What?"

"Sure you do. Think."

"*No Susan*," they shouted in unison and laughed.

"Yep, no more Susan in my life. She's all Tony's problem now."

"Speaking of Tony, he was in talking with Graham."

"And?"

"He confided that Jane and him hooked up a while back, couple of times. He's sure the baby was his."

"Wow."

"I thought you might want to know."

"That's so sad." Lauren shook her head.

"Jane told him about the pregnancy. She was excited."

Lauren digested the news in silence.

Claude checked her phone. "I'm meeting Roberto for lunch. Why don't you join us?"

"No thanks. I want to pack up and get out of here before I run into you-know-who."

"I can stay and help carry these boxes for you."

"Thanks, but Gunner already offered."

The two friends stood by the door, then Claude reached over and gave Lauren a gentle hug. "I'll text you later."

The boxes were full and the office now bare. Lauren phoned Gunner. She wanted her luck to hold out and not see Susan. It did.

Chapter Forty-Four

Lauren placed the cactus on the windowsill in the kitchen. There was one more thing she needed to do. "Maverik, you stay here."

The boards on Twila Nash's front porch creaked. Lauren heard Percy's barks from inside the house. The door swung open before she had a chance to knock.

"Hello, Mrs. Nash." Lauren bent, gathered up the little dog and hugged him.

"Don't just stand there, come in. You're letting all the heat out."

Lauren stepped into a mirror image of her own house. Twila closed the door behind her.

"We were just getting ready to have our afternoon coffee. Stay for a cup?"

"Um, sure."

"Milk and sugar okay? I don't have any of them fancy

flavors you young people like."

"Milk and sugar is fine. Thank you. *We?* Am I interrupting anything? Do you have company?"

"Oh, no. Sit down. I'll be right back." The old woman shuffled off to her kitchen.

The first thing that caught Lauren's attention was a brown plaid throw on one cushion of Twila's yellow and blue flowered print sofa. She sunk into the worn cushion next to it. Percy jumped out of her arms and went over and sat on the throw.

"I see you've got your own spot. Has Old Lady—Has Twila been spoiling you?"

The cloth arms of the sofa were faded to a soft sheen. The carpet had a matted path from the recliner to the kitchen. The room smelled of lemon furniture polish. An end table with a lamp next to the recliner held today's newspaper and a word search puzzle book.

Twila came out of the kitchen with a cup of coffee and a small saucer. She handed Lauren the cup and placed the saucer on the floor next to the recliner. Percy jumped off the couch, went to the dish, and lapped up coffee.

"Don't look so surprised, young lady."

"I had no idea Percy liked coffee."

"Oh, he does. I only give him a little, of course, since he's just a little thing himself." After retrieving her own cup from the kitchen Twila slowly lowered herself into the recliner and set her cup on the newspaper. Percy jumped onto her lap, circled two times and lay down.

The coffee tasted weak but hot.

"We was just getting ready to watch *Ellen*. You like *Ellen*, don't you, Percy?" Twila recounted the numerous "adorable" things Percy had done that week, and told Lauren of the other TV shows her and the Papillon watched together.

"*Wheel of Fortune* is his favorite." Twila kissed the top of his head.

They sat in silence drinking their coffee. Lauren studied the old woman with Percy snuggled into her. She held her cup on her lap and cleared her throat. "Twila, before all the craziness that went on at my house last week, I had been looking for a permanent home for Percy." She took a deep breath and continued. "I know this is asking an awful lot, but do you suppose there would be any way you could possibly keep him? You'd be doing me such a big favor. Having two dogs in the house is just too much. I can see he likes it here, and it would be such a relief to me knowing he found a loving home."

Twila rocked in her chair. With her liver-spotted hand she stroked Percy. "He has been a good watch dog. He lets me know when anyone is at the door. And he does mind me." She stopped rocking. "I guess I could help you out. On a trial basis that is."

"That's a good idea, a trial basis."

"What do you think, Percy?" Twila looked at the dog.

Percy answered by licking Twila's very wrinkled cheek.

"But remember, it's just a trial."

"Of course. I'll come by later with his toys and the rest of his food." Lauren made a mental note to run to the store to pick up another bag of kibble for Mrs. Nash.

"And if it's okay with you I'll bring Maverik over once in a while and they can run around together. I think they'd both like that."

"As long as they run around in *your* yard. I don't want that big dog of yours making a mess in mine."

"Of course."

Percy jumped off Twila's lap, and she eased herself out of the chair. "Well, that's settled then."

They walked to the front door. Lauren picked up the small dog and gave him a hug. "You be good." She handed him to Twila and the women said goodbye.

When Lauren reached the sidewalk, she turned and waved. Twila stood there with Percy, his breath a little circle of steam on the storm door. Twila waved back and smiled.

Lauren glanced up at the unblemished sky, remembering Jeff's words from the other day. No, there were no pigs flying.

"I know, I said I would be right back, but good news, I think Percy found his forever home." Maverik sniffed Lauren. She went into the kitchen to fix herself a real cup of coffee, not satisfied with the watered-down version Twila served.

"Ar-roof."

"Are you agreeing with me?"

"Ar-roof, ar-roof, ar-roof." Lauren put her finger to her lips to quiet Maverik.

"Ar-roof, ar-roof."

"Now that it's just you, that means more one-on-one training. That's right, you and me." Lauren made a V with her fingers, and motioned back and forth from Maverik to herself.

Maverik ran to the front door and barked. Lauren parted the curtains in the living room. "Damn you have good ears." She was smiling as she opened the door. "Hi."

Detective Overstreet stood there, his coat collar pulled up. He returned the smile. "I take it that means you're happy to see me?"

"Private joke with Maverik." She laughed. "Come in."

"Am I interrupting anything?"

"No, not at all. I just got home. I was packing up my office."

"I heard the news. That's tough."

"Well, compared to almost going up in flames, literally…" Lauren gave a small shudder "… being out of work is a minor inconvenience. These past few weeks have given me a new perspective on life."

"I stopped by Jack and Kate's. Jack told me you had gone home this morning. I wanted to see how you were doing. Now that my end of the paperwork is taken care of I can finally catch a breath."

"You deserve it. I was just about to make some coffee. Care to join me?"

"Sure, thanks." He followed her into the kitchen. "I also wanted to give you an update on Capshaw, let you know she's going to plead."

"She is?"

"Yes."

"It's really over? This nightmare is finally over?"

"It really is over." The detective glanced around. "Hey, where's Percy?"

"At his new home. Old Lady Nash—I mean Twila, my neighbor, has agreed to keep him. On a trial basis that is."

"I'm a little surprised."

"I went there to pick him up, but after seeing the two of them together, I really think Twila needs him. And he loves it there. Besides, with him right next door I'll see him all the time. And he's going to get to come over and play with Maverik."

The detective nodded.

Lauren reached up into her cupboard to grab two mugs and winced. "I keep forgetting I'm not supposed to be lifting my arm yet."

"Here, let me." Detective Overstreet reached around her, brushing her shoulder with his outstretched arm. He set the cups on the countertop.

She inhaled the scent of his aftershave. It was then that she noticed the white bakery bag in his hand. She cocked an eyebrow.

"For you. And Dominick sends his regards. Says to tell you he misses his favorite customer."

Lauren laughed, then peeked inside the bag. "Ooh, cheese danish, my favorite. How did you know?"

"Seriously? You have to ask?" He laughed. "A certain baker told me. Where are your plates?

She pointed to the cupboard by the stove.

He set out two plates and removed two pastries from the paper sack. "You sit. I'll pour." He filled their cups with coffee and joined her at the table.

She bit into the cheese danish. "Mmm. This is *so* good. Thank you, Detective."

The corners of his mouth turned up. His dark eyes softened. "Sam. Call me Sam."

THE END

Acknowledgements

I want to thank the Nite Writers of Cheyenne: Anna Lane, Dave Lerner, Rene Minder, and John Schultz. Each of you, in your own very unique way, helped me grow as a writer, which, in turn, made my story come alive. If I were not part of this amazing group of fellow writers, *Silent Gavel* would never have seen the light of day. You're the best.

To Mary Billiter, for coming to the Nite Writers' meetings. Your critique of my book, along with your encouragement, have been invaluable.

Thank you, Tim Green and Dean Jackson, for your expertise on police matters, and Lynn Boak for your expertise about alpaca life. If I have gotten any factual elements wrong, that burden is on me.

Chris Rhatigan, thank you for editing my manuscript, and giving me advice and suggestions on how to make it better.

And to Mick and Gabby, thank you for believing in me.

About the Author

Merissa Racine was born in the Bronx, and grew up on Long Island, New York. When she was a teenager her family moved to Miami, Florida, where she lived for several years. Missing the change of the seasons, she left the Sunshine state and settled in an even sunnier place, Cheyenne, Wyoming, where she grew to love the open spaces that the High Plains offers, and views of the Rocky Mountains.

She became a court reporter while living in Miami and continues to be a freelance stenographer in Cheyenne. Merissa's career in the legal profession provided the authentic flavor to Silent Gavel. She is busy working on her next mystery.

When not working or writing, she loves spending time with her three grandchildren; trying new recipes and baking, gardening, and hanging out with Roz, her rescue dog, and Zelda, her not-quite-feral cat.

CPSIA information can be obtained
at www.ICGtesting.com
Printed in the USA
LVHW04s1724041018
592410LV00002B/526/P

9 780999 303306